DEADLY SILENCE

KYLIE HATFIELD SERIES: BOOK FIVE

MARY STONE

BELLA CROSS

Deadly Silence, the fifth and final book in the captivating Kylie Hatfield Series, is a pulse pounding emotional roller coaster of a ride.

DESCRIPTION

Silence can kill...

Babies are going missing. Mothers are being killed. Because these women are poor and alone, no one seems to care.

Now that Kylie Hatfield's dreams have come true—she's married to Linc, the man of her dreams, and she's a real PI with her own business—everything should be smooth sailing.

Just as she's settling into married life and getting a foothold in the business, a pregnancy test and its little plus sign throws a wrench into her plans.

They were going to put a hold on kids, and for good reason. With ten puppies and a business that needs to turn a profit, this isn't the time for the added pressure of a baby. Plus, Kylie's work can be so dangerous.

But when a big case comes across Kylie's desk, one she simply can't turn her back on, Kylie has to decide what is most important to her. And just how far she'll go to protect the things she holds dearest.

1

September 1975...

PATRICIA HASTINGS FIXED her traditional white nursing cap over her stick-straight blonde locks before jumping into her little Dodge Dart. The cap was vintage, worn by her mother and grandmother before that. She didn't want a new one. She loved that her cap had been witness to so many years of helping others.

Sipping at a cup of coffee, she turned up the radio loud, grooving to Captain and Tennille's "Love Will Keep Us Together" as she headed out onto Rural Route Three toward the little town of Jolivue, Virginia.

As she drove, she patted her fringed bag, making sure she'd remembered the card to go along with the New Mother diaper basket she gave all of her patients. In the card, she'd written, *Best of luck to one of my favorite new mothers. Please don't hesitate to call me should you and your beautiful daughter ever need anything!*

Under that, she'd written her home phone number, which she rarely gave out. Her patients usually called her through the Staunton Midwife Service, which was customary procedure. She'd also stuffed a bigger pile of diapers in the basket than usual. She had a feeling this client would need the extra supply, and she couldn't deny that she'd miss this client more than her others.

Maybe it was because Renee Best, the spunky little kid, reminded Patricia of her own daughters, now grown. Poor Renee. Not yet twenty with no husband, no money, no support system, but so strong and brave. The young woman had an uphill battle in front of her, for sure, whether she realized it or not. Being left by one's significant other with no means of support would unhinge anyone, let alone a nine months pregnant, hormonal mother-to-be.

But not Renee.

Every time Patricia stopped by for one of Renee's prenatal check-ups, Renee would welcome her with a big hug, put a kettle on for tea, then the two would talk like old friends. She lived in a rust-trap of an old trailer, right off the highway, probably not the best place to raise a child. She was always alone. And yet every time Patricia showed up, Renee would be there, belly a little bigger, excited to show off some new find she'd gotten at the thrift store or crocheted herself.

A nurse midwife for twenty years, Patricia had seen all kinds of cases, but never anyone so excited to be a mother as Renee. A small blessing considering the hard road ahead of her, the delivery had gone like a dream. No complications whatsoever. Six hours of natural labor, and out popped Lyra Rose. It was women like Renee who made Patricia love her job.

And the baby? Adorable. Healthy, chubby, a regular Gerber baby, but with a halo of inch-long red hair the color of a new penny. Patricia had never seen any mother look at any baby with as much love as Renee had, the first moment she was placed into her arms.

Patricia smiled as she pulled off the two-lane highway, onto the dirt road leading up to the trailer park. She'd become a midwife because she loved helping women with what many would consider the most important day of their lives.

And she cared for all her young mothers. Sometimes, too much. Goodbyes were always hard on her heart, but she couldn't stay in their lives forever.

Her kids said she always had trouble with the moving on. It was why she still hadn't thrown out her daughters' stuffed animals and kept each of their rooms untouched, looking exactly as the day they flew the nest, even though they'd been out of the house for years.

But she loved babies and children, couldn't wait to have her own grandkids. Maybe, one day, she'd get a letter from Renee, thanking her for her friendship through this difficult time. Maybe she'd learn one day that little Lyra Rose had become a success and gone on to do great things. A doctor. A famous actress. Maybe she could say, one day, that she'd played a small part in that. After all, one of the first babies she'd ever delivered was now a quarterback for James Madison University, and there was talk of him being recruited into the NFL.

All in all, a very good life. But she'd thought it would get easier, saying goodbye to the babies she delivered. Unfortunately, it never had.

The radio had just begun blaring the news of the day, the sensational story of how that heiress, Patty Hearst, had been captured and arrested for armed robbery in California. *What a crazy world we live in these days,* Patricia thought as she flipped the radio off.

As she neared the trailer park, she saw something she'd never seen in these woods.

Flashing blue lights.

A police car.

No, two of them. Three.

Born and bred in this small town, Patricia had never seen three police cars congregated anywhere in Jolivue. Were there even three police officers in Jolivue? Nothing ever happened here.

But something was definitely happening now. Something bad.

She slowed to a near stop, creeping down the curving dirt road. When a loud horn blasted behind her, she nearly bit her tongue in surprise as she looked in the rearview mirror to see a large white form with flashing red lights bearing down upon her.

An ambulance.

One thought sprang to Patricia's head. *The baby. Lyra Rose is ill, or hurt, or worse.*

Pulling to the side of the road to let the ambulance pass, Patricia decided this was all her fault. Renee was a new mother, had so many questions, and likely hadn't had anyone to ask once Patricia had gone away. What if Renee had made an error of judgement? A serious one? And Patricia hadn't been there to help her.

Patricia's eyes drifted to the diaper basket, and the card she'd written out. Too late.

Maybe if she'd given it to Renee sooner, she wouldn't have felt like she had to handle this all on her own. After the birth, she'd told Renee she would make herself available if she was needed. But Renee was a sweet girl, overly accommodating and always saying she didn't want to be too much trouble. Maybe Renee hadn't wanted to bother her?

And now…now something horrible had happened.

Patricia threw open the door to her Dart and rushed through the crunching leaves toward a small gathering of grim-looking police officers as the paramedics filed inside the rusty old Airstream trailer. As she approached, an older officer with a salt-and-pepper moustache and a tired face turned to her and held up his hands. "We'll need you to stay back," he said gruffly.

"Is Lyra Rose okay?" Patricia asked desperately, trying to peek over the officer's broad shoulders to see the new mother. "The baby?"

"Baby?" His eyes narrowed as he studied her. "Were you friends with Miss Best?"

Were?

Patricia's blood ran cold at the use of the verb tense. Not *are.* If she hadn't been so alarmed, she would've explained exactly who she was, but instead she said, "Yes. Did something happen to her?"

He nodded. "I'm afraid so. There's been a suicide."

"Suicide?" Patricia said the word aloud to try to get it through her head. Not Renee. Not that peppy young thing who always had a smile on her face. "That's not possible. I was her midwife. I delivered the baby two weeks ago. Everything was fine. It's just...not possible."

"I'm sorry. A neighbor reported not seeing her or her baby for a couple of days and asked that we check up on her. It appears she overdosed on prescription medication."

Patricia recoiled. Prescription meds? How did she even get those? Renee had been insistent about natural childbirth. She didn't want any medication in her bloodstream. "Prescription medication?" Patricia repeated.

"Yes." His gaze grew even sharper. "As her midwife, did you notice any signs of postpartum depression? Did she talk to you at all about being sad or blue or wanting to kill herself?"

"N-no." Her voice cracked, and she cleared her throat, swallowing down the tears threatening to take over. "Not at all. Not even once. She was very happy, and she was thrilled to be a mom. I didn't have the slightest concern."

"Well, how often did you visit with her?" he said, eyebrow cocked in doubt.

Patricia crossed her arms, suddenly cold on this warm autumn day. "Once a week. That's per usual. If I saw any reason to visit more often than that, I would. But I had no reason to." She still couldn't get over the feeling that this officer was blaming her for missing key signals to Renee's condition, so she added, "Look. I've been doing this for twenty years, and I've seen many women who suffer from postpartum depression, and I can tell you right now that Renee Best wasn't one of them."

"I see." He sounded unimpressed.

Patricia sighed and looked up as the paramedics wheeled a stretcher toward the door of the trailer. "Where's Lyra Rose?"

Ignoring her question, the officer pulled out a pen and pad and jotted something down. "What's your name?"

"Patricia Hastings," she murmured, watching as the paramedic went inside the small trailer. Her eyes trailed down to her feet, where she saw something pink among the leaf-cover. With her toe, she moved the leaves away and realized it was a little pink bootie that Renee had knitted for the child. She'd been so proud of them. She said it was her first knitting project, ever.

Patricia reached down to pick it up, then froze when the officer barked, "Don't! Please, don't touch anything. When did you see Miss Best last?"

"A week ago," she said, desperation settling over her. She tried again. "Where's the baby?"

He wrote something else down. "Where do you live?"

She sighed, getting annoyed. "I'm sorry. Am I a suspect or something? What's—"

"No, Mrs. Hastings. These are just routine questions. Renee's baby is missing, and as of now, you may be the last person who's seen her."

Patricia's stomach dropped. "Missing?"

"There's the possibility that the mother killed the baby prior to committing suicide. It's often the case when someone feels hopeless. They may take it out on the innocent child. If that's the case, she may have buried the child nearby."

"Renee?" Patricia gasped as he rounded up a couple officers and asked them to search the vicinity. "Oh, no! Never!"

There were several other trailers around, all in various states of disrepair. At one of them, Patricia saw a couple of children's faces peeking out from behind a dirty window.

"Loneliness often drives people to do terrible things," he said, shaking his head with regret. "She clearly had money troubles and no way of supporting herself."

"She may have been alone," Patricia argued, her voice rising with each word, "but she wasn't hopeless. She'd been so happy the last time I saw her. Yes, she might've been low-income, but she was really excited about her future, and she loved Lyra. The last time I spoke to her on the phone a few days ago, she was looking into subsidized daycares so she could start working again. She was *looking forward*. She wasn't even a little bit sad about her situation."

The officer shrugged. "I suppose you never can tell. She might not have appeared sad because she'd already made the decision to end it."

So much was wrong with that, Patricia didn't even know where to start. "No. That's wrong."

He gave her a look that said he was not amused and didn't really care to hear her opinion. "I'm sorry, but you'll have to leave now," the officer said, pointing down the driveway. "We can't have people uninvolved in the investigation loitering around here."

She took a step back and started to turn, her mind still awhirl, when the paramedics appeared in the doorway with a stretcher containing the black body bag of the young mother. Nausea bubbled in Patricia's throat as they wheeled it through a square patch of dirt. Only a week ago, they'd shared tea in the little kitchenette, and Renee had talked about how she was planning to make a garden for fresh vegetables so she could make her own baby food.

Renee. Dead.

Suicide.

How could this have happened?

Patricia backed up, tripping over a tree root before righting herself and scrambling back into her car. As she turned the key in the ignition, she looked over at the diaper basket filled with the extra diapers and even a little bunny pacifier that Patricia had chosen just because Renee had loved the snuggly looking creatures.

Tears flooded her eyes, and by the time she'd made a three-point turn and pulled out onto the main road, she was sobbing. Those poor babies. The two of them. Renee was really just a baby herself. Naïve. Maybe she'd had a flash of clarity and realized just how hopeless her situation was.

But even if Renee was feeling hopeless, how could a mother kill a child? Or just abandon her somewhere? How could a mother not feel at least some motherly instinct toward a baby?

Patricia gripped the steering wheel tightly, knowing that she needed to only turn on the evening news to see how a mother could do such a horrible thing.

Not Renee. Patricia just couldn't believe it. The moment she'd given birth, she'd cradled that baby to her breast and

Patricia had seen them bond. That's why none of this made any sense.

But how well did she really know the women whose babies she delivered? Even Renee. Seeing her a couple times a month didn't make them best friends. Maybe there was a darkness within the young mother that Patricia hadn't detected.

That just didn't seem right, though. She thought she was a good judge of character. Renee hadn't been even remotely depressed. And why would a woman care so much about not harming her child during her pregnancy and childbirth, and then kill the helpless infant weeks later?

Patricia reached over and rolled down the window of her car, grabbed her Virginia Slims from the glove compartment, and lit one up, her hands still shaking. She sucked on the filter, trying to calm herself, and blew out a cloud of smoke as she entered downtown Staunton, where she lived.

Stopping at a light, she set her cigarette down in the ashtray and pulled the card from the basket with the cute little chick on the front. *Welcome Chickadee!* the front proclaimed.

Reading her message inside one last time, she tore it in half, then in half again. She wiped at her eyes, tossing the papers to the passenger's side of her car.

Rolling down her window for some much needed air, she froze, her ears picking up a sound. A baby's cry. An infant, from the sound of it.

Patricia craned her neck to see an impeccably dressed woman in the passenger seat of the fancy sedan next to her. She was rocking an adorable little pink wrapped bundle to her chest, looking exasperated.

Patricia blinked. Then blinked again.

Was she going insane?

Because that little baby looked almost exactly like Lyra Rose.

Her eyes weren't what they used to be, though. She waved away the cloud of thick cigarette smoke, softly pressed the gas, and slowly rolled up so that she was now in line with the window, striving to get closer. She leaned her head out the window so she could get even nearer.

Yes. It could be.

All newborn babies look the same, her husband, Al, had once said to her.

And while that was true—they all kind of looked a little pruny and odd—by their second week of life, they started to distinguish themselves. A week ago, Patricia had remarked to Renee that Lyra Rose had the perfect little nose, and what's more…an adorable dimple in the center of her chin.

No question. This baby had that dimple.

And how many babies had dimples like that? Week old babies with perfect noses? What were the chances?

Lyra Rose also had one ear that was slightly smaller and stuck out more than the other. She'd recommended to Renee to get the baby's hearing checked, because deformities of the ear often meant hearing issues. If Patricia could see both ears close enough to compare, she felt for certain she'd know.

And that hair.

If only the baby wasn't wearing a little cap, she would know for sure.

When Patricia was practically hanging from her driver's side window, the woman holding the baby noticed her. She smiled at first, but the smile soon faded as Patricia continued to scrutinize the child with narrowed eyes, willing the woman to turn the baby more fully toward her so that she could see both sides of her head.

Then, without warning, the driver stepped on the gas,

and the car surged ahead, making a left turn, leaving Patricia at the green light. Behind her, a horn blared.

Heart pounding in her chest, she made the split-second decision to follow, nearly side-swiping another car as she swerved into the left lane, making the turn. More horns blared. As she followed the sedan, she told herself she'd just get one more glimpse of the baby, to be sure. The car was a late-model Buick, bright blue, and from what she could see, though her eyes weren't so good anymore, the first digits of the license plate were W4B or WAB.

She tapped her trimmed fingernails on the steering wheel as she watched the car go into a place with a sign that said Yorkshire Terrace. Another new development that hadn't been here a year ago. The shingled roofs of gorgeous new homes were visible among the trees.

Patricia turned in, following from a safe distance as she watched the car slowly make its way past children playing basketball in the street, their bikes strewn over the grass and sidewalks. The driver of the car beeped cheerily, waved, and said something to the kids as they passed. High-pitched laughter filled the air, and on the other side of the street, a child wheeled by on a tricycle.

About six houses in from the entrance to the neighborhood, the car pulled into the long driveway of a gorgeous, sprawling, brick-front split level. A dwelling that looked rather like the house in the *Brady Bunch*, that show Al was obsessed with.

As Patricia slowly inched by, the kids playing on the street regarded her like exactly who she was: a stranger interrupting their game. Once she passed them, she pulled to the curb and watched as the mother stepped out from the Buick. She was wearing a smart plaid dress and matching shoes, holding the baby in her arms. A well-dressed man in a striped tie came around from the driver's side, and they started to walk up a flower-lined path to the front door.

Patricia sighed. They looked like the picture of the All-American dream, the pinnacle of human aspiration. Where the radio constantly blared about Patty Hearst and Watergate and Vietnam, all that was awful in the world...this family was everything that was right with it.

The baby couldn't have been Lyra Rose. This had to just be Patricia's imagination running away with her. Her grief was simply interfering with her logic.

She'd been watching too much Ellery Queen on television, Al would probably say. Had this well-to-do couple kidnapped the baby and murdered Renee? No. Of course not.

But Patricia found herself jumping from her car, nevertheless.

Until she made sure, absolutely sure, she would never sleep well at night ever again.

Skipping into a run, she made it across the street as the man and woman reached their front door. "Excuse me!" she called to them, stepping onto the sidewalk and starting up their wide two-car driveway.

They both turned. The baby cried harder, its little face bloodred now. The corner of the woman's eyes wrinkled in recognition, and she clutched the baby closer to her chest. "Yes?"

"I'm sorry. I saw your baby back there, at the light," she said, realizing she hadn't come up with any story ahead of time. Obviously, they'd think she was insane. Or worse, a kidnapper. After all, she'd *followed* them. "And—"

"I know. I saw you in the car back there at the light. You... you followed us home?" Although the woman's voice was more confused than accusing, she still snatched the screaming baby even closer to her chest.

"Well, yes," Patricia said, blushing as she crossed over

their manicured green lawn, hoping to get a closer look at the newborn's ears. "I'm sorry, this is so presumptuous of me, but I've never seen such a beautiful child."

The man smiled proudly, unaware of anything being wrong. He touched the baby's red cheek, and the baby turned its head instinctively, searching for food. "Yeah, she's a peach, isn't she?"

"Oh, yes," Patricia said, staring hard at the child. "What is her name?"

"Jennifer," the woman said, her voice and body language still hesitant.

Right. Well, of course she wouldn't be named Lyra.

"She's…beautiful," Patricia repeated, still trying to get a look at those ears. And the hair. But the baby was wearing a tiny pink beanie. If only she could… "Could I, perhaps, hold her?"

The couple looked at one another, and for a moment, Patricia thought they'd agree. The man opened his mouth, but the woman took a step back. "Oh, Frank…"

Finally sensing her concern, the man stepped in front of his wife. "You know, maybe not. Kid can be kind of skittish if she ain't with her momma. You know how babies can be."

Patricia shifted her eyes to the woman, who was staring at her cautiously. *Was* she the mother? She looked remarkably trim and well-rested for a woman who'd just had a baby, but some women were known for springing back like that.

"Oh. Of course." She tittered a bit, rubbing her damp hands down the front of her uniform. "The bond between a mother and child is powerful."

The man laughed and cleared his throat. "Well, yes. We were blessed to have Jennifer come into our lives just yesterday, so we're still getting used to all of—"

Come into their lives?

"Was she adopted?" Patricia blurted, then quickly lowered

her voice. She sounded like a maniac. "That's so wonderful." She desperately wanted to have a look under that hat. She craned her neck, noticing the bulge of the ear, but that didn't say much.

If only you could talk, baby, you'd tell me. Did I deliver you?

"Well, it was nice meeting you," the woman said curtly, turning her back to Patricia.

"Yes," Patricia said reluctantly, taking a step back. "Best of luck with your precious new addition."

"Thanks, ma'am," the man said, giving her a hard look before turning toward his wife.

But she couldn't bring her feet to move from the spot where they'd been rooted. She couldn't simply walk away. The baby was the right age, the right sex, and she had the dimple. And she'd been *adopted*. That was enough.

"Actually…" she said loudly. The couple turned toward her. "I hope you…I mean, I'm not exactly sure how I should put this to you, but you see, I'm a midwife. And well, one of my clients was just found to have committed suicide, and her baby is missing." She swallowed and motioned to Jennifer. "Your daughter looks very much like that child. Where did you adopt her from?"

"W-well, I-I-I…" the father stammered, his face reddening. "There's got to be some—"

"It's a very reputable agency!" the woman snapped, turning with the child to keep Patricia from looking at her. "I'm sorry, whoever you are, but you're mistaken. And I want you to leave. Get off our property. Now."

"But—"

"Now!" The father barked, and Patricia apologized as he opened the door and allowed his wife to go in first. With a final glare, he stepped inside and slammed the door with a resounding bang. The moment it was closed, the lock clicked home.

She sighed.

Well, what could she expect? She'd all but accused them of stealing the child. If she'd been in their shoes, she probably would've reacted the same way.

She walked back to her car, and as she looked up at the house, noticed the vertical blinds dip in an upstairs room. They were watching her. On the street, the boys had stopped playing basketball and were now frowning at her like she was worse than a stranger—more like a criminal. Likely, they'd heard the whole tense exchange.

The boys weren't the only ones watching, either. From a car parked by the sidewalk, someone stared at her, although she couldn't see them very well.

Patricia hung her head, suddenly very embarrassed by her actions.

What was she doing?

Swiping a stray strand of her blonde hair back, Patricia gave the kids an apologetic wave that they didn't seem to accept. She climbed into her car and willed herself to put the horrible day out of her mind. Al would be home from work soon. She needed to stop playing Columbo, get back to the house on the other side of town, and make him dinner.

She'd talk to Al about these things as they ate. He was usually her voice of reason. He'd be honest and tell her if she was flying off the deep end which, most likely, she was. She had a history of obsessing about things, especially anything related to babies.

But that sweet little baby didn't leave her mind. She always thought it'd be hard to forget Lyra Rose, but now, she knew that as long as she lived, the memory of that child would be engrained in her mind. While she drove to the Safeway at the Staunton Mall, while she was loading the groceries for that evening's dinner into the trunk, even when she started the oven for the pork chops, she was thinking of poor Renee and sweet little Lyra Rose.

She didn't need to ask Al. She couldn't let this go. She needed to do something. Just in case.

Even if she was mistaken, it was better to be safe than sorry.

She was putting the butter back in the fridge and had just made up her mind to go to the police with her fears when the doorbell rang.

She checked the clock on the kitchen wall. Five-thirty. They rarely got visitors on their rural street—even Avon ladies found it too remote to be worth it. This had to be Al. He had a terrible habit of forgetting his key.

She'd forgive him, though, since he was right on time. The pork chops were ready, just the way he liked them. With applesauce on the side.

Wiping her hands on the dishrag, she threw open the door to their modest little rancher. "Al, you'll never believe what happened to—"

Bam. Bam.

The two bullets that slammed into her chest rocketed her back into the wall. Her legs gave way, and she sank to the floor as two legs appeared in her line of vision.

She opened her mouth to speak. Say something. Anything.

Please, her mind screamed when her lips refused to work. *Don't. Please don't.*

But when she looked up, all she could see was the black barrel of the gun staring back at her.

"Please…" she whispered. "Please don—"

Bam.

2

P *resent day...*

"WELL…?"

Kylie Hatfield Coulter looked at her husband of three whole months, her phone still pressed to her ear. His question was repeated on his face. The raised eyebrows, the inquisitive gleam in his eyes. The genuine curiosity and hope that she'd just landed a new case…a new, *safe* case.

But Kylie had a bigger question, a bigger curiosity, burning through her mind.

Sure, she'd love a big, fat, juicy case, safe or not. Her new role as an official—business card and all—private investigator was all well and good, but it usually involved dull day-to-day grunt work of conducting background checks and workers' comp surveillance. Nothing too exciting. It was the big crimes that rarely happened that really got Kylie's heart pumping. And, to be honest, the woman who'd just called sounded like she had a case that would get Kylie's blood flowing.

But...

She looked at the bathroom. The same bathroom she'd lost her stomach lining in just a few minutes ago before being forced to come out and take a phone call. The same bathroom holding a little stick she'd just peed on. The same bathroom that held the answer to the question burning in her mind.

Positive?

Negative?

"Kylie?"

Linc's look of concern was a reminder that she needed to speak. She needed to tell him about the phone call she'd just taken. The new case. Something.

She needed to say something.

But before she could, one of the ten puppies playing and rolling around on the floor in delighted puppy glee squatted and a pale circle of puppy pee spread around him. Or her. Kylie still couldn't tell them apart at first glance.

"No!"

The word came from her mouth more sharply than she'd meant to say it, and all the puppies looked at her in abject terror. Feeling immediately regretful, Kylie picked up the guilty one and hugged him—or her—tightly, burying her face in the soft fur while Linc swiped a few sheets from the roll of paper towels they now kept in every room.

Wincing against the sound of all the barking, whimpering, yipping, and growling, Kylie looked around the squirming sea of furry puppies scattered about their living room as she wiped dog drool from her fingers.

If this wasn't hell, it was pretty darn close.

Coulter Confidential, the new business venture she'd

started with her husband, Linc, was anything but conventional, that was for sure. It was less of a private investigations firm, and more of a…madhouse.

But with this most recent bout of nausea, she had a feeling that it was about to get a lot madder.

She'd woken up with it, had some coffee and toast, and felt better. But now it was back. And that was not good. Not good at all.

"Let's go, guys," Linc said to the dogs, and they all scrambled after him as he led them to the fenced in yard.

Blessed silence.

"Guess what?" Linc said as the screen door slammed. A moment later, her beloved husband reappeared in their makeshift office area at the front of the house, where they had two desks arranged front-to-front, so the newlyweds could gaze lovingly at one another.

Though she really hadn't been doing much of that lately. Right now, even Linc Coulter's handsome face wanted to make her puke. "What?"

"Fixed the handle on your door."

That was amazing. The thing had only been busted since the last case, when Vader chewed his way out of her Jeep to come to their rescue. "Really? Did you do it yourself?"

He nodded. "Wasn't so hard."

"Then I don't know why it took you forever." She tamped down the nausea and smiled at him sweetly.

He blew on his fingernails and pretended to polish them on his chest. "Pure genius takes time. How's work in here going?"

She looked around at the accumulating pile of papers on her desk. "It's going. The little monsters are at it, though, as usual."

He shrugged. "That's nothing new."

"Did you train them at all today?"

"Best I can. Puppies are hard. They're coming along, though. Slowly. But I can tell they're smart. They just got a hell of a lot of energy. They'll make good SARs, though, one day."

Right. She knew that. Just now…they were a little hard to handle.

A lot hard.

Actually, everything was. New company, new puppies, new husband…and here she'd thought that once she got married, things would settle down. Instead, she felt like there was a knot in the middle of her chest, tightening every time a new wrinkle popped up. Right now, she was so wrinkly she felt like an old lady.

That wasn't like her. She'd never been able to concentrate for long on one thing, but as she was ping-ponging around, she'd normally been so glass-half-full. So happy.

But now…it felt like her emotions were all over the place. Happy one minute, freaking out the next.

She didn't need any more wrinkles to show themselves. And she wasn't sure that Happy Kylie would ever come back.

Because of the summer heat, Linc had been walking around in nothing but gym shorts all day, and she had to admit, looking mighty fine doing it. They'd just celebrated their three-month anniversary, and she was still as excited to look at him as she ever had been. She laid a hand on her stomach to quell the butterflies.

Nausea climbed up her throat again, reminding her of what was waiting for her in the bathroom. Not that she needed a reminder.

He leaned back and placed his hands behind his head. "So, you going to spill about the case or what? I know I'm only the second in command around here, but I hate being kept in the dark."

She balled up a piece of paper and threw it at him. "For the last time, you're *not* second in anything. We're equals in this venture. Remember? And I was just going to fill you in. That was Elise Kirby."

His face darkened with confusion. "You say that name like I should know it."

"Well, that's because you should. Elise Kirby from the Sunset Diner? The waitress who always remembers that I want extra butter with my toast?"

He squinted at her. "*I* don't even know you want extra butter with your toast. Is that a thing?"

She simply shook her head. Men could be so thick.

"Of course it is. They give you those tiny little pats of butter, and it's never enough. You know I'm a butter fiend and—"

She stopped. Why was she arguing about butter with him when there was a pregnancy test cooling in the bathroom cabinet, waiting to reveal its contents? Did pregnancy tests go bad? If she waited too long, would it give her the wrong answer? But Linc was waiting on her to explain, so it wasn't like she could just call a break and go check, especially considering she'd *just* been in the bathroom less than two minutes ago. If she hightailed it back there now, he was bound to get suspicious.

"Anyway," she said, sitting on her hands to stop from fidgeting with them, "Elise says she wants to possibly hire me. She said something about a phony adoption agency, but I think she might be a little confused. Something about a baby she thinks is missing."

"She seemed…" He touched the side of his head. "Am I right?"

Kylie nodded. Elise Kirby was what some people might call a little slow. It might have been an intellectual disability, but she also walked like she was moving through molasses, with a little bit of a limp. And when she spoke, it usually took her quite a while to get the words out.

"But she's so sweet. I really like her, so I agreed to meet her this afternoon." Kylie wiggled her eyebrows at Linc. "Now who thinks it was a dumb idea to put the ads for Coulter Confidential on their placemats?"

Linc raised his hand, grinning at her. "I still do. Just because some waitress hires you for what could or could not even be a case doesn't mean that you're going to recoup the three-hundred bucks a month you put into it."

Kylie's face pinched. She'd really been proud of that advertising coup, especially when she'd finagled an extra month free out of the ad exec. "You just wait. Anyway. We should probably clean up this sty before she gets here."

"Wait." He looked down at the balls of fur floating around like fuzzy tumbleweeds. "You're meeting her *here*?"

"Yeah. She said it was a personal matter. She didn't want anyone at the diner hearing about it."

He considered this. "About an adoption agency?"

Kylie nodded.

"Interesting." He pushed up off his chair and grabbed a training leash. "Going to see if I can't do some one-on-one training with Beatrice. She's the most promising. If she gets it, maybe her siblings'll fall in line."

Kylie smiled wide at him, trying not to shoo him away. She was anxious to get rid of him because of what waited in the bathroom cabinet.

"Have fun," she said to him, still sitting on her hands. *Get moving, bud. I got things to do. Life and death things.*

The second the screen door slammed, all the pups but Beatrice hustled back inside, yipping and sliding on the wood floors.

She cursed, then rushed to the bathroom as if her pants

were on fire. By then, she was sweating and nauseated again. A few more dry heaves later, she grabbed the wand, and saying a little prayer, raised it up so that she could read her future.

3

Something was definitely up with Kylie.

If only Linc knew what it was.

He'd known Kylie for over a year now, and that was the thing about her. She was always optimistic, even on the worst days. And now...not so much.

He took a few breaths in the bracing mountain air. It was still summer, and yet the weather was comfortable this high up. He'd grown up here, on this hill, preferring the tranquility of his grandparents' vast oasis to his parents' stuffy mansion in Biltmore.

Kylie was turning out to be a different story. Oh, she said she loved the farmhouse, but she sometimes grouched whenever they had to drive a half-hour to get to the supermarket, remembering fondly the days when she could walk right out of her downtown Asheville apartment and grab everything she needed at the market next door.

Once they were married, Linc thought they'd become the type of couple who read each other's minds and completed each other's sentences.

Fat chance.

With Kylie, he'd quickly learned that was impossible. She was, and always had been, all over the place. Just like Vader, her Newf. Two peas in a pod.

Not like Beatrice here, Linc thought, petting the pup's side. She may have looked like Vader, but inside, she was all Storm, his well-behaved German Shepherd, and until an injury sidelined her last year, one of the best SAR dogs in the state. Bea, who Kylie had named after one of the rescuers who'd been murdered on a case she'd solved, was calm. Even temperament. Not prone to any Vader-like outbursts of insanity.

Kylie may have had a definite case of ADHD, but what made him able to tolerate her was that, like Vader, Kylie was always, always positive. Happy. Infectiously so.

Now…Kylie's unpredictability was rearing its ugly head even more. Because now, he couldn't even count on the happiness.

"Come on, girl," he said, leading Bea into the fenced yard. When he closed the latch, he let her off the leash and started out with the basic commands.

Talk about insanity. Ever since Kylie'd started this venture a month after they'd gotten married in May, she was up one minute, down the next. She was so invested in getting it off the ground, spending long hours transitioning every-thing from Greg, that she'd barely had time to breathe. Prob-ably just stress, but she'd quickly gone from high-strung yet upbeat to high-strung and moody.

That's why he'd decided it'd be better to remove himself from her hair. They didn't fight much, but when they did, it could get real ugly, real fast. She didn't stop until she'd figu-ratively pinned him to the floor, and he didn't like confrontations.

He'd quickly learned that it was easier to either let her win or walk away.

When Beatrice lifted a paw when he asked her to shake, he smiled. Good dog. She'd gotten all the basic stuff already.

Now, it was time to introduce some basic SAR lessons.

As Linc was about to get her started on scenting, the back door opened, and a crazy parade of dogs barreled straight for him, barking and intent on creating a little havoc.

What the...

Whenever all the dogs got together like this, all the training lessons pretty much went out the window. There were too many of them to adequately train as a group.

"I can't clean anything with them in here!" Kylie yelled, her head poking through the door. "Elise'll be here any minute. You're the dog whisperer! You deal with them!"

Well, okay then.

He opened the gate that led to the yard, closed his eyes and rubbed his temples as several of the more Vader-like dogs jumped at him, wanting to play. All right. So, training would have to wait.

He threw a ball for them to chase, thinking of his wife.

It wasn't supposed to be like this. They were married. She was his. He was hers. All those relationship head games were supposed to be behind them. Wedded bliss, right?

Then why was she acting like this? Was it really the stress of the job, or something else? He'd thought the anxiety of starting the new business would let up after a couple months, but if today was any indication, it only seemed to be getting worse.

Just this morning, she'd been so happy. What the hell had made her turn on a dime like that? If he talked to his brothers, they'd have probably told him she was on the rag, but that was the reason he never went to Craig and Erik for marital advice, even though both of them were much older and no strangers to married life.

What it was, probably, was too many changes too soon.

Marriage. All the puppies. The new business. Mountain farm life.

Her old life had completely transformed into something different, and she needed time to process all the changes. She had a reason to be stressed right now. The best he could do was hang on for the ride.

And something that he wasn't really all that great with. Communication.

Yeah. Kylie was big on communication. Really big. She never stopped talking, wanting to share feelings, but as the strong, silent type, that was hard for him. She had been rather closed-off lately, probably because she was too busy trying to keep all of her balls from dropping.

Maybe that's all he had to do. Open up the lines of communication.

He'd go in there and talk to her until she spilled whatever was bothering her. She'd seemed like she wanted him out of her way, but maybe he should've offered to clean up with her. Maybe he should've told her that if there was anything she wanted to tell him, he was all ears.

Right. That was it.

He threw the ball again, then bounded up the back steps and went into the kitchen. As he was opening the door, he caught sight of Kylie, sitting at the kitchen island, phone in front of her, holding something he couldn't quite see in her hand.

As soon as she looked up, she snatched the thing behind her back and scowled. "What are you doing in here?"

Wow. That was a tone of voice he hadn't expected. Had she ever sounded that annoyed with him before? "I just wanted to see if you needed me for—"

"I needed you to keep the dogs busy while I cleaned up in here," she snapped, fisting one hand on her hip while keeping the other behind her back. What was she hiding?

He leaned against the doorframe, studying her closely. She looked a bit flushed. Had she been crying? "Are you sure you're okay? You've been acting a little—"

"I'm fine!" She bit the words off in a way that proved the opposite. Not at all fine. Before him, she took in a really deep breath, closing her eyes as if praying for patience. When she opened them again, she smiled. A big, fake smile. "I'm sorry, honey. I was just googling my newest client to see if there was any info on her. I like to go into my meetings prepared."

Kylie was usually the very opposite of prepared, but he didn't argue with her. She had been getting better, doing the things that were necessary even when they weren't necessarily fun. Research would be one of them.

Even so, she'd been trained by the best private investigator in Asheville, Greg Starr, who'd been at the business for forty years before he took Kylie on as a lowly filing clerk...at first. But she'd shown that she had so much spunk, grit, and determination that she'd quickly risen in the ranks before he decided to place the business and all its assets in her capable hands and fish his way into retirement.

All right. If she insisted.

But she must've seen the doubt in his face, because she added, "I know, it's not *The Red-Headed League*, but we've all got to start somewhere. And I do feel bad for Elise. She sounded really worried."

"I'm sure you can help her." Working on new cases, helping people, always made Kylie happy.

But what the hell was behind her back? Why was she hiding things from him?

They were married. Secrets and hidden things were not supposed to happen between them. He walked around her, but she spun with him, facing her back away from him.

Definitely. Definitely hiding something.

The more she spun to face him, the more curious he got.

He had the urge to lunge over to her and grab it from her hand, whatever it was.

"I *hope* I can help her," she said, ignoring his curious looks. So that was it. Deflect, and maybe he'd forget about whatever it was she was hiding. "It'd be nice to have a good case that's not from Greg. Then I can really say the business is taking off."

"You'll do great." He wasn't really paying attention.

She picked up her phone and slid off the stool, still facing whatever was behind her back away from him. "I'm telling you. Those placemat ads? Pure gold."

Deflect, deflect, deflect.

He stared at her as if he could see through her, to whatever she was keeping from him. "I guess."

She nudged him. "Come on! Admit it!"

Now, she was teasing him? All right then. "Okay, okay. It was a good idea."

She gave him a triumphant smile, and then reached into the garbage bin, grabbed the overflowing bag, tossed whatever was in her hand in there, and tied it up tight.

"I'll take that out," he said, sensing his one and only chance.

"It's okay. I'll do it." She was already heading toward the front door, where she could get to the trash cans they kept near the barn.

He sighed. Even if she'd let him take out the trash, would he really have pulled open that bag to see what she'd thrown away? Didn't he trust her?

Yeah. He did. And that's why no…he would not go snooping on his wife. He trusted that if she had something to tell him, she would. "Hey, Lee?"

She stopped and spun to face him.

He'd practiced what he was going to say to her, and outside it had made sense, but now it seemed awkward. "If

there's anything you have to tell me or want to talk about…
I'm here."

She gave him a look like he was a many-horned thing that had crawled out of the pond out back. "Uh. Thanks."

Then she turned and pushed out the front door, letting the screen door slam behind her.

Scratching his head, he went to the back door, where the dogs were all pressing their noses up to the glass, wondering where he'd gone.

Heading outside, he groaned. As much as they said Coulter Confidential was their shared venture, it was really Kylie's baby. She loved it, just as he loved working with SAR dogs. She wanted desperately for it to succeed. So, if her three-hundred-dollar investment in placemat ads was going to get her where she wanted to be, he was all for it.

He just couldn't bring himself to be as invested as she was. He was invested in the sense that he wanted it to make her happy. But if it didn't? Then he had his job. It didn't make oodles of money, but eventually, when he had the dogs trained, he could sell them off, and that would probably net them enough money to live comfortably for the next few years, with or without Kylie working.

Besides, in another few years, he wanted kids. Actually, if he'd had his way, Kylie would be fat and pregnant right now. He was thirty-three. It was time to start a little brood of his own. But when the prospect of taking the investigations business over from Greg landed in her lap, they both decided to put starting a family off for a few years, to get the business off the ground.

Or at least, Kylie decided. He went along with it, because he wanted her happy. And the business? It made her happy unlike anything else. Even, sadly, sometimes him. He'd never seen her looking so alive as she did while she was in the throes of researching one of the big, important cases. She loved the thrill, the hunt, the adventure, the danger.

So, maybe being a private investigator wasn't the greatest job for a mom to have. Especially considering how Kylie always got herself embroiled in some heavy shit. In the past year, she'd been kidnapped, shot, had her car torched, and more. Kids didn't fit into that job description.

So, yeah. Waiting.

He took a deep breath, sucking in more of that mountain air and tried to relax. The dogs were fun, sure. He loved playing fetch with them. But he couldn't help thinking what it'd be like to be throwing a ball around with a little boy. His son.

Then he turned around and realized that half of the brood had disappeared.

"Damn it all to hell," he murmured when he went to the fence where he'd last seen them and noticed a small hole, like some animal had chewed through the wire.

Fantastic. The run he'd made for the dogs was about a football field's length in size and went from the back of the house down a long, grassy hill. But, apparently, that wasn't enough space for his spoiled pups. They wanted to explore.

Something told him that he'd be up late tonight, picking burrs out of fur. Wonderful.

Bending the wire to close it up, he told Beatrice, the good girl, and Britt, the good boy, to stay, and motioned for Storm to come with him. "Where'd they go, girl?" he asked her.

Once she got free of the fence, she tore off like a bolt of lightning toward the woods, surprisingly fast considering she'd lost a leg not that long ago. Linc had a sneaking suspicion that Storm's beau, Vader, the rebel, was at the helm of this particular prison break. He'd never been keen on setting a good example for his kids.

As Linc climbed down a sloping embankment, he saw the

pups between the trees and cursed. There was a small creek that ran through the property, the edges of which were mostly mud…thick, black mud.

And yes. Burrs. Lots and lots of burrs.

Even from several dozen yards away, he could see that most of the pups had gotten themselves good and dirty with all that nature had to offer them. They were rolling around in it, without a care in the world.

Shit. Kylie would be furious. She'd just love to finish cleaning the house, only to have these nightmares trailing mud and wet fur through it.

"Dammit!" he muttered under his breath, then shouted, "Come!"

Of course, Storm obeyed, moving swiftly in spite of her disability. The rest? Fat chance.

Linc slid down the embankment toward the rest of the muddy pups, getting his jeans coated in the dirt. When he got closer, he realized that Vader wasn't all that dirty. In fact, he was running around the pups, barking at them, nudging them with his nose. It was almost like he was trying to get them to behave.

"Vader, come," he said, and the enormous Newfoundland mix listened. He came, head down, looking immensely sorry. Linc patted his side but couldn't help feeling a flash of jealousy for the dog having pups to look after. Linc would've liked any pups, even misbehaving ones.

That would probably be a really nice feeling, to have a little someone to teach, to mold, to love. He was a traditionalist. He wanted that. Marriage. Kids. Maybe even a whole brood like the dogs had, one that would require a massive minivan. Their own freaking baseball team, or a clan that they could tote around to school events, a kid in every grade, and everyone would say, "Ah, here comes all the Coulters. All twelve of them."

But no. He wasn't going to tell Kylie that he'd made a mistake by agreeing with her that they should wait to start that family. She needed to feel comfortable in her job first.

All in good time.

"Come on, pups," he said to them, starting to walk back toward the house, hoping they'd be tired of the mud and the playtime and follow.

No surprise. They didn't.

4

Kylie was sitting out on the porch, practicing meditative breathing when the old, rusting Honda Civic came puttering up the hill.

She'd gotten control of herself.

More or less.

The house cleaning mission was a failure. It still looked like a bomb had been dropped in the very center of the living room, which happened to be Coulter Confidential's world headquarters. Actually, it looked worse than it had before she started, as if that was even possible, thanks to some unruly pups who'd decided to go inside directly after Linc hosed them off and get their muddy footprints all over the hardwood floors.

But even before then, she'd known cleaning was a lost cause. She couldn't so much as inhale the scent of a Clorox wipe without getting ill. She'd been spontaneously retching every few minutes, ever since she'd looked at that wand, confirming that, indeed, she was pregnant.

Pregnant.

There was a tiny baby growing inside her. By next spring, she'd have a child.

Try as she might, she couldn't wrap her head around it. It touched every little area of her life. As she was trying to go about her business, something new would occur to her, making her stop dead in her tracks. Did she have to go to the doctor now? Where would the nursery be? Had that glass of chardonnay she consumed last night fucked the baby up for good?

And then there was the big thing: Linc.

What would he say?

This wasn't supposed to happen. She should've known, though. She always said she would plan and research and really try to learn before she was thrown into something, but it never actually ended up working that way. More exciting things tended to sidetrack her.

Her life was about trial by fire. So, while she'd planned to read everything there was about being a mom before it actually happened, she didn't know the first thing. Didn't know a single thing about being pregnant or having a baby. Heck, the only time she'd ever held a baby was for a friend, two years ago, and she'd been stiff and scared to death, like it was a grenade about to go off in her face.

So cleaning was out of the question. Trying to give herself a break, she'd told herself it was a nice day, and she'd just meet with Elise on the front porch. That way, she could spare Elise the horror of the mess that was their house, and they could enjoy lemonade and the fresh country air from the porch swing.

Then it had started to rain, and a cool mountain wind had started to blow in from the west.

From the way Linc had been casting her worried glances and walking on eggshells around her, she got the feeling she was already going off the deep end, with the stress from everything. So she was determined to be her normal, cheery self where Elise was concerned.

As the car approached, windshield wipers arcing steadily, Kylie waved frantically, smiling as big as she could. The car stopped at the front steps, the passenger-side door opened, and Elise slowly emerged, despite the rain falling on her face.

She took her time, holding the railing of the staircase as she helped herself up, step by step. By the time she got to the porch, her long blonde hair was drenched.

"Hi, Elise!" Kylie said brightly. "Glad you're here."

"Hello, ma'am," she said, wiping raindrops off the end of her nose.

Ma'am? Kylie suddenly felt like a grandma.

"Please, call me Kylie." Kylie squinted to see beyond the rain-spattered windshield. "Does your…driver want to come out?"

Elise looked back. "Nah. That's just Cody. My boyfriend. He's fine out there."

"What's Cody's last name?"

Elise waved at the car. "Miller. Cody Miller."

"I thought we could…" Kylie stopped, looking back at the porch swing. The rain was now blowing in sideways, and the rocking chairs were wet too. And poor Elise's waif-like body was shuddering from the dampness. She was just wearing a tiny tank and shorts, and they were soaked through. This wasn't going to work. She grabbed the screen door. "Um. Let's go in."

She opened the door and let Elise in first, cringing when she saw all the puppies racing for the two of them, a tidal wave of fur.

"I hope you don't mind, but we have quite a few—"

"Oh!" Elise gasped, and at first, Kylie was worried she hated dogs, but then she crouched and let them all start licking her face. "They're so cute! Oh!"

They started to consume her, like locusts, and she giggled, clearly loving every minute of it. Pretty soon, she was on the floor, then on her back, letting them have at her. And have at her, they did.

Before Kylie could tell them to back off, the young woman squealed, "This is so fun!"

Kylie watched for a moment, wondering if they'd ever get down to business, with the puppies stealing the show, when Linc came out of the kitchen. "I thought you were—"

"It's too wet out there. Can you take the puppies somewhere else so we can talk in peace?"

He nodded and whistled for Riot and Roxy, the two mostly Vaders, who were starting to get in a fight in the middle of the living room right by her desk. "Yeah. Sure. We'll go out to the barn."

As he left, holding the door open so all of the puppies could tumble out onto the porch, Elise giggled. "They're so cute. How many do you have?"

"Ten puppies plus their mom and dad."

"Oh my goodness," the blonde girl said as Kylie led her to a seat beside her desk, which was overflowing with paper. "I've always wanted me a puppy, but Cody says we can't afford it."

The skeletal girl perched on the edge of the chair, her back straight, looking carefully at everything with a frown. She shivered, and Kylie wondered if it because she was cold or because the place was such a mess.

"Sorry that this place is a disaster."

"Are you kiddin' me? This place is great!" Elise exclaimed with a bit of a lisp. "Cody and I just live in a small apartment downtown. He calls it a dump. It's not bad, though. Overlooks the railroad, and I used to wake up ever time a train went by. Now, I guess I'm used to it."

She shivered again.

Kylie smiled and played hostess. "Would you like something to drink? Coffee or tea? Something to warm you up?"

"You got any milk?"

Milk. Strange request, but yes, they had that.

Kylie went to the kitchen and poured her a big glass of one percent milk. When she came back, Elise had her hands piled in her lap, and Kylie was sure she was trembling, despite it being pretty stuffy and warm inside. She wasn't sure if it was a chill or her nerves, but she brought a towel so the girl could dry herself off, just in case.

But if it was nerves, that was okay. That was where Kylie excelled. Greg had told her as much. She had a way of putting people at ease and making them open up—clients, witnesses, everyone. It was an important skill for her line of work, where people were often spilling their deepest secrets.

Kylie sat down on her chair and pulled her knee up to her chest, trying to be casual. "So, you said you had a possible case you needed help with?"

Elise's eyes widened, and her body crumpled. Her eyes volleyed around the room. "Well, I saw your ad, you see. On the placemat? And you seemed so nice whenever I waited on you two guys. I thought if anyone could help me, maybe you could?"

Kylie smiled. Placemat advertising had been a freaking fabulous idea. She made a mental note to make sure Linc knew that.

"Sure. I'd like to try. If you tell me what the trouble is."

Elise looked at the glass of milk cupped between her hands. "I'm not sleepin' well at night. I keep tryin' to, but it's real hard. Not because of my schedule. I take pills, ones that I got over the counter, not drugs." She finally looked up and met Kylie's gaze. "I don't do drugs," she insisted. "Just the sleep ones, but even they don't do nothin' for me anymore..."

Kylie shifted on her seat, listening, trying to understand

where the need for a private investigator would come in. Maybe Elise was confused. She spoke so slowly and in circles that even Kylie, who was usually a good listener, found her attention flagging.

She shifted her gaze to the window, where the dog whisperer was trying to round a bunch of soggy mutts into the barn and having a hell of a time doing it. They'd just managed to get the dogs cleaned up after their earlier mudbath. And now they were as bad, if not worse. Kylie smiled as two of the pups chased each other's tails in a circle around him.

What a disaster.

"…and I just don't know when it's goin' to end. I need my sleep. I don't get my sleep and someone at the diner ends up with key lime pie in their lap."

Kylie refocused on the woman and sighed. Gently, she said, "Elise, you do know I'm a private investigator, right?"

Her blue eyes widened again. "Oh, yeah. I sure do."

"And that's what I do. I investigate things for people who need me to help them."

Elise nodded vigorously.

"And, well…have you spoken to a doctor, maybe? One who specializes in sleep disorders? Because if you're having trouble sleeping, there are doctors who can prescribe you something to help. Unfortunately, I'm not sure if I'm the right person to help you with your problem."

Elise stared at her, mouth slightly open, her grip gradually loosening on the full glass of milk. Kylie noticed it before Elise did, but by the time she reached out to steady it, it was too late. The glass slipped from the girl's grip. It fell to the floor, spilling across the hardwood as the two women jumped to attention.

Before Elise could apologize, Kylie ran for the ever-present roll of paper towels. "Not a problem," she said, grabbing it and crouching to wipe up the spill. "You know what they say. No use crying over—"

"But she's out there," Elise said in a small, child-like voice. Tears flooded her eyes. "Somewhere. Without me. And you're the only one who can maybe bring her back."

Kylie stopped swabbing the mess and looked up, thoroughly confused. "Bring who back?"

"Daisy," the girl wailed. "My baby. I can't sleep because she's not with me. Because I don't know where she's at."

Kylie gradually rose to her feet, holding the glass and the wet wad of towels. "Your…baby?"

It might have been that Elise seemed too child-like herself, but Kylie had never imagined that such a tiny little fragile waif could have her own baby. She'd known her for a year at least, and nothing about Elise's infantile demeanor, slim hips, and nonexistent breasts suggested that she was a mother. Surely, she was speaking of something other than an actual baby. A beloved family pet who'd run away?

Elise nodded. "Well, she probably ain't a baby anymore. But…" she reached into her tiny denim purse and pulled out a photograph of a couple-days-old baby, the kind of mug shot that's usually taken in the hospital, "I can't stop thinkin' about her, ma'am."

Kylie let the "ma'am" slide this time because she was too eager to hear the rest of the story. She tossed the glass in the sink and the paper towels in the trash and rushed back to the girl, lightning fast. "She's beautiful. And she's your baby? I'm sorry, I didn't realize you were a mother. Can you start at the beginning?"

Elise opened her mouth to speak, but then stopped when a car horn blared outside. The two of them jumped, and the dogs started to bark. Elise straightened, an expression of pure fright on her face. "Um. Maybe I should just go. I mean, Cody told me this was shit-stupid, me comin' up here. He told me it was a waste of my time, botherin' you guys like this, since I don't got no money."

"No, no! Please!" Kylie begged, urging her to sit back down. "I'd like to hear what happened to your...Daisy, you said?"

Elise nodded and slowly sat down. "Cody's probably right. I mean, he told me these private investigators are expensive, and I don't got two pennies to rub together, like my ma used to say. I been saving up, but I still don't got enough. And if the police say she's gone, then she's gone."

"All right. But that's okay." She put a hand on the girl's arm. "Don't worry about that. Just tell me what happened from the very beginning and don't think about the money. Okay?"

The horn blared again. That boyfriend of hers, Cody, was being an asshole. Kylie wanted to run outside and stick the horn up his ass.

Elise shook her head. "I should—"

Kylie gritted her teeth. "Wait."

She went to the window and spotted Linc standing in the driving rain. Whatever whisperings he was using on the dogs was obviously not working since he was drenched through and they were frolicking like drunken college students at a frat party—even the so-called good ones. From his hunched posture, hands in the pockets of his cargo shorts, it looked as if he'd given up. She pushed open the window with the heel of her hand and motioned him over.

His hair slicked down in his eyes, he loped over to her, looking nothing short of miserable. His t-shirt was plastered to his muscular frame and the water was running in rivers down his face, spouting off his chin like a faucet turned all the way up. As he got closer, he sneezed.

"God bless you," she said automatically. "Could you do me a favor and entertain Elise's boyfriend?"

He ducked his head under an eave for a momentary reprieve and raised an eyebrow. "Entertain?"

"Yeah. I'm in the middle of the consultation with Elise, and I'm trying to listen to her story. I'd really like to get to the bottom of this, so I need a few more minutes."

Linc shifted his gaze toward the front of the house, where the beat-up old Honda was idling. "What do you want me to do? My soft-shoe routine?"

"No," she said, trying not to smile. She'd known he'd say something like that. "I don't know. Think of something. Show him the llamas. He's getting ants in his pants, and I really just need five more minutes with her. Please?"

He grunted and headed to the front of the house, his boots kicking up mud in the deep puddles. She was going to owe him big-time later. Probably in bed, knowing him. Could pregnant women have sex? She'd have to research that later.

Oh, god. She was pregnant. In the excitement of Elise's case, she'd almost forgotten.

Forcing that little notion away, Kylie sat down again and pulled out a pad and pen. "All right. Now, where were we?" Elise was gnawing on her lip, clearly reluctant, so Kylie decided to push her along. "Tell me about Daisy?"

Elise shook her head. "I don't...oh!"

Just then, they were interrupted by Britt, the shiest puppy of the litter. Somehow, while Linc was herding them all outside, Britt must've been overlooked, as he often was. Though she had a hard time telling the dogs apart, she knew Britt because he was only about three-quarters the size of the other dogs. He was more German Shepherd than Newf, with a trimmed beige coat and little ears. When he licked at Elise's flip-flop, she wiggled her purple toenails and giggled.

"Oh, who's she?"

"He. That's Britt."

"Britt!" Elise reached down and lifted him up, regarding him at eye-level before bringing him into her arms. "He's so cuddly. Oh my gosh, he's the cutest little doggy."

Kylie smiled. "He's a good boy," she said as Elise stroked the fur between his ears, completely enamored. "So, about Daisy…?"

"Daisy. She was my…baby," Elise said, her voice full of child-like delight, as if she was cooing a bedtime story to the puppy. "Cody ain't the father, so maybe that's why he don't care. I got pregnant when I was seventeen." She finally took her eyes off the little dog and glanced up at Kylie, shame like a mask on her face.

Kylie leaned forward and covered her hand with hers. "It's okay. Just tell me what happened."

Tears came to the young woman's eyes, and she hugged the pup closer to her chest. "Wasn't good in school so I fell in with a bad group. We partied a lot. Drinking and doing things we shouldn't of. One night, I went drinking, passed out, and woke up with a man on top of me."

Kylie barely stopped herself from gasping. "Who?"

Elise shrugged. "Don't know who. I think it was one of my friends' fathers. My mom kicked me out when she found out I was pregnant, so I went to live with my older brother, Hal. But he went off to be an army man and left me alone in his trailer. I was scared and mad and sad. All these feelings inside me…and a baby too."

Kylie moved her pen to the paper, feeling sad to her very core for Elise. And anger. And helplessness. And through all those emotions, she couldn't stop thinking about the life inside her.

This sweet young woman had been serving her and Linc for over a year, always smiling, always happy. It just went to show that everyone was struggling with their demons. It made Kylie feel bad for stressing over her situation. She had a husband who loved her, which was more than a lot of people had.

"Nine months later, I had Daisy," Elise said, smiling so brightly that Kylie couldn't help but return it. "She was perfect. Everythin' just seemed to fall into place, you know? I stayed home from the diner for six weeks, just me and Daisy, bondin' and all that. I swear, it was the best time of my life. I loved that little girl with every inch of my heart."

"And then?"

Elise leaned down and planted a kiss on Britt's wet nose, and Britt licked her chin in return. She giggled. "Well, I don't got no trust fund, so I knew I'd got to get back to work because I was already three months behind on the rent, and Hal hadn't sent me any money from the army to pay, so I was up shit's creek."

Kylie's heart began to pound, the spidey sense she relied on stirring deep in her belly. "What happened, Elise?"

"I had a neighbor with a grandkid who said she'd watch her durin' my shift. But then I got back home after a shift and Daisy was gone. So I ask where the baby was, and she tells me that my aunt came and picked her up. I said I don't got no aunt, don't got any family 'cept for my mom who didn't want to see me and my brother who was off who knows where, but Agnes just insisted it was my aunt, and that's that. I—"

Elise sniffled, buried her face into the pup's soft fur, and started to sob.

Kylie blinked rapidly, trying hard to not break down herself. "So, this woman who babysat...she said your aunt took Daisy, but the woman wasn't your aunt?"

"Yeah. Agnes. She's an old lady. And I don't got no aunt. My mom was an only child and my dad..." She shrugged. "I never knew him, so it had to be someone pretendin' to be my aunt, I guess? I don't know. But she took my baby and disappeared on me. And I didn't know what to do."

Kylie reached over and plucked a tissue from a dispenser, handing it to the girl. "Did you call the police and report Daisy missing?"

Elise nodded, then blew her nose, long and loud, into the tissue. "Yeah. They looked for her, but not too hard. They searched my trailer and had these dogs search all around." She sniffed harder, pressing a new tissue to her eyes. "Dogs for dead people, but they never found nothin'."

Kylie blew her own nose, still trying to pull herself together. Hormones were no joke.

"I'm so sorry. That's awful." She wrote a few notes and began her line of questioning. "When did this happen?"

"Two years ago."

Kylie froze and just stared at the young woman, her heart sinking down into her toes. "Two...*years*?" When Elise nodded, all shreds of hope Kylie had harbored over finding this child suddenly fell away. "And you're just looking into it now?"

"No, like I said, the police are suppose to be lookin' into it for me. But they ain't doin' much." She leaned forward, lowering her voice. "They kept askin' me if I'd killed her or gave her away, but I kept tellin' them I loved my little Daisy and would be doin' nothin' to hurt her. I don't think they believed me, but they didn't put me in jail either, so..." Elise shrugged, her shoulders coming up to her ears and staying there for long moments.

Kylie said, "Ah," though she was pretty sure that case had to have been buried and filed away in some Unsolved Cases folder months and months ago. As much as she hated to think it, they were probably stringing Elise along because she was low-income and slow. Jerks. "If I can be honest with you, I think they've probably stopped looking, if it was that long ago."

Elise nodded, her eyes flooding with tears again. "Cody

says it's cause we're white trash and nobody cares about white trash. He told me that if I was the governor's daughter, they would've found her by now. Because I'm not the governor's daughter, I thought I better save up and get myself a real investigator but getting the money for that wasn't workin' out. So, I told myself I should just get over it. That's what Cody said to do."

She was smiling, but it was the most miserable smile Kylie had ever seen.

"So I tried to," the girl went on, "but it's like there's a hole inside me, just getting wider and wider with each passin' day, you know? Every time I see a baby, I swear, for a minute or two, I think it could be Daisy. And I think I won't be able to get past it and get some real, good sleep unless I figure out what happened. When I saw your ad, I...I..."

She buried her face in her hands and cried softly, dabbing her face with the used tissue.

This time, Kylie brought the box of tissues close, and joined in. She didn't care if it *cost* her money to investigate this case. She was in; ready to bring out the contract and sign her name on the dotted line, no matter what.

5

Linc shivered as he walked the stalls of the modest little barn he'd recently had rebuilt after a devastating fire. As he did, introducing his two llamas to the newest guest, the dogs swarmed his legs, putting him off-balance.

Wiping his hot forehead, he sneezed. His head ached with the action, making his teeth hurt. He braced himself against the wooden gate to avoid pitching himself into a stall. Over the course of the morning, he'd felt more and more like shit.

Damn sinus infection coming on. At least that was what it felt like. Nothing infectious, at least he didn't think so.

Cody, Elise's boyfriend, was nice enough, a little jittery, but damn. Linc had never been much of a conversationalist, but now his tongue felt thick in his mouth. Yeah. He felt definitely shitty, and damned if he hated being sick.

But he'd deal. If it meant Kylie getting a new case and helping her business grow, then he'd stand out in the rain for a week talking to this moron.

"I told her it was damn stupid comin' up here," the kid muttered as he kicked at some straw. He had on a backwards baseball cap, a t-shirt for a band that Linc had never heard of that clung to his wiry frame, and jeans that were dangerously close to puddling at his feet. He also smelled like tobacco, mixed in with a little pot, and Linc was pretty sure those were track marks on his skinny inner arm.

Which was sad, considering that the kid looked to be all of twelve. Seriously. Was Cody a tween, or was Linc just getting old?

He felt old. He actually felt like his head could pop off, and he'd praise the idea of being rid of it.

"But you still drove her. That was nice of you," Linc said, rubbing the back of his sweaty neck. He was burning up. And he needed another haircut. He'd do that...whenever. After Kylie'd nearly shaved his head bald the one time he'd let her get near him with some clippers, he knew he'd never trust her again with a pair of scissors, so he'd have to find the time to get down the mountain and get to the barber...somehow.

For the first time, he found himself agreeing with Kylie. Sometimes, it was a pain in the ass being so far away from everything.

Cody shrugged and rubbed his nose with the back of his hand. "She's schitzin' over this thing that happened to her years ago. If I hear her nag me on it one more time, I'm gonna go mental, you know? Move on, you know?"

"Yeah? What happened to her?" Linc reached for a pitch-fork and dug the forks into the dirt, leaning on the wooden handle to keep himself upright.

"Eh. I dunno. Somethin' about a kid she lost."

Linc raised an eyebrow. A kid? Lost? That sounded serious.

"It could be bullshit. It was before my time, so who knows? Lise is always tellin' stories. She ain't all there." He stuffed his hands in his pockets. "This whole place yours?"

Linc frowned at the insensitivity of the man but accepted the change of subject with a nod.

The kid whistled as he looked around, eyeing another pitchfork on the wall. He picked it up, hefted it for a few seconds, put it back. "Must be nice. So, what? You a farmer?"

"No. I train search and rescue dogs," Linc said. He'd normally have said it with pride, but now he couldn't infuse any emotion into his voice.

"Cool. You mean for like, finding cadavers in the woods and shit? That's hardcore. You ever find anyone like that?"

"Like…what? You mean, dead?"

Cody nodded, super-interested now.

Linc had, many times. More times than he could count, but he was already feeling like shit. He didn't need to recall those times and feel even shittier. "Yeah. What do you do for a living, Cody?"

"Little of this. Little of that. My dad works at the garage downtown, so sometimes I help him out, doin' oil changes and shit," he said, reaching into the pocket of his jeans and pulling out a pack of cigarettes. Linc hoped to hell he wasn't thinking of lighting it, not considering he'd spent most of the summer rebuilding the barn. Instead, the kid just tapped the pack on the rail and sighed. "Elise and I have it pretty good. She works hard. Gets really good tips because she's hot. Sometimes I wonder if she's giving her customers a little something else on the side, if you know what I mean, 'cause they're so good. But nah. She's just good at what she does. Takin' care of people. She's a good girl. Keeps me honest. That's why I look out for her."

It was the first thing he'd said that didn't smack of immaturity, and Linc found himself warming to the kid.

Or maybe that was the fever.

He opened his mouth to ask the kid if he wouldn't mind sitting down on the porch, since he was having a hard time standing on two feet, when they heard the screen door slam.

They walked together to the barn doors. Suddenly, Linc felt even sicker.

Elise was standing there, cradling little Britt in her arms. "And you're sure I can have her?" the slip of a young girl was saying. Her limbs were all bare and as pale and thin as skeleton bones.

"Him. It's a him," Kylie was saying, nodding. "Britt. Yes. Of course. He's all yours. I can see he really adores you."

What. The. Hell.

"Aw, shit!" Cody groused as he fixed his baseball cap down on his head. "I told you, Lise. No pets. What the hell are we going to do with that little monster? Guess I'm gonna be the one looking after his little ass, picking up his shit and stuff while you're at work."

For a minute, Linc was glad of the kid's protests. Maybe they wouldn't want the dog after all. But then Elise stuck her lower lip out and said, "But he's so cute. Cody, look."

Britt did the kiss of death; licking her face. No human with a soul could resist such charm. Cody ran through the rain and climbed the steps to the porch, two at a time. He touched Britt's nose, and Britt leaned into his hand, clearly in heaven. "Yeah. I guess he's cute."

And...sold.

Dammit

What the actual...hell? He thought that he and Kylie had a tacit agreement to discuss things before they went and separated the litter. After all, Kylie was fond of *discussing,* and would sometimes do it until they were blue in the face. It was her number one hobby. For her to make this arbitrary but major decision on her own? What the hell was his wife doing?

But Kylie's eyes were glazed. She didn't even bother to look at the eye daggers he was trying to shoot her. Actually... she looked more like she was about to burst into tears.

Who was this woman, and what had she done with the real Kylie?

Kylie said her goodbyes to the Elise and the puppy and told her she'd be in touch. They hugged like old friends. Linc always marveled how he could know someone his entire life —family even—and always keep them at arm's distance, but Kylie could meet someone once, and suddenly they were the type of buddies who hugged and kissed and got all touchy-feely.

The two kids climbed into the Honda and set off down the puddle-filled drive, *with his damn puppy,* and since the rain had let up, Kylie watched them, waving the entire time.

"You gave them Britt," he said, trying to keep his voice even.

"Yeah. I had to."

"*Had* to?" He blew out a long breath. "Britt was one of the good ones. He was catching on faster than all of them, maybe except Beatrice. He would've made a great SAR."

Not only that. Of all of them, Britt was his favorite. The runt of the litter. Beatrice, like Storm, knew she was a champion, but Britt had no such attitude. He was also the most mellow. Kind of like Linc.

Kylie wiped at her face. "Geez, Linc. Life is not all about SAR," she snapped, whirling and stomping inside.

What? Okay, life wasn't all about search and rescue, but it was pretty damn important. It might not have been all of his life, but it was *most* of his livelihood, the thing that kept a roof over their heads. He thought she understood that.

Apparently not.

He stood there for a long time, his throbbing temples and dizziness forgotten. Sure, they fought. But hell, now it seemed like that was all they were doing.

He took a breath and opened the screen door, closing it quickly behind him so the pups wouldn't follow him in and trail mud in the house, making her angrier yet. He found her, sitting at her desk, her face in her hands. At first he thought that she might've had a headache, but then he heard a soft sob.

"Kylie." His voice was gentle.

She didn't stop.

He tried again, louder. "Kylie."

When she still didn't answer, he decided she was just ignoring him, so he went to his desk across from hers and sat down, waiting for her to stop. When she finally did seem to quiet down, he said, "You want to tell me what this is all about?"

She looked at him through her hands, her eyes red-rimmed, her nose running. "Not really. I'll be fine. I just need a moment. It's just…that poor girl."

"I get it, Lee. You always get invested with your clients. But I got to tell you, if you get so invested that you put their needs ahead of yours, we're going to end up in the poor house. You need to draw a line between business and your personal feelings."

She lowered her hands to her thighs and let out a moan. "You're right. But I can't help it. It was such a sad story. I told her I'd take the case pro bono, and—"

"Pro bono? Seriously? Lee!" he said, exasperated. "What were you thinking? First, you give up my dog, and then you—"

"Your dog? I thought they were *our* dogs." Her voice was hollow.

"They are ours. But they were our cushion. You do realize you just gave away twenty-thousand dollars. Right?"

She looked at him, confused. "What?"

"Yeah. A trained SAR dog is priceless, but I can usually sell them to handlers for about twenty K. That litter, properly trained, is our future, Lee."

She blinked. "Wait. You were going to…sell our dogs?"

He'd always thought that went without saying. Before Kylie'd arrived on the farm, he'd had dozens of litters of SAR dogs, which he'd trained, then happily sold off to other handlers. It was part of his business, the reason he was able to afford nice things.

But now, looking at the horror in her face, he wished he had another answer. "Did you really think we were going to keep all the dogs around here? This place would be a madhouse."

"No, but…yes. Actually. You don't just get rid of family. They're family."

He couldn't believe what she was saying. She was always complaining about the dogs being underfoot. "And what's Britt?"

She gave him a wounded look. "Elise needs him more than we do. After what she went through…besides, she said she'd bring him back to visit. I was looking at it as an open adoption. We'll still see him."

His vision swam, and he closed his eyes to ward off the dizziness. In the house, with darkness falling, he was starting to feel hot and feverish again. "All right. But, Lee, please don't bend over backwards for this woman. I know you want to help her, but you've got to think of yourself too."

"I know. But the baby…"

He thought of what Cody had said. *Something about a kid she lost.*

"Baby?"

Kylie swallowed, and she looked like she might burst into tears again. "Elise had a baby two years ago. She went to her job at the diner and left her with a babysitter, and then the child just disappeared. She hasn't seen her since. Can you imagine?"

He leaned a shoulder against the wall. "Are you serious?

Jesus." Maybe she was right about Elise needing that puppy. But then he remembered the other thing Cody said, about his girlfriend making up stories. "Are you sure she's telling you the truth?"

Her eyes flashed to his. "What? Of course."

"Cody said she likes to tell stories."

"What, like make something like this up? Why?" The disgust was thick in her voice. She pulled out a photograph that Linc could barely see, a photo of a few-days-old baby with a thick mop of black hair. "If you heard her talking about Daisy, you'd know it wasn't a story."

"Okay, but what does she think you can do about it after two years? That's a lot of time to pass before taking action. Why'd she wait so long?"

Kylie shrugged. "She had the police looking into it, and then she was trying to save up the money, and then she saw my ad."

So, his beautiful and compassionate wife had paid three-hundred dollars for placemat ads so that she could pick up a bunch of free work? Kylie had gone through a lot of majors at UNC, but he got the feeling business wasn't one of them. He massaged his temples.

"I'm not sure what I can do," she continued, scribbling something on her notepad. Probably ideas for the case. "But I can do a little digging. Maybe try and find out if anyone else witnessed this woman leaving with the baby."

"Not too much, though," he warned. "Remember, you have paying clients. They need your attention, especially since they're *paying*."

"Yeah. I know. It's a cold case, so it's not going anywhere. It can just be my hobby. My thing to do when I'm not busy with my other work."

He wasn't sure he liked the sound of that. *He* wanted to be the thing she did when she wasn't busy with the investigations work. But she had that excited "alive" look to her now, the one she only got when she was working a big case. He saw how much it meant to her, so he decided to let it go.

Besides, he had to help himself to some sinus medicine before he wound up kissing the floor.

As he climbed the stairs, feeling like shit, it occurred to him that Kylie hadn't noticed that he was getting ill. She usually was the first to bring him chicken soup and take his temperature when he was feeling low.

But Kylie wasn't even looking at him as he went upstairs. No, instead, she was staring at the photograph of a days-old baby, with her dark, spiky hair, a ruddy face, and tiny pink arms spread out like a goalpost. The missing baby.

The baby that, Linc knew, in the coming weeks, would be the source of many of his wife's sleepless nights.

6

It felt damn good when everything was going to plan.

Unfortunately, I'd been in this business for far too long to expect that. Half a century of making family dreams come true had proven one thing to me. This business was havoc. Wrenches got thrown my way often in the process, usually in the form of an incompetent hospital worker, or an intermediary getting too greedy. Sometimes, local law enforcement got too close for comfort, which was never a good thing. Just as babies were unpredictable, so was the business of adoptions.

Today, I leaned back in my busted pleather chair and took a moment to appreciate this.

This moment, when everything was going exactly the way I wanted it to.

I read the email again and smiled. Blonde and blue-eyed. That, we could do.

Hell, we could do anything for half a million dollars. Or die trying, as my dear old husband had been fond of saying. RIP. Dead for twenty years now.

As I opened an email to respond, the door opened, and

my assistant popped her head in. She was one of those high-maintenance, just-out-of-college millennials, with a too-short skirt and a useless sociology degree, who thought she was making minimum wage bringing my coffee today, and ruling the world tomorrow.

I closed out of the email quickly and said, "Honey, didn't I tell you to knock?"

"Yes, I know, but…" she flipped her blonde hair off her shoulder and gnawed the bright red lipstick off her bottom lip as she shuffled in the doorway excitedly, "your twelve is here."

"Ah."

Well, that explained her overeagerness. There was always a degree of excitement whenever one of the children being shuttled through the foster system found a forever home. I stood up and followed my assistant to the conference room, where the anxious new parents had brought all sorts of gifts for their newest family member.

Shaking hands with them, I said, "Tom. Gerri. So wonderful to see you again. It looks like you're ready to become a mom and dad, huh?"

They nodded, nervous laughter all around.

"Jared will be here in a few minutes. We sent a car to pick him up."

The new, young parents nodded and thanked me, sitting down at the table and twiddling their thumbs in anticipation. This particular case, Jared Watts, had been born to a heroin-addicted mother ten years ago. Though Jared had grown up in foster care, his mother had fought for custody, which had been granted, up until the time she was found in the back of a Walmart bathroom with a needle in her arm.

She had been given a second chance at least three or four times, and each relapse was worse than the last. After that, there was a lengthy court battle where she eventually wound up relinquishing rights, and Tom and Gerri Marlowe, who'd fostered Jared as a toddler, stepped up to make the situation permanent.

A happy ending. I lived for those. Jared was a cute kid. He deserved a good life.

And that's what I delivered to kids. Day in, day out. The dream of a happy life. Though there was plenty of heartbreak in the child welfare system, I felt privileged to play a part in the act of uniting families. Of making the dreams of childless couples and orphans come true.

Yes. A very noble cause indeed. I had a wall in my office full of awards and commendations, all shining and sparkling and reminding me why I'd gotten into this business. I'd started as an RN working in obstetrics, but when the situation arose, I'd gotten my master's in social work. I lived to serve the children of not only this community but other communities around the country.

I couldn't have been prouder when the door opened and little Jared peeked his head through. Once a scared little boy, his big brown eyes were now full of joy, and his smile lit up the entire room. He ran to his new parents, and they heaped together, hugging and sobbing.

Next to me, my assistant tucked her visible red bra strap back under her blouse and wiped a tear from her eye.

I reached over and handed her a tissue. There was a reason our office had cases of Kleenex delivered every month. Most of the tears, though, were happy ones.

I made sure of that.

My assistant offered them our standard congratulations basket—full of little goodies, and a gift card to Applebees so that the family could have a nice meal together. Photographs were taken, with Jared holding a little wipe-off board that said, *Adoption Day!* and the date. Hugs all around.

A cake was brought in that said *Congratulations, Marlowe*

Family! I let them make the first cut, and then my assistant went around doling fat pieces to everyone in the office. There was never a shortage of parties here. It was a wonder we all weren't fat as pigs.

When the crew said goodbye to the new family, I walked back to my office, rolled my busted chair close to the desk, and opened the email again.

Some families, like Jared and the Marlowes, came together easily.

But in other cases, a little finessing was needed.

After fifty years in the business, first working in hospitals and now in social work, I knew all the shortcuts, all the loopholes. Sometimes, crafting a perfect family for a child required a few risks. But in the end, the child would be happier. And that's all everyone wanted, wasn't it?

Some families were so eager to adopt that they threw money at us; especially if it meant they could be placed first on the list and avoid the usual years-long waiting period. It wasn't unusual for them to offer up hundreds of thousands of dollars in "fees," no questions asked, for the chance to become mommy and daddy.

The cut I took of the adoption "fee" was nice too. I'd never be able to take my yearly cruise vacation if I'd had to survive on the director's salary. Social workers were paid peanuts, even high-level ones like myself. And my stupid husband had died and left me with very little in the way of a retirement pension. I had to do this all myself.

I reread the email on my private account. It was written in code so that anyone looking at it wouldn't be able to decipher it, but by now, I read the code as if it was written in everyday English. It said: *Hello, Looking for a blonde, blue-eyed infant for a high-ranking government official. $500k if you can deliver by the end of the month. K*

I smiled again.

That was the most I'd ever been offered for one baby. Party time, indeed.

I knew my contact only as K. The emails always came from kfy1674@gmail.com. He or she was my marketing guru. Whoever K was, he sourced the people looking for children and passed the information on to me. When I received the goods, I usually dropped them off at whichever clinic was arranged ahead of time, to be united with the adoptive family. I'd never met K, but from what I'd heard, he fielded requests for these adoptions daily on the dark web. I was only a small cog in his operation.

I'd lost count long ago, but this little baby would be close to two hundred, plus or minus a few.

A cause for celebration.

Two hundred sweet children I'd saved from poverty and neglect. Two hundred little souls who now had the chance for happiness and prosperity. Two hundred men and women who attained the blessed goal of being parents...because of me.

I placed both hands over my heart and smiled. My life's mission fed my soul.

Digging through my desk, I pulled out the burner phone I used only for this contact and pressed the call button, then smiled when the line was answered almost immediately. Mark Lamb. One of the best obstetrics nurses in the business, he'd been on the job for twenty years, working at one of the little Podunk hospitals in some backwoods town in Mississippi.

"Well, hello, Mark."

"Hey, I haven't heard from you in a while," he said, clearly pleased that I'd called. That was good. "Beginning to wonder if I'd fallen off your radar. It's been, what...two years?"

It had been three, but who was counting?

"Feels like much longer," he went on, his voice deepening.

Was he flirting? I was nearly twice his age. Well, two could play at that game. I'd been around the block long enough to know when a man was using his charm to try to get somewhere with me.

No, he wasn't flirting. He wanted more money. That was always the case with these people. I'd dealt with it enough to know.

"As you know, sweet boy, I have to spread myself around as much as possible. You understand, I'm sure."

He laughed, playing the game. "Yeah, I do. How can I help you today?"

Small talk was over.

"If you can manage it, I have another opportunity that has come up."

"Okay. What are the details?"

"Blonde, blue-eyed if possible. Sex doesn't matter. Your cut will be given to you upon delivery to me."

He didn't even pause. "Actually, this is perfect timing. I know just the candidate. Mother came in a few hours ago. Fits your requirements perfectly."

"All right. Let me know when you think you can have it ready for me, and I'll arrange the details."

"Will do," he said, and I smiled. Sometimes, it was like taking candy from a baby. "But as for the compensation…"

Oh, no. Here it came. "Just as before. Twenty percent."

He made a noise, low in his throat. "It was pretty tough last time. I almost got caught. And I don't have to tell you that I'm risking my entire life on this. My career, my reputation, not to mention that I could get put in jail for years."

I rolled my eyes. This was the most common wrench, but not one I wasn't used to dealing with. People getting greedy. As if $100,000 wasn't more than he made in an entire year. "Yes, yes," I said dismissively. "And I'm very grateful to you for the help."

"Are you grateful to the tune of fifty percent?"

I nearly choked. Hell no.

"You understand that I only receive twenty percent, same as you?"

This was a lie, but I found that this line usually helped put an end to the negotiations rather effectively.

"Yeah. Well, maybe you should be asking for a raise as well," he muttered.

I didn't have time for this. I had another meeting at two, with a couple of potential adoptees looking for an older child. "Fine. Twenty-five is the most I can offer you."

"All right. Twenty-five," he said. "You've got yourself a deal."

I gritted my teeth. This was bullshit. He might've been sticking his neck out, but I had a lot more to lose than he did. And the people I worked with should've counted themselves lucky to get a call from me. Not the other way around. I had enough connections that I didn't need Mark or anyone else.

"Just...get it done right. I'm expecting no more bullshit from you."

"Always." He sounded cocky. That was always a problem.

I didn't say goodbye. Suddenly, I didn't really care for Mark that much. Greedy bastard.

I hung up, opening an email to my contact. *Not a problem. Will contact you when ready so you can give me details on drop-off.*

I loved hearing when my contact had a potential candidate. Sometimes, it could take months. But Mark was good at what he did. The last time I worked with him, he'd done well. No problems. I had dozens of other contacts in the hospitals all over the United States, but I only worked with them two, three times at most. Any more than that, and people started to get suspicious. My contacts got cocky. In the nineties, I'd sourced three from one hospital alone in a matter of a couple years. That had been reckless. I'd almost gotten caught.

But this would be my last time working with Mark.

This was a win-win situation for everyone involved. Well, the mother would lose…lose the responsibility and expense and effort a child took. A baby was likely something she hadn't wanted to begin with. Another complication in her already difficult life. I'd be doing her a favor, taking a baby off her hands. That was the way I saw it. And the baby would grow up in a life of privilege, instead of a trailer somewhere with pot-addicted, lowlife parents.

Because of me. Because of my efforts to make the world a better place.

Yes. It certainly was nice when things went to plan.

7

A very Boone would have adored being in labor, if it wasn't for the pain.

"Get me some ice chips," she said to whoever would listen after the last contraction subsided. "Please! Thank you!"

She'd been in active labor for just over four hours. From her three hours at the hospital, she'd quickly learned that these people in scrubs had been assembled to do her bidding.

Since being waited on hand and foot sure beat working at the local grocery for minimum wage, she was making the best of it. She didn't have insurance, but one of her friends had told her that doctors had to treat her, so not to worry about it.

So, she didn't.

First, some pain meds in her IV, followed by a few sips of Sprite. Now, ice-chips. If she asked one of these nurses to wipe her forehead with a wet rag, or even feed her grapes, they'd probably do it.

This was the life.

Avery was sure she was meant to be rich. After spending a twelve-hour shift on her feet behind a cash register, getting yelled at by annoying customers whenever she had to do a price-check, having people wait on her as she lounged on the bed was heaven. Plus, the hospital bed was so big she could stretch out in it. She didn't have to worry about Billy rolling over and smacking her in his sleep as he was fond of doing.

She'd take whatever pleasure she could from it now. Especially since every person she came up against told her that having a baby meant that she wouldn't rest for the next eighteen years straight. *Enjoy the high life now, baby, because it ends the second they wheel you out those hospital doors.* She planned on milking it for as long as they would let her.

A nurse came in with a cup full of ice cubes and set one on her tongue. She sucked it, looking around at the people assembled around her hospital bed, all dressed in scrubs of varying pastel shades.

All of them were strangers.

Of course. The produce manager at the grocery had driven her here after her water had broken in the parking lot, but he must've hightailed it out of there the second she got through the Holmes County Hospital's front doors. Probably didn't want to be accused of being the father, since Avery was only sixteen and he was probably forty. Maybe fifty. Old.

And of course, no Billy. She couldn't count on that dead-beat to do a damned thing right. He was the reason she was here, putting her body through this ridiculousness, since it was his condom that had broken. Probably a cheap one he'd gotten at the dollar store. Moron.

She never should've trusted him. Likely, right now, he was somewhere playing Fortnite, maybe with a needle in his arm. Maybe screwing Cathy, that little slut. Her best friend. Correction…ex-best friend. Ex ever since she discovered that the two of them had been sexting each other regularly, and who-knew-what else.

Avery had dropped out of school and gotten a real job at

the grocery store to try to make a good living so that they could be a family. Meanwhile, her belly had just kept growing until even Billy looked disgusted by her.

It would be nice to look human again. Put on one of those short skirts and the stilettos that had gotten her into this trouble in the first place. But of course, she'd be more careful next time. She'd lose the baby weight and drive the boys wild —making sure they could look but never touch.

She wouldn't do it for Billy, though. Screw Billy. When she got out of here, she'd leave him. Never look back. He'd never cared about being a father. She and the baby would be better off without him.

As she sucked on a chip, letting the cool liquid slide down her throat, another contraction ripped through her. As it ramped up, she dropped the cup between her legs and tightened her hands on the bed rails, wincing and moaning until it was over.

That was the worst one yet.

"Oh, that was a good one," the nurse said with a grin, studying the monitor.

Avery scowled at her. *Sure it was a good one. Because you didn't have to feel it. Fuck you, bitch.*

She turned to the television set, which was on some old television sitcom she'd never seen before with a bunch of middle-aged, unattractive losers living in an apartment. She wished she had Netflix. Of course, Netflix and chilling with Billy in the living room of her family house was what had gotten her here to begin with.

She'd been so stupid. Buying all his dumb lines last summer. To think, at the beginning of the school year, the only thing she had to worry about was making sure she looked good in that tiny cheerleading skirt so she could make assholes like Billy drool.

Dumb, dumb, dumb.

After the pregnancy test came back positive, her mother had flipped, and her father had hounded her nonstop, asking why she hadn't kept her legs together. She couldn't take their constant bitching, so she'd left. She'd told her parents that she didn't need them and dropped out of her junior year of high school, intending to get a place with Billy. But apartments were super-expensive, he couldn't get a job, and so she'd been living at Billy's dad's house, in his basement bedroom. The only good thing about that arrangement was that Billy's dad was rarely home and usually let them do what they wanted.

Usually, that entailed sex, smoking pot, Fortnite, and more sex. At least, when she wasn't at work.

But what she wanted most, now that she and Billy were no longer a thing was to get away from him. He wouldn't miss her.

It was time to move out. She and the baby could probably go somewhere. A house for unwed mothers or something. That was a thing, wasn't it? She could hang with all the other moms, bond over diaper changing and feedings and shit.

A man who looked like a television doctor with a stethoscope around his neck and a confident, easy gait strode into the hospital room. Ignoring her, he asked the nurse, "How are things with this patient?"

The nurse told him that she was fifty percent effaced, whatever that meant, as Avery glared at the man. Why did all these people ignore her like she wasn't even there? It was especially hard, because he was kind of cute. Where once, she drove boys crazy, now, they looked at her like some kind of head case. She couldn't flirt her way out of a paper bag anymore.

"Are you the doctor?" she asked him.

He shook his head as he snapped on a pair of rubber gloves. "I'm the head nurse here. The doctor on-call will be here shortly. Am I right in reviewing your paperwork that this baby has had no prenatal care?"

Avery let out a huff and crossed her arms. "I was busy. I meant to, but I don't got insurance so…" All these excuses came pouring out of her mouth at once, and she found herself blushing from shame. Maybe she *would* want to get out of here, sooner rather than later.

The nurse-man didn't roll his eyes, but he might as well have. "All right. Let me have a look."

He moved forward. He had one of those stubbly, sexy jaws, and was cute, even though he was probably old enough to be her father. An older man would probably know how to take care of a woman. Damn, she wished she had a sugar daddy.

He wore a nameplate that said M LAMB, and he smelled like the antiseptic wash he'd just used to clean his hands. She squirmed. It was bad enough, the female nurses practically sticking their entire hand inside her, but this guy was a judgmental prick. An *attractive*, judgmental prick. And none-too-gentle, either. He shoved her legs apart and stuck his hand up her hoo-ha like she was some kind of farm animal. As he felt around in there, she groaned at the dull pain in her abdomen.

He pulled out just as quickly and snapped off the gloves, then said to the nurse, "Looking good. Shouldn't be long now."

"Is everything okay?" Avery asked him.

He turned, as if surprised to see she actually had a mouth. He nodded. "All as it should be, so far. Now…Miss…" he glanced at her name on the wipe-off board on the wall, "Boone. I'm assuming you have no birth plan for the child. What pain relief options have you chosen?"

She frowned. Birth plan? "What's that?"

He let out a sigh, like, *Do I really have to explain this common term to you, dumbass?* "It's a plan that tells us things like if you want an epidural." When she still looked at him dumbly, he went on, "It's an anesthetic that we'll administer directly to the spinal cord to help with the contractions. Do you want to be numbed to reduce the pain?"

She wanted to say no, she didn't need it. She didn't need anything where his smug ass was concerned. But it already hurt like a mother and would probably get worse if what she'd seen on television and in movies was true. "Oh. I guess so."

He looked at the other nurse. "Get the anesthesiologist down here."

She wasn't sure if she'd made the right decision. No pain was good, but she had no clue what she was in for. A well-meaning friend had bought her a copy of *What to Expect When You're Expecting,* but she'd used it as a doorstop. She hadn't wanted to face the reality of what was happening until the last possible moment. It was all so scary.

The man-nurse continued, "And…as far as what happens after the birth. Have you planned that?"

"After?" She wished all of this didn't sound like a foreign language. It seemed so easy. What did he think happened afterwards? She went home with a baby in tow. The end. What else would happen? They didn't expect her to stay in the hospital for the rest of her life, did they?

"Yes. If you're interested in exploring adoption, or if you'd like to talk with a counselor."

Oh, of course. That was it. She was young, and all alone, so they were already stacking the chips against her that she wouldn't be able to cut it as a mom. Everyone was always against her—her mom, her dad, her teachers, even Billy. But she was set to prove them all wrong.

"No. I'm not giving the baby up for adoption, thank you very much," she said, lifting her chin with pride.

Nurse-man nodded, but she was sure there was doubt

clouding his eyes. "All right. But we noticed that you left the next-of-kin off your paperwork. We need to fill that out, should we need someone to make decisions for you."

"Why would I need that?"

"It's just a precaution."

She flattened the sheet over her enormous belly. "Well. He's not really related to me, but you could put Billy. My b…" She stopped. They kept breaking up and getting back together, at least twice in the last month, so she wasn't sure where they stood at that moment. "The baby's father."

She rattled off his phone number, and he wrote that down. "Sounds good," he said as a gray-haired, portly guy with a white coat, who looked kind of like a gray Teenage Mutant Ninja Turtle appeared in the doorway.

"Who's having a baby?" He grinned goofily.

Avery rolled her eyes. Adults everywhere either treated her like she didn't exist, or like she was three. She wished she could press fast-forward on this entire day. She just wanted to meet the creature that had been growing inside her for the past nine months and get this over with. And maybe get the hell out of there. Forget about milking a longer hospital stay. These people were douches. "So, you're the doctor?"

He nodded. "That's what they tell me."

She wasn't sure she wanted this jokester anywhere near her baby. But half the personnel in this hospital had already been between her legs, so she figured, why the hell not. If it got her out of here faster, bring it. She spread her legs apart and let him have a feel too.

"Looking good," he said, feeling around a little more gently than Nurse McDreamy Asshole. "Anesthesiologist's here. Let's get you all numbed up and feeling fine, shall we? Next stop, cloud nine!"

She hated the needle for the epidural, and she didn't really feel like it did much good. They'd put it in her back, dammit, probably messing up the tramp stamp she'd gotten last year. Her first tattoo, one she'd had to forge her parents' signature for. She'd gotten three more since then, since Billy's best friend was a tattoo artist. Birds on her shoulder, thorns around her ankle, a hollow heart with the word *Billy* written in curly letters on her hipbone. That one had hurt like a mother, but he loved to kiss it every time he went down on her.

She still felt the pain as she pushed. Maybe it was worse because she didn't have anyone there that she knew or trusted. All these nurses and doctors yelling orders at her, and not one of them actually *knew her* or cared what happened to her. Not really. They were all just here to do their jobs.

Right before the baby made its appearance, she began wishing she and Billy hadn't fought so much, so that maybe he could be there, with her, holding her empty hand.

But then she heard the baby's cry, and all of those thoughts went away.

"Congratulations," one of the female nurses said as she wiped a sweat-soaked tendril of magenta-dyed hair from Avery's face. "You have a beautiful boy."

"A big one too. Ten pounds, three ounces," someone called from another part of the room.

A boy, she thought excitedly, thinking of the name she'd wanted. Billy had never wanted to talk names. In his mind, she wasn't sure he even *got* that he was going to become a dad. She whispered the name, almost to herself, "Diesel Warren Boone."

Warren after her dear grandfather, who'd died a year ago. Diesel because she just liked the way it sounded. Tough, like he was going to be. She'd give him a baby mohawk for his first haircut. And later? She was going to make sure he had a

Harley. All the girls would go crazy for him, the little heart-breaker.

Though she was exhausted, she managed to peel her top half off the delivery table so that she could try to get a glimpse of the baby as the nurses crowded around him, tending to him at a station in the corner of the room. The cries were loud, but the most beautiful thing she'd ever heard.

"Is he okay?" she asked.

"Oh, yes. Perfect," one of the nurses said to her. "What a beautiful little man you have."

"Can I hold him?" she asked, reaching out her still empty hands.

"Just a moment, and he's all yours," the nurse said. Avery smiled at the thought of that. *All mine. Yes, that's right. ALL mine.*

McDreamy Asshole stepped back into the room, his hands in his pockets as he approached her bed after stopping to take a good long look at the perfect little boy she'd created.

"Congratulations," the nurse-man said and tapped his finger against the line of her IV.

Avery stiffened. It wasn't that he was necessarily doing anything wrong. He was a nurse, after all. He just seemed… nervous, maybe. His eyes kept darting over to where the other nurses were still toweling off her baby.

Between her legs, the doctor was doing something she couldn't feel, but she kept her eyes on the nurse. She didn't trust the creepy man.

Little Diesel screamed, shifting her attention to the bloodred infant. They'd jabbed his little heel and were squeezing blood from the wound, none too gently. No wonder the darling boy was so unhappy. Avery was in the process of opening her mouth to tell the witches to be more careful when her vision began to blur.

"Wha…" was all she could manage.

Avery closed her mouth. She couldn't remember what she was going to say.

The male nurse walked away, his hands still in his pockets as her baby's screams grew dull and the room swelled into darkness.

Avery blinked, squinting against the bright lights overhead. She shifted in the bed she was laying in and immediately winced. Her va-jaja felt like it had taken a beating.

She looked around, noting the clean gown she was wearing and morning sun streaming through the window. Where was she?

More importantly, where was Diesel?

Probably in the nursery, she decided, and she must be in one of the recovery rooms on the labor and delivery floor. Trying to peek around the curtain separating her from the door, she spotted another patient just a few feet away. She suspected it was another mother who'd just given birth. From the balloon bouquet at the foot of the other patient's bed, it was clear her roommate had more fans than she did.

But that didn't matter so much. She had Diesel, and he had her. She couldn't wait to see her beautiful baby boy, now that he'd been cleaned up.

A nurse walked in and smiled, though the gesture seemed a little…sad? "Oh, you're up."

Avery tried to sit up in bed, and the nurse rushed over to help her. She winced again. Wow. The space between her legs seriously burned. Was she wearing a diaper? A cold diaper? "What's going on down…"

"You have an ice pack down there, to help with the pain and swelling."

"Oh." As she sat up, the curtain behind the nurse wavered, and Avery spotted an old, frail woman in the other bed.

In maternity? What was going on?

She looked around, confused. She was sure that the wallpaper in the maternity wing had been a rose color, and there'd been pictures of babies on the walls of the other room she was in. But this room was blue and covered with ocean scenes.

"Am I still in the maternity ward?" she asked.

The nurse shook her head, the sad smile returning. "We thought it was better to move you to intensive care."

Intensive care?

A beeping in the room sped up as her heart rate increased. "Am I all right?" she asked, looking down at herself. She felt a little woozy from the epidural, a little nauseated too, and there was that dull pain and burning below the sheet, but she figured that was normal for what she'd been through. "I mean, I feel okay."

"Oh...yes," the nurse said, wrapping a blood pressure cuff around her arm. "You're fine."

As she pushed a button, making the cuff contract on her arm, Avery said, "Well, can I see my baby now? Is he in the nursery?"

The woman didn't answer. Just great. Another one who treated her like she didn't exist. The woman wrote something down on her tablet and said, "The doctor will come to see you now."

Avery blinked and sat up even straighter, pulling the sheet up over a belly that now looked like a semi-deflated beach ball. "Is everything okay with the baby?"

The nurse opened her mouth as if she had something to say but closed it again as if she had no idea how to say it. She cleared her throat and tried again. "One moment. I'll let the doctor explain everything to you."

As promised, the doctor appeared a moment later. The jokester. She expected some lame joke, but he did not look in a joking mood right now. He came up close to her and took her hand. "I'm sorry, Miss Boone. There were…complications."

Avery swallowed, her heart beginning to pound. "He's all right, isn't he?"

The doctor bowed his head, then shook it almost imperceptibly. "I'm sorry. No, he's not."

"He…you mean, he…" She couldn't get the word out. When she did, her voice cracked. "Died?"

With a single mournful movement, the doctor nodded.

"But how? He was so healthy. He cried so loud! That's got to be wrong!" Avery shouted, ready to tear off the sheets and find the nursery herself. Surely, they were saying this to the wrong mother, because Diesel had been perfect. *Perfect.*

"Sometimes these things happen to newborns," he said. "He was fine after the initial examination, and then he went into cardiac arrest, and could not be revived."

She stared at him, sure this was a nightmare, and any moment she'd wake up and find her baby in the crook of her arm. *Diesel. Diesel Warren Boone.*

"I don't believe it." She looked around the intensive care room in which she'd found herself. "Why am I in here? None of this makes sense."

"You stopped breathing," the doctor told her. "You actually died before we were able to bring you back."

She had…died?

Avery shuddered. "When did Diesel…" she almost couldn't say the word, "die?"

The doctor coughed into his hand, his face growing red. He was getting emotional too. "It all happened at nearly the same time. You stopped breathing and almost all attention went to you, trying to save you. The baby went to the nursery while we stabilized you. A moment later, the child went to cardiac arrest." He coughed again. "He couldn't be saved."

Avery just stared at the doctor, her heart breaking with its every beat.

"We can do an autopsy to—"

Horror filled Avery from the top of her hair to the tips of her toes. "No!" The thought of them cutting into her child. Pulling out his brain so that it could be weighed? Bile filled her mouth, and she was forced to swallow the noxious liquid. "Do you have to?"

The doctor's hands went into his pockets, stirring a memory she couldn't fully see. "No, you don't have to, but it might help you come to peace with why the baby died."

Avery thought about that. Did it even matter? Diesel Warren was dead and nothing, no explanation would bring him back.

She didn't know what to do. For the first time in forever, she wished her folks were here. She wished an adult with adult experience and knowledge could tell her what to do.

Just then, Nurse McDreamy Asshole stepped into the room, but this time, he didn't look so assholeish. He looked sad. She nearly cried he appeared to be so filled with compassion.

"I'm sorry for interrupting, doctor, but you're needed in room seven."

Frowning, the doctor tried to smile at Avery. "Again, I'm sorry," the jokester said. That's what he'd been before, the jokester, right? Maybe all of this was just some sick joke. But he stepped back behind the curtain without revealing the punch line. "I'll be back to visit you again later."

She didn't want him back, but said, "Okay."

After the doctor left, the nurse-man she met before stepped closer. "I'm so very sorry," McDreamy said, taking her hand. He handed her a small box. "I made a memory box for you. When you're ready, you'll find a lock of hair, hand and footprints, pictures, things to help you through this terrible time."

Avery held the box to her chest, tears pouring down her cheeks. "Thank you." She looked at the door where the doctor had exited. "They want me to do an autopsy."

McDreamy frowned, but only for the slightest moment. "How do you feel about that?"

"I…I don't know."

He leaned forward. "Want my advice?"

She nodded vigorously. She really couldn't believe she'd thought this man was an asshole at first. He was so nice. "Please. What should I do?"

"Don't let them cut him up." Avery shuddered at the thought, and McDreamy patted her hand. "We can offer cremation, and you'll be able to keep his urn with you forever."

The thought pleased her greatly. But…

"I can't afford a funeral or anything like that."

McDreamy nodded solemnly and lifted a clipboard he'd been carrying onto the bedside table. "We have funds that can cover the whole cost for situations like yours."

She blinked. "Really?"

He looked so compassionate that tears sprang to her eyes again. "Really. I've already set the wheels into motion to make sure I'm not offering you something I can't give. But, if you'll sign this paper, I'll take care of everything."

He handed her a form that seemed to have twenty pages, written in the tiniest font she'd ever tried to read. She gave up almost immediately.

She was so tired. So devastated. She simply didn't want to think about it anymore.

Flipping to the last page, she scrawled her name and

thrust the clipboard back at the nurse. "When can I see him?" She wasn't fully sure if she wanted to. Did she want to see the beautiful baby she'd had inside her for nine months...an empty shell that would never grow up, never get his first haircut, never have a first girlfriend, never take his first motorcycle ride?

The compassionate smile faltered a little. "Are you sure you want to?"

Avery sucked in a breath but couldn't get enough oxygen into her lungs. She saw bright spots in her vision. The room was closing in on her. This wasn't really happening.

McDreamy moved to her IV pole, started fiddling with the tubing. "I'm just going to give you a little something to help with your nerves."

Avery couldn't breathe. Something to help with her nerves sounded really good, so she didn't argue with him.

She hadn't had a birth plan when she'd come into the hospital, but she'd formulated one since. And *this* wasn't in the plan. She was supposed to leave here, not alone, but with her child. She was going to go back to Billy and tell him it was over, that she and Diesel would be just fine without his lying, cheating ass. She was going to raise Diesel to be a motorcycle badass, without his stupid father in the picture. It would be hard, but they would be fine, because they would be together.

"There you go," McDreamy said in a low, lilting voice. "Night, night. Sleep tight. I'll take care of everything."

The room tilted onto its side.

She thought of her baby, her beautiful *Diesel Warren Boone*, the child she'd never gotten a chance to hold, lying cold, in a morgue, maybe a few floors below.

And now she really wanted to leave. Get away from this awful hospital. This awful place.

But she was so sleepy.

McDreamy's face filled her field of vision. He was smiling as he got closer…closer…

His lips pressed to her forehead.

She tried to push him away, but she couldn't lift her hands. She couldn't move.

"Thank you, Avery," he said against her forehead. "Try to make better decisions next time."

At least that was what she thought he said. She couldn't be sure because everything in her world went dark as he stepped away.

THE LIGHTS of some seedy strip mall sign shone down upon the wide, empty parking lot as I paced back and forth between the cart returns. *Fucking Mark Lamb.*

From some faraway tree, an owl hooted. A homeless man crouched in front of a massive dumpster, his back against a different garbage can. Other than them, I was alone. The store had closed two hours ago, and though a couple of night restockers had come in, they hadn't noticed me as they drove to the back of the massive store.

It was getting cooler here in…actually, I wasn't sure where I was. Somewhere in between Mississippi and home. Some little town at the very northeastern tip of Tennessee, where there was nothing around but cows and rolling farmland. East bumblefuck, a great place for the business at hand.

I had to make it back home, and soon. Before the sun came up would be best. If I did, I could make the special delivery to the clinic, collect my fee, and wipe my hands of the whole thing.

Twenty-five lousy percent. I was still bitter about that. Maybe I should have argued with him. Mark Lamb. Definitely not one of my favorite people to work with.

And now he was late. Yes, this would definitely be the last time working with that cocky bastard.

I pulled my cardigan closed and readjusted my fake glasses and wig, hugging myself as tires screeched in the distance. I looked up to see a blue muscle car careening into the lot.

I crossed my arms as he screeched to a stop in front of me and rolled down his window. "That was great. Why don't you kill the kid on the way over here?" I said as he shot me a mock salute. He had a thick head of hair and was unshaven, as was the style of kids today. Still wearing scrubs and Crocs, with a little black pea coat over the ensemble, he jumped out and sauntered toward me.

"Hello, sweetheart," he said with a leering grin, hands in the pockets of his coat like a sulky teenager. "How've you been?"

I didn't answer him.

He mock-pouted. "No kiss, grandma?"

Scowling at him, I walked to the car and looked in the back to see a tiny thing in a blue hat. A boy. Despite the rollercoaster ride he'd been on, the baby was sleeping soundly, in what looked like a cardboard box full of rags. "What the hell did you put him in?"

"It's not like I had a car seat," he said as I opened the door and lifted the tiny thing out of the box. I inhaled the newborn smell on his tiny head as I scrutinized him closely. No obvious defects. No skin tags, odd birthmarks, funny deformities that could break the deal. Good. Just a perfectly nice little baby.

I, on the other hand, did have a car seat. I had more than one, for any age, in the trunk of my car. With my business, I was always transporting children. Earlier, I'd set up the seat for the tiniest of newborns, but this one wasn't so small. He may have been a ten-pounder.

"Get the back door to my car," I ordered Mark, cradling the baby's tiny head.

He stood firm. "Wait. What about my money?"

Of course. That's all he cared about. I motioned with my elbow to the pocket of my cardigan. "It's all there."

"Yeah? All of it?" He reached in, grabbed the folded white envelope, opened the flap, and began to count the bills.

"It is," I insisted, nudging him. "Now open the door before this little one catches a cold. I can't deliver a sick kid to them. You know if he's had his shots?"

He nodded, opened the door, and reached into the back of the car, pulling out a card. He held it up to me. The baby's immunization schedule. Vitamin K, Hep B, erythromycin eye drops...yep. All there. Passed the APGAR test with flying colors."

"What about the parents?"

"Mother is a teenage girl. No father. She came in alone. I created a, um, medical emergency and substituted a stillborn from the morgue. No one suspects a thing." He blew on his fingernails and pretended to buff them on his coat. "God, I'm good."

"They better not suspect anything," I said, settling the little boy down into the waiting car seat. I had to adjust the straps for his bigger body. He squirmed and fisted his little hands as I buckled the five-point harness but didn't make a sound.

Good.

I'd brought extra formula and diapers in case they were needed, but I wanted to get on the road as quickly as possible. This was the most nerve-wracking part of the job— during the hand-off, when the baby was in my possession.

I climbed out of the back of my car. Mark Lamb was extending his hand to me. "Nice doing business with you, sweetheart. Take it easy."

I shook it lightly with my gloved fingers, wondering how a guy like Lamb could have become a nurse. Nurses cared about people. That's why I'd become one. This man only cared about one person—himself. "Goodbye, Mr. Lamb."

"No kiss, baby?"

I rolled my eyes and walked away from him. When I last looked at the bastard, he was busily counting his new wealth. He'd probably blow the funds on another muscle car, and I momentarily considered running him over. But...cameras. They were such a nuisance nowadays. One never knew where one of the damned things would be hidden. Besides, I'd never see the smug little bastard again. He could live, and I'd never have to think of him again.

I yawned as I got into my car and checked the time. I was getting too old for these late nights. Slightly under three hours until sunrise. I could make it. And then that money would be mine, and I could start thinking of where I wanted to go on my next cruise. Caribbean maybe. That would be nice. I'd heard good things about the ABC islands.

As I pulled to the light, I peeked at the newborn in the rearview mirror. "You'll have a picture-perfect life now, sweetheart," I told him, smiling. "You'll see. It will be wonderful. I know you'll be very happy."

8

Maybe it was just too much togetherness.

But now, as Kylie sat hunched over her computer, watching Linc fiddling with the dishwasher in the kitchen, she wanted to shove a fork down his throat.

He'd kept insisting that there was something wrong with it, even though it was fine with Kylie. It cleaned their dishes, which was what they wanted, right? But Linc thought it was making a weird noise and had noticed earlier this morning that one of his favorite coffee mugs had come out chipped.

So now, he was on his knees, his upper half buried in the thing, making some rhythmic banging noise with a wrench.

Ping. Ping. Ping.

She groaned loudly. He'd been sick with a sinus infection the past few days, so while she usually would've tended to him, she'd done her best to try and stay away. She wasn't sure if her being sick would harm the baby.

She made him chicken soup and delivered gallons of orange juice to their bedroom, but she'd slept downstairs in the spare bedroom with the dogs.

Grunts and groans emanated from the dishwasher. Now

that he was better, he was trying to take on too much, as usual.

Some of the dogs, thinking it was playtime, kept trying to get in there with him and help, and some of them were getting into little scuffles from boredom, especially since he hadn't really given them a good workout in several days, due to his sickness. It'd be nice if he did what he was supposed to do. Go out and train them and get them—and himself—out of her hair.

But no.

She grabbed her phone, plugged in her earbuds, and tried to listen to some calming music as she went over the month's financials. But even Enya couldn't take away the headache that was spearing her right between the eyes.

Her eyes nearly crossed as she stared at the Excel spreadsheet. Whatever Linc had been saying about them ending up in the poorhouse? He wasn't exaggerating. For yet another month, they were in the red.

The results made her shiver.

It had been fine the first few months. She'd told herself she just needed time to get her footing, and there was a lot of added expense in transferring all the assets to the farmhouse. The moving van, the new computers, new desks, new software to get Greg's hopelessly behind-the-times outfit into the twenty-first century. But now? She'd expected to have been turning a profit by now. Or at least, breaking even.

But they weren't. Not even close.

That business lunch? What a waste. She hadn't even secured that client, despite plying him with thirty-dollar scotches. And what the hell? Forty dollars for paper clips? What were they, solid gold? She'd have to ask Linc about that one later. He'd ordered them online.

As she tallied a column in her Excel file for the twelfth

time, expecting a different, better result, she heard it, clear as day above the groove of "Orinoco Flow."

Ping. Ping. Ping.

She ripped the earbuds out of her ears.

"Linc?" she called to him, her voice crackling with bitterness. She forced herself to soften it. "Sweetheart?"

"Yep?" His voice echoed in the cavern of the dishwasher.

"Can you…" *kindly get the hell out?* "…maybe take a break? Go outside with the dogs? They're getting restless."

"One sec. I almost got this."

Ping. Ping. Ping.

She slumped against the back of the chair and smashed her teeth together, studying that big red number on her spreadsheet.

If only that was the only thing on her mind today.

But this morning, when the day was bright and new and everything felt like a fresh start, she'd promised herself she'd have a different attitude. Be the old Kylie, the one who constantly looked at everything in a positive way. It was only because she was stuck under a mountain of responsibilities that she'd been down, so she had the distinct feeling that if she made her to-do list her priority, she'd be happier. She'd tackle the day, get the monthly financials done, work on some of Greg's cases, be productive. Oh, and she'd call her OB-GYN.

She'd decided, early that morning as she laid awake in bed, that she wouldn't tell Linc. Not just yet. After all, pregnancy tests were fallible, weren't they? Maybe she had nothing to worry about. She'd go to the doc and get the real diagnosis first.

Deep down, though, she acknowledged that she was putting it off because she was just buying herself time to process it. She still hadn't wrapped her head fully around the fact that she could be knocked up.

Also, she knew Linc. She knew he was kind of over-bearing and protective, and he'd only be more so if he knew. He'd put her on lockdown, and she'd probably never breathe on her own again.

Almost on cue, her stomach tightened, and the nausea returned. She reached into a hidden drawer in her desk and pulled out a cracker to nibble.

Ping! Ping! Ping!

"Shit!" Linc wailed.

She narrowed her eyes. Something was afoul in dish-washer-land. That probably meant his one second was now one hour. Dammit to all hell.

He stood up and wiped his hands on his jeans. "One minute. Got to get something out of my toolbox."

She sat back, fighting the urge to lunge across the room and strangle him. "Oh...so now it's one minute?" The sarcastic comment was out of her mouth before she could stop it.

"What?"

"Before, you said it was one second," she reminded him, softening her voice and giving him a smile. She really did love him. He didn't deserve her foul mood.

"Oh." He shrugged, failing to see how close he was to a grisly death as he walked past her, slamming the door as he went to the shed where he kept his tools.

She was still sitting there, glowering at that figure in red on the monitor, when he came in, carrying a bigger—and probably noisier—wrench. He glanced at her and frowned. "You okay?"

She nodded, knowing that she looked the very opposite of okay. She knew her face was red; she felt it burning. She was hot, and bothered, and almost *shaking,* she was so...well, she didn't know what she was, but she was most definitely *not* okay.

He touched his chest. "You got something…"

She looked down. Cracker crumbs had fallen across the shelf that was her bustline. She plucked her tank top up and let them scatter.

"Are you sure you're—"

"I'm fine," she said, keeping her voice calm. She was losing it, on the very verge of crying.

It was so tempting to tell him everything and lay all her problems on his strong shoulders.

But…

She needed to do this on her own. She couldn't tell him about the deficit because he'd really get on her about taking the Elise Kirby case on pro bono. Mr. Forty Dollar Paper Clip. She'd just have to handle buying the office supplies right now. And make sure she didn't buy any potential clients ridiculously expensive scotch.

Even looking at the black hole that was their finances, she didn't regret taking Elise on as a client. She was glad, too, that Linc hadn't gone off on her too much about it, even though his disappointment was evident. If he had given her shit about it? She hated to think about what her hormonally ridden body might have done.

She didn't have the temper to deal with him now.

Linc held his hands up in surrender, a regular position for him now. "All right. Sorry."

She slumped in her chair. So much for having a happy, positive, Old-Kylie day.

"You look tense. Is there anything I can do for you?" he asked and wiggled his eyebrows. "Back massage?"

She checked the clock on her computer and stood up. She'd normally loved cuddling with him, but right now, she was so tense she thought she'd go off like a live wire if anyone even tried to put a finger on her. "No. I've got to go.

I'm meeting with…" she wasn't sure how to finish and fibbed, "a client."

"Oh, yeah? I didn't see the appointment on your calendar," he said, heading back to the kitchen. "I guess I'm on my own for lunch?"

"Yes, sorry." Not that he was helpless in the kitchen. He was the one who normally cooked for her, but she hadn't mentioned this appointment because, contrary to what she'd told Linc, in the past few days, her little "hobby" case, the one she promised she'd work on only when she had extra time, had been consuming much of her thoughts.

When Linc had been out, she'd called Elise a few times, gleaning more information. And now, she had a meeting with Agnes Mott, the woman who'd been babysitting Elise's child when the kindly "aunt" came to take her away.

As she went upstairs to change, she heard the *Ping, Ping, Ping,* and a surge of guilt overwhelmed her. Or maybe that was nausea. She had to run to the upstairs bathroom and barely made it to the toilet before she retched the two saltine crackers she'd managed to get down.

She tried to be as quiet as she could, and thankfully, from all the noise going on downstairs, Linc hadn't heard her.

She stared into the toilet, willing herself not to crack. She loved Linc. They'd only been married a few months, and yet all she kept doing was piling up more and more secrets. It wasn't fair to him. And not only that, she transformed into a world-class bitch whenever he was around. And he was just trying to be good, fixing the dishwasher, offering to give her a back massage. He was the husband most women would kill for.

She was being an awful, terrible wife.

Forcing those thoughts away, she changed into a blouse and her favorite pair of black slacks, noticing that they were a little tighter around the waist. Despite losing the contents of her stomach almost daily, she felt bloated in her middle. Scraping her hair into a ponytail and applying lip gloss, she piled her things into her bag and ran down the stairs.

"You want me to come with you?"

She jumped and found him behind her. She was usually jumpy, but why was she even more so now? "Thank you, but that's okay. I'm sure you're busy after being sick the past few days." One of the Vader pups peed in the floor, and she glared as she snapped a few paper towels off the roll. "Besides, you have the dogs to train. They really want to get out."

He took the paper towels from her hands. "Okay. Suit yourself. I just thought you might want company."

The crazy thing was…part of her did. She felt insane. She wanted to be with him, and yet, two minutes later, she was annoyed by his very being. Was this just normal pregnancy hormones? Or was she on the verge of a mental breakdown?

Grabbing her keys and her phone, she lifted onto her toes to press her lips to his, glad she'd remembered to brush her teeth.

"I'm sorry I'm being crazy," she said, and tears washed into her eyes.

His hand moved to her cheek before he pulled her into his arms. "You know you can talk to me, right?"

The offer nearly broke her resolve, and she just held him close as she willed the tears away. "I'm good. Promise." She rose to her tiptoes again, letting this kiss linger a bit longer. "Got to go."

He patted her bottom as she turned away, and she was actually smiling as she headed out to her Jeep. But the smile had faded by the time she'd driven to the end of the driveway, and she stopped long enough to tap the little call button on her phone.

"Asheville OB-GYN!" a chipper receptionist answered.

"Hi, this is Kylie Coulter. I'm a patient of Dr. Ling's," she said, gnawing on her lip. "And I think I might be pregnant."

The receptionist didn't waste time. "Congratulations! How long since your last period?"

"Um…well…probably about five, six weeks?"

"And you've been to the office before. Your name again?"

"Kylie…well, you have me under Kylie Hatfield, but I've since married. I'm Kylie Coulter now."

"Ah. I see. You haven't been to our office for a routine exam in several years."

And she thought she couldn't feel any more guilty.

"Yes. Well, I've been busy. I meant to get in, but with the wedding, and—"

"Is all your health history the same?" the receptionist asked, obviously not interested in her excuses.

"Um. Yes. Well, except for the baby I think's inside me."

The woman laughed. "No major surgeries or…?"

"Well. Actually. I did have surgery on my shoulder last year."

"Oh. Arthroscopic, or…"

Kylie gripped the steering wheel tighter. "Actually, it was for a bullet wound."

"Ah." For several seconds afterwards, the nurse seemed to be at a loss for words. She probably wasn't going to win any Mom of the Year awards for that admission. "Is this your first pregnancy? No abortions or miscarriages in your past?"

"No. None."

"We have an opening tomorrow at eleven. Will that work?"

"Yes, that's perfect. Thank you."

Kylie hung up, and only then did she realize that Linc would probably look on her schedule and wonder exactly where she was headed, just like he'd done this morning. She

decided she'd have to make something up, another mysterious client appointment, and then felt guiltier yet.

AGNES MOTT LIVED in a trailer park in a remote, wooded
area outside of Asheville, in a little town close to the
Tennessee border. It was the same place where the baby had
been kidnapped, and where Elise had once lived, although,
when she started dating Cody, she'd left the trailer park and
moved into his apartment in downtown Asheville, which was
closer to her employment at the Sunset Diner.

As she drove along the wooded highway, Kylie spotted
the Luxury Acres Trailer Park from the road. Several of the
homes butted right up to the road, though there were some
scraggly looking pine trees set up at intervals on the side of
the street, which were trying and failing to provide privacy.
There was also a sign that said, FOR RENT, LUXURY
HOMES, but the trailers weren't exactly luxurious. Most of
them were rusted and broken-down, with windows covered
with bits of fabric and dirty, holey screens. They were all
arranged in a circle, and there was a little girl in a bikini
sitting on the side of a bald tractor tire, playing with a hose,
surrounded by a mud puddle.

Kylie parked on the side of the driveway and walked
around a white fence, to where the child was squealing in
glee, all skinny arms and legs. Her bathing suit was too small;
the top was riding up over her tiny chest, not that she cared.
She appeared to be the only person around.

"Excuse me," she asked the little girl, nearly hopscotching
on tufts of dried grass to avoid the mud. "Could you tell me
where Agnes Mott lives?"

The girl regarded her warily, flipping her sopping ponytail over her shoulder, then pointed to a powder-blue trailer

with red flowers— undoubtedly plastic—in the window boxes.

"Thank you."

She walked across the courtyard, being careful not to step on the child's muddy toys, which were scattered amidst the puddles. It was a little like a minefield. She climbed the small wooden staircase, rapping on the metal door.

"Come in!" a gravelly voice called.

Kylie turned the handle and pushed, but nothing happened. She pulled, and nothing happened either. Finally, after jiggling it some, she managed to yank it open. She walked inside and immediately smelled burned toast mixed with something medicinal, what she thought was Bengay. It was stuffy and unbearably hot too.

For a second, she wondered if she'd forgotten her saltines, but then she remembered sticking a whole sleeve in her purse the night before.

When her eyes adjusted to the darkness, they fell on an overweight woman with gray-white hair that resembled a mop, who was sitting at the kitchenette in a ratty pink housecoat. To add to the ensemble, she wore striped sports socks pulled up to her knees, and the skin of her upper arms was covered in giant freckles.

She squinted in Kylie's direction. "Who's there?"

"Hello. I'm Kylie Ha...Coulter," she said, speaking loudly because the woman had been hard of hearing on the phone. She moved through a narrow opening and into the kitchen area. "Ms. Mott, I'm the private investigator who was hired by Elise Kirby. We spoke on the phone, if you'll remember."

"Yes, yes, hello, Kylie Hacoulter," she said, patting the bench. "You sit right on over here and we'll talk."

In her phone conversation with the old woman, she'd gotten the feeling that Agnes Mott was very lonely. She'd kept Kylie on the phone far after they'd arranged the appointment, just talking about, well, nothing. The weather, which was much hotter than it ever was when she was a kid. The sorry state of kids today, who had no respect. How everything about the world was going to hell in a handbasket.

Based on that experience, Kylie expected this meeting would probably drag on well into the afternoon. As a chatterbox herself, Kylie didn't think she'd mind, but now, she felt uneasy. Sweat was pouring down her ribcage, her stomach was queasy and unsettled, and now she had tomorrow's appointment to think about, and of course, the guilt and uncertainty she felt about keeping it from Linc.

She squeezed into the bench seat across from Agnes, noticing the woman's large cleavage was resting on the table. Actually, on the plate that was there, filled with toast crumbs and little globs of jelly, which were already staining the front of her housecoat. She reached over and pulled the plate a few inches away. Agnes didn't seem to notice.

She pulled out her notebook and smiled. "Nice of you to meet with me!" she yelled.

"Oh yes. So, what are you selling? Is it cosmetics?"

Kylie blinked. "No. I'm a private investigator, remember. Elise Kirby secured my services. I was hired to—"

"Oh, that's too bad. I was looking for something to get rid of this." She unzipped her housecoat a little, and Kylie could see that she wore nothing underneath as she showed Kylie a large, brownish mole on the pockmarked flesh of her collarbone. That, and waaaay too much cleavage, considering this was their first meeting.

"Oh, um…" Mentally shrugging, Kylie leaned forward, studying the mole. "You know, that could be cancerous. Melanoma can be bad. You should have it checked by a dermatologist."

The woman waved the idea away. "Well, then, let it take

me. I ain't going to no doctors." She sipped her coffee, making loud slurping sounds. "Now, what *are* you selling then, dear?"

Kylie inhaled a deep breath, then wished that she hadn't. Ms. Kirby needed a bath. "I'm not selling anything. I'm a private investigator looking into the disappearance of Daisy Kirby."

"Daisy...Kirby?" The woman scratched at one of her chins. "Now, why does that name sound familiar?"

She looked down at her bag, and then realized that the woman's eyes were still trained on the floor. Was she...blind too? And Elise had trusted her baby to this woman?

"Uh, you babysat little Daisy? For Elise Kirby? About two years ago?"

"Ah! Yes," she said, and then her face fell. "Oh. That was not a good time. I'd rather not talk about that. I felt terrible. Are you sure you're not selling anything?"

Kylie sighed. She wished she had a little tub of Vaseline in her purse. She'd give it to the woman so they could get on with it. "Well, I'm hoping I can ask you a few questions about it?"

Agnes nodded, but the gesture was slight. "I wasn't as broken down as I am now, you see. I could move a lot better, hear a lot better, see a lot better...but I've gone downhill since that baby went away. It really hurt me, you see. I guess you could say I blame myself every day, and that guilt's taken its toll."

A tear appeared in her eye, and Kylie reached out and touched her arm. "Oh, you shouldn't think that. It's not your fault, Ms. Mott. How were you to know?"

The woman hung her head in response. "It's just that she had looked like a very respectable, wealthy, important woman, so I just assumed..." She wiped at her eyes with a paper towel. "I suppose I should've called Elise and asked, but

I knew she was always so busy at work, what with that diner, and this was the middle of the dinner rush."

Kylie positioned her pen to take notes. "Can you tell me exactly what happened?"

"Yes. I'd been with the baby since the early afternoon, since Elise was going to work the dinner shift. She came over from her trailer, which was that yellow one right over there." She tilted the blinds and pointed to one across the courtyard. "It was actually her brother Hal's trailer, but he went off to the army. When he left, she lived there alone. Last I heard, Hal was back, but he'd gone off somewhere else. Don't live there no more."

The trailer was smaller, falling apart, like the rest of them. There was a BEWARE OF THE DOG sign in the window. Kylie studied the trailer more closely, almost pressing her nose against the screen until she realized how dirty it was. There was a spider weaving a web in the corner of it. She quickly backed away.

"Daisy was asleep, so I just put her down on the bed at the back of the house, and off Elise went to work. We'd gotten into a little groove, that Little Miss Daisy and me. She was an easy baby, that girl. Mostly just slept, right back there." She extended her fleshy arm behind her.

Kylie craned her neck to view the bedroom in the back of the trailer. Everything was dark-paneled wood, so it made the insides very dark, but she could just make out an unmade bed down the narrow hallway, past a small living area with a sofa and an old television set.

"You'd babysat for her before?"

"Yes. Only about a dozen times by then. Daisy was about two months old. Smiley little kid." She wrapped both hands around her mug and stared into it. "Well, it was about four hours later that a woman came knocking on the door. I answered it, and she told me that Elise was going to be late at work, but she'd just gotten back in town, and Elise had told her she could watch the baby. I said I didn't know anything about that, but she said it was fine, her flight had gotten in earlier so that's why Elise didn't know, and not to bother her at work. Elise always works so hard, she said. She said she lived right down the street and she'd watched the baby before. So I said okay. She went and collected the baby, and then off she went in her fancy Mercedes, quick as that. Never saw her again."

"What did she look like?"

"Well, that was the thing. She was so sweet and grand-motherly looking, she looked like she couldn't hurt a fly. She was wearing a nice suit, heels, rich looking, you know? Lots of expensive pearl jewelry. Platinum blonde hair, done up in a lot of spray. And she smelled like a perfume store. She was older, but she had pretty, young-looking hands with bright pink nails, so long and pretty like she'd never worked a day in her life and had servants to do everything for her. So, I thought, this woman's grandmotherly and rich, she ain't gonna harm the kid." She shook her head sadly. "I was wrong. I guess appearances can be deceiving. And now, come to think of it, I doubt Elise would have an aunt like that. So rich and pretty and fancy looking like that."

Kylie scribbled down the description in her notebook: *Rich-grandmotherly-suit-heels-pearls-perfume-long   fingernails.* "What do you mean?"

"Well, Elise'd lived here for a while with her brother, Hal, when her momma kicked her out after getting pregnant. Then her brother went off and enlisted and left her alone in the trailer. She kept saying she was all alone and was worried about what she'd do with a baby. Never mentioned an aunt, let alone a rich one who lived nearby. I should've questioned it."

Kylie absently stroked her stomach. It was flat now, but

even just having life inside her made her feel for Elise. Right now, Kylie knew nothing about babies. But at least, she had her mother and Linc and so many other people to help her out. Poor Elise. "It's not your fault. You said this woman drove a Mercedes?"

She nodded. "Or something like that. All shiny and silver, like a million dollars. She looked like one of them ladies that sits in the front pew at church. All done up. And she had the car that says, *I'm someone*."

"I see. And she didn't strike you as the babysitting type."

"No. Not at all. In fact, when she came to pick the baby up, it seemed almost like a business transaction."

"A business transaction?"

"Yes. Cute little baby makes everyone smile, right? She didn't smile. Not once. The baby was sleeping, but I remember that she woke when the woman lifted her up. And she started to cry. But rather than comfort little Daisy, or make silly faces, the woman just kind of went along with her, almost like she was holding a piece of meat. I found that odd. Detached. You know?"

Kylie wrote that down. "And you'd never seen the woman around here before that? Perhaps snooping around or at the supermarket?"

Motts shook her head. "Would've noticed her. Would've stuck out like a sore thumb 'round here."

That was Kylie's reason for asking. She tapped her chin, thinking, but before she could ask whether Elise had had any other visitors, Agnes added, "But honestly, I don't go out much. The sun disagrees with me. And I have a bad ticker. And I don't do my own shopping. Elise used to go out and do that for me, but now I have Edgar next door. He helps me out. I'm not a snoopy snooper, like some people around here are. Always looking through windows."

That was probably a shame. A *snoopy snooper* would come

in really handy right then. She looked down at the paper, where she'd written the kidnapper's description. "Is there anyone else around here who might have been living here during that time? Who might have seen something?"

The old lady shook her head, her jowls jiggling. "We get pretty high turnover around here. I'm the only old-timer."

"Oh. Okay. Right," Kylie said, trying to think of anything more she could ask. Her mind was a blank. "Well, I think that's all I have to ask you for now."

"Are you sure you aren't selling anything?" the woman asked, looking hopeful as she rubbed her hands together. "I'd like to get some of those scented oil warmers. You know the ones? They make the air smell so pretty. I like the ocean ones. Been a long time since I got to the ocean. Used to go to Myrtle Beach with my sister, oh, about twenty years ago."

It was almost like she was creating some reason to get Kylie to stay longer, which broke Kylie's heart. It was so tempting to just give in and stay much longer, just to give the woman some company.

Ignoring the tug of her heart, Kylie closed her notebook and slipped out from behind the table. "Yes, Myrtle Beach is beautiful, but I'm sorry. I'm not selling anything." She pushed a business card over to her. "If you do think of anything else that could help me, please call."

Agnes nodded, sadness filling her expression. "Nice meeting you, sweetheart."

Kylie swallowed and said, "You too," then pushed hard to open the door before stepping out into a mud puddle from the little kid who was still playing with the hose. She looked down and realized her pants were streaked from knee to ankle with grime. Great.

Although a bit irritated, she smiled at the little girl as she walked to the car. When she slid into the driver's seat, she took off her shoes and grimaced, pitching them into the passenger floor. Before tossing her notepad onto the seat beside her, she scanned what she'd written down. It wasn't much of anything. The description of the aunt was pretty good, but there were about a million Southern Belles in this state who looked like that. There was nothing to lead her anywhere else, no threads of a lead to grasp on to.

She decided she should go and see Elise. Maybe there was some more info she could give her to help her search. It was just after lunchtime anyway. She was starving, and her nausea had begun to come back.

Kylie turned the key in the ignition and realized she had a message on her phone from Linc. It was sent only a few moments before. It said: *Had to go into town to get a part for the dishwasher. If you're done early, maybe we can meet up for lunch?*

She pressed her lips together, thinking. She'd been feeling guilty about being so short with him earlier. If they went to the Sunset, she could casually ask Elise questions without making him think she was spending too much time on the case. Probably.

She typed in: *I'm done now. Sunset?*

His response came in a few seconds later: *Be there in ten. Love you.*

She smiled. He was such a good husband. He'd make a good father. She was so lucky to have him. She needed to remember that and stop getting annoyed by every little thing he did.

Love you too, she typed in, then threw her car into reverse.

As she was driving, it occurred to her that there were probably angles to the case that she was overlooking. She decided to put in a call to Greg, her former boss and mentor. Now retired and living in a condo on Lake Norman, he'd always been able to help her out when she was stuck.

She thumbed in a call to him, and when he answered with a garbled, "Yello," she could already tell he was drunk. He was either *really* enjoying his retirement or else in the process of drinking himself to death.

"Are you okay?" she asked, genuinely worried.

"Hey, short stuff. What's up? How's the investigations business without me?"

This was where they'd normally shoot the shit for an hour. But after the frustrating day Kylie was having, first blowing up on Linc, then learning her business was falling apart, then making no headway on her investigation, she came right to the point. "Oh, it's going. But I have some questions to ask you, if you're not busy."

He snorted. "Busy? Hell. I just got in from fishing with the guys. It's a beautiful day. I was going to sit out on the deck and enjoy it. That was my agenda for the rest of the day."

"That sounds nice. Listen," she licked her lips, "this case is giving me some trouble, and I thought you could point me in the right direction?"

"Sure, kid. Shoot."

She had a flash of nostalgia for the old days, when they used to sit in the office that used to be a vacuum store in downtown Asheville, trading barbs at one another while they worked. Back then, she was a filing clerk, and the most she had on her mind was collecting a paycheck and whether or not that stoic but insanely hot dog-whisperer guy actually liked her or just her dog.

"Well, one of my clients had a baby, left it with a babysitter, and it was kidnapped while she was at work. I interviewed the babysitter, but it wasn't much help, and I'm kind of banging my head against the wall right now. You have any suggestions?" she asked, her voice running a mile a minute.

"Whoa. Slow down. You said her baby was kidnapped while she was at work? Were there any witnesses?"

"This happened two years ago, so it's hard to find anyone who might have seen what happened."

"Shit. Two years?" There was a pause. "There's not a lot that you can do that the police probably haven't already done, but who knows? I'm assuming you got the police report?"

Kylie opened her mouth and then snapped it shut. Of course, the police report. That was rule number one in any investigation. How could she have forgotten that? Face heating, she said, "Well, I'm going to."

"Take a look at that and see if that'll lead you anywhere. Maybe you can talk with the lead investigator and see what he remembers. If it's not an active case, he should be pretty forthcoming with the information because there's no chance you can step on any toes."

"Right." Kylie suddenly itched to go ahead and get that report. God, she'd been so dumb. What was she even thinking? That was the first thing she was supposed to do. You'd think she never investigated a case before. Her mind was definitely going. "Thanks, I've got to—"

"Hey, Kylie?"

She stopped. "What?"

"Calm down."

She sighed. How could he, on the other side of the state, see that she was so stressed? Were the vibes she was giving off that powerful? "I am calm," she lied.

"Yeah. About as calm as a rattlesnake that's about to get stepped on." His voice leaked doubt. "You okay? The business is good? No problems?"

"No, no problems," she said lightly, or at least she tried to be light, but it was hard, since at that moment, her mind flashed back to the bright honking red number on her Excel spreadsheet.

"Okay." His voice said he didn't believe her. "You take it easy. Go get that police report. Have a good day, Kylie. And if you need me at all, just call. Okay?"

Tears pricked at her eyes and her sinuses burned as she held the phone tight against her ear. Greg Starr was precious to her. Her own father hadn't been present in her life. Greg was like the dad she'd never had, and she hadn't seen him in months. It only occurred to her when she heard his voice how much she missed the grumpy old man. "Ye-ah," she said, her voice cracking.

When she hung up, she pulled into the diner parking lot. *Keep it together, Kylie. Go and have a nice lunch with your husband and be happy!*

But when she looked around for Linc's pickup, she realized he wasn't yet there.

She took a deep breath. Then another one.

Then she found a secluded spot back behind the diner, parked, turned off the ignition, put the phone back in her purse, slumped over the steering wheel, and finally allowed herself to cry.

9

The Sunset Diner was Linc and Kylie's go-to place for lunch whenever the two of them found themselves downtown. It was always crowded, served just about any type of food a person could want—from Louisiana gumbo to Vietnamese Pad Thai—and the service was excellent.

But Linc really hadn't cared where they went to eat. He just wanted to see his wife and talk to her. He'd been tidying up his desk while he made the call to see if the hardware store had the part he needed, and that's when he'd seen it. It was right on her computer screen, so he couldn't ignore it. A rundown on Coulter Confidential's revenue for last month.

And it was dismal.

Maybe that was why she was acting so strange. She didn't want the company to fail. She said they owned the company equally, but it was really her baby. And no matter how many times he said she didn't need to work in order for them to get by, she wanted the business to succeed for more than just the money. She loved the work, loved helping people. She probably felt that there was so much pressure on her to make it all turn out the way she wanted.

He understood why she'd kept it to herself, though. He hadn't exactly been supportive of her idea of taking things on pro bono. But that's what she needed to see: She couldn't be a bleeding heart when her business was on the line.

He thought that if he took her out and they discussed it rationally, maybe he could help her see that. After all, she didn't have to work. Without her job, he could bring in enough money for both of them to get by on, if they didn't make any wild, extravagant purchases. But if she was going to insist on keeping this company chugging along and let it continue to drain their finances, though, whatever cushion he'd amass for their retirement would probably be gone.

They needed to discuss it sooner rather than later. Calmly. Without judgment.

That meant, in public.

When she stepped out of her car, he had to wonder how her client meeting had gone, especially since her pants were covered in mud. Her shoes were clean, though, and he recognized them as the extra pair she usually kept in the Jeep. "What have you been doing?"

She looked down. "Oh, nothing."

He frowned. It hadn't rained since that storm a few days ago, when she'd first taken on Elise's case. Since then, there'd been a lot of blistering hot days. Since mud was in pretty short supply nowadays, he had to wonder what kind of client she'd been meeting with...and where. But he didn't want to ask too many questions. Too many questions seemed to get her on edge, especially now.

When the two of them walked in, he spotted Elise Kirby immediately. The blonde was behind the lunch counter in her blue dress and apron, pouring coffee for a customer. When she saw them, her eyes lit up, and she waved.

As the hostess seated them, Elise came up and clapped her hands excitedly. "Hi, guys! I'm supposed to be waiting the counter right now, but I spoke to my boss and she said I could wait on you! Isn't that great?"

Kylie smiled at her. "That's fantastic. How are you doing? How's Britt?"

She grinned from ear to ear. "Oh, he's the best. I snuggle with him in my bed each night. Right between me and Cody. Cody's getting jealous."

Linc had to admit that as much as he hadn't wanted to sacrifice Britt, the girl seemed different from the one who'd visited them at the farmhouse. She had color in her cheeks and didn't seem quite so nervous, but that might've been because she was in her element here at the diner. Linc wondered how much that had to do with the dog.

"He'll need to go to the vet," Linc pointed out. "He's due for his next round of shots in a couple weeks."

Elise's face fell, and her eyes widened. "The vet?"

Over the table, Kylie shot eye-daggers at him.

Fine. He was just trying to ensure the health of his dog. A very important thing. "We've taken him to Asheville Veterinary in the past," he said. "Out on 11? If you just tell them you're with me, they'll put the charges on my bill."

Kylie's face softened, but Linc could only think that their combined generosity was dragging them closer to the poorhouse. "I'm so glad you're enjoying him," Kylie said. "He's a great boy."

"Oh, I am," Elise said, looking down at her pad. "Oh, stupid me. If I keep blabbing all day, I'll forget to take your order. What can I get you to drink?"

"We're ready to order," Linc said. Despite the tome-sized menu, the two of them always got the same things. He looked at Kylie, who ordered the club sandwich on wheat and an iced tea. "And I'll have a water and the cranberry walnut salad with the balsamic vinaigrette dressing on the side."

Elise practically beamed at them. "All right. Let me get that in for you."

Linc drummed his hands on the table as she left. He leaned toward his wife, who was unrolling the napkin to release her silverware. "How was your meeting?"

She shrugged. "Good."

Linc raised an eyebrow. It wasn't like Kylie to give a one-word answer to, well, anything. The woman could talk to a wall. Either she was angry or stressed.

"Muddy?" he prompted.

"Yep." He watched as she peered out the window. Despite the sun, rain had begun to fall, a sudden cloudburst. Maybe she had been caught in the rain wherever she'd been. "I wonder if there'll be a rainbow."

"Maybe. I trained the dogs," he said, trying to make conversation. "They're good and tired now. I think some of them are getting it."

"That's terrific." She laced her fingers in front of her. "What was wrong with the dishwasher?"

"Nothing I can't fix. I'll get the new part installed when we get back, and I think it'll be good as new."

She sighed dramatically. "Good."

Elise arrived with the drinks, sparing them more inane conversation. As she set them down, Kylie turned toward the girl. "Elise, I have some questions about your case I want to ask you."

Ah. No wonder she'd been so distracted. Her mind was on her pro bono case. Which was why she'd suggested the Sunset. Kylie, always on the job. If she didn't quit stressing over these things, she'd probably implode one day.

"Sure," Elise said as Kylie scooted over on the bench to let her sit beside her.

Kylie pulled out her pad and pen and flipped it to a page with a bit of writing on it. Linc strained to see what was scrawled there as Kylie said, "I'm having a little trouble trying to figure out where to go next. I'll get the police report, but I was wondering if there was anyone else who might have seen the woman who took your baby?"

"Well...Agnes," Elise said, twisting her fingers together.

"Yes. You gave me her name before. Anyone else?"

"Did you meet with Agnes?"

Kylie's gaze shifted toward Linc. He saw guilt there. "Yes, but do you have anyone else?"

Linc shifted in his seat. So, that answered that question. She'd been investigating this case, the case she'd said would only be a hobby. And she'd been deliberately keeping it from him.

Not good.

"A neighbor? Anyone?" Kylie sounded more exasperated with every passing second. Her face was getting redder too.

Linc leaned over. "Kylie..." he said softly, sensing there was a bomb about to explode.

She waved him away frantically as she waited on Elise's answer.

Elise shook her head. "No. Nobody."

Kylie let out a big breath and tossed her pen down. "Well, that's just *great*."

Linc stared at her. He'd never seen Kylie look quite so defeated. Next to her, Elise hung her head, like she'd failed her friend somehow. "I'm sorry."

Kylie blew out a breath, and Linc could see her physically calming down. Her voice gentled. "I'm trying to help you, Elise. Really, I am. But how am I supposed to when there is so little to work on?"

Elise put her elbows on the table and buried her head between her hands. "I know, I know, I wish I remembered more."

This was where Kylie would normally sense Elise was

feeling bad and tell her it was okay, but she didn't. She picked up her pen, tapping the cap against her notepad. "All I have is a description of the kidnapper that could be any number of women. I only hope the police report will tell me more."

Linc looked over at Elise and tapped on her arm. "Hey, it's all right. You're doing your best."

Kylie blinked and immediately put her arm around the woman. "Oh, yes. Sorry, Elise. It's not your fault. I'm just a little frustrated. I really want to get your daughter back for you. You know, so you can sleep at night."

Elise smiled, but it was a more guarded one now. "Thanks, Kylie. I don't mean to cause no trouble for you."

"It's no trouble. I'm sorry for snapping at you," she said, patting Elise's shoulder like the old Kylie would have. "I've just been having one of those days. It's nothing to do with the case."

Then what does it have to do with? Linc wondered.

It had to be something, and not just PMS. She'd been going around like a ticking timebomb for the past week. The finances. It had to be that. She'd bitten off more than she could chew, and now this business was starting to wear on her.

"Okay," Kylie said, looking up from her pad. "One more question. Daisy was two months old when she disappeared. Can you tell me all the people you had contact with from the moment your baby was born?"

Elise's eyes widened, and Linc gave her a doubtful look. How did she expect this poor girl to remember all that?

"Well…" Elise began, her eyebrows furrowed in thought. "Wasn't that many people. Um, the nurses and doctors at the hospital. I don't know their names. Agnes. And…well, that's it."

"No visitors?" Kylie asked.

No one coming to see the baby did seem strange. Even if

she didn't have any family, people gravitated to newborns. It was just normal.

Elise shook her head.

"Did you go anywhere with your baby during that time?"

"No. I didn't have no car." She shrugged. "Sometimes I'd use Agnes' 'cause she never used hers, but not then. I was kind of scared to go anywhere with a new baby."

"How did you get home from the hospital?" Kylie asked.

Elise's eyes widened. "The people at child welfare brought me."

Linc leaned closer, as did Kylie. "Child welfare?"

Elise, realizing her mistake, turned a bright shade of crimson. "Oh, I'm sorry. You asked if I saw anyone. I saw my caseworker. She came in every week the first few weeks to check on the baby."

Kylie's face brightened. "Do you know her name?"

Elise shook her head. "Um…"

"What about the agency she was from? Do you remember that?"

Elise shook her head slowly, like a child who wanted to please her mother. She was clearly afraid to disappoint Kylie again. "The government just sent her. I didn't pay much attention."

Luckily, Kylie had gotten control of her emotions by now. Linc could see that she wanted to erupt, but she took a cleansing breath and laid a hand over Elise's. "Thanks. This is helpful."

Behind the counter, a bell dinged, and a gruff voice shouted, "E, your order's up!"

Elise jumped to her feet. "I think that's yours."

As Elise walked away, Linc looked at Kylie, mentally urging her to talk about what had gotten her so riled, but she was scribbling in her notebook. "So," he said gently. "Just looking into this case when you don't have anything to do?"

Kylie turned a bit pink. "I had some time, so I made the appointment." She shrugged. "It's not eating into my paid work."

"I didn't say it was."

She lifted her chin. "But you're insinuating."

He was prepared to deny, but Elise came back with the food, and a bottle of ketchup for Kylie's fries. They thanked her, and she walked away to help another customer. Kylie nibbled on one thoughtfully as Linc said, "You don't seem like yourself."

She bit into her sandwich and shrugged. "I'm fine," she said, mouth full.

"Are you sure?"

She widened her eyes and nodded, mouth still full, in a way that said, *Back off.*

He let out an exasperated breath. "Geez. Kylie. Level with me. I know what's going on."

She froze. She even stopped chewing. Then she started again, slowly. "What do you mean?"

"The financials for last month. I saw them."

She swallowed, and he could almost hear the gulp. "Wait. You were going through my desk?"

"Of course not. The spreadsheet was on your computer screen, which you left on despite me telling you that you should shut it off in case we have a thunderstorm and a power surge. I was going to shut it down when I saw it."

She swiped another fry through her ketchup. "There's a little deficit, but we expected that when we took the company over. We knew we wouldn't turn a profit at first."

"'*At first* is over," Linc pointed out, dipping a crouton into his salad dressing. She looked at him like she was about to explode, so he held up his palm to her and quickly added, "It's okay. I know you've been trying your hardest. We both have. But I really think you and I have to seriously look at the business and how we can cut expenses and increase profits. I'm not trying to make you feel bad. I just want to figure this out. Together."

"Maybe it has to do with your forty-dollar paper clips," she muttered.

"What?"

"I saw them on the sheet. You spent forty dollars on paper clips."

He just stared at her before remembering. "Oh. Yeah. That was a mistake. I ordered the wrong quantity. So, we'll have paper clips for the next sixty years."

"So?" She gazed at him like this was all his fault.

"So…it won't happen again. But you have to admit, forty dollars isn't the sole reason we're in the red."

She sighed.

"There are other things that we can look at. It means cutting out pro-bono cases and increasing paid work." Her eyes fell to her lap and she nodded as he added, "Especially if you don't want me to sell the dogs."

Her gaze flashed to his. "You won't sell them?"

"Not if you don't want me to. I mean, the house'll be a zoo, but they're half yours too. If you don't want me to let them go, I won't."

She smiled, tears springing to her eyes. "Thank you. I really love you, you know."

Sometimes, lately, he wasn't so sure.

"I love you too. We're a team." He glanced around the diner and spotted Elise at the counter, then leaned forward, lowering his voice. "This case with Elise…it's probably the last pro-bono one you should take."

Kylie lifted her sandwich but nodded before taking a big bite. "I agree. I decided that when I saw the numbers. But it's the first real case I've taken that isn't some carryover from

Starr Investigations. And it's been pulling at me. You know how I get when a case is pulling at me. Right?"

He knew it well. When a case involved an injustice against the poor, defenseless, or voiceless of the world, Kylie could scarcely think of anything else.

"All right." He surrendered to his own curiosity. "It sounds like you're running into roadblocks."

She sighed. "Yes. Once I get the police report, I hope it'll open up some new avenues to explore. I called about getting a copy a little bit ago."

"You ask Jacob to put a rush on it?" Jacob was Linc's best friend and a Buncombe County detective.

"No. It happened in Haywood County, not Buncombe."

"Ah."

Her eyes drifted to the back of the diner. "I feel bad about being snippy with Elise, though. It wasn't her fault. I hope I didn't harm our relationship, both business and personal."

"She'll be okay," Linc said, although he honestly wasn't sure. Elise seemed like one who carried her heart on her sleeve. "Who have you met with so far? You said the babysitter?"

"Yeah, in Luxury Acres. You know it?"

It sounded familiar, but he couldn't quite place the location. Slowly, though, an image came to mind, of a place on the side of the highway that looked like a refugee camp. When he was growing up, he and his friends used to ride for miles, all over the area. He used to ride past that place on his bicycle, and there were rumors that every pedophile and miscreant in the state of North Carolina was sent there when they went on parole.

She couldn't mean that Luxury Acres, could she?

"Whereabouts is that?" he asked, taking a sip of his water.

"On 11. By the old mill."

So, it *was* the same place he remembered. "Wait. You went there alone?"

"Of course." She visibly bristled. "You know I went alone. It was fine."

"Fine? That place is where criminals, especially sexual predators, go to die." He couldn't help his voice from rising in alarm.

"What?" She looked at him like he was crazy. "That's where Agnes Mott lives, a blind, almost deaf old lady. I think I was pretty safe, considering."

"Yeah, but did you see some of the other residents there? You don't know what kind of criminals you could've been surrounded by."

The hint of a smile he'd worked so hard to achieve disappeared in an instant. But she was being stupid again. It was like she went looking for trouble. "It was fine."

"This time, maybe. But you don't—"

"I handled myself perfectly fine for nearly a quarter of a century before you came along," she said and stabbed one of his tomatoes with her fork. He got a feeling she'd been wishing for another, more human, target. "Believe it or not."

"Yes, but back then, you weren't—"

"Can we drop this, please?" she said a little too loudly before clearing her throat. She crossed her arms over her chest. "You're not my warden, you know?"

"Me, wanting to make sure you don't die, isn't being your warden," he responded calmly, crossing his arms to mirror her. "It's not like you haven't been in life-threatening situations before. I'll save you as often as I have to, but I'd rather you not be in that position in the first place."

Her expression turned mutinous. "You don't always have to be there to save me. I'm not helpless. Sure, I've been in tight situations before, but those are rare. This is my job, whether you can deal with it or not. And this wasn't even remotely dangerous, Linc."

"You don't know that. That's what makes it dangerous." She was still gazing at him defiantly, so he dragged his hand down his face and decided to let her win this one. "Fine. What did the babysitter say?"

She studied him closely, seemingly surprised and pleased that he'd dropped the subject. "Well, she gave me a description of the kidnapper, but not much else. Grandmotherly, platinum hair, wealthy. Sounds like any one of a million people out there."

"Anything else?"

"Nothing much. Oh. Just that she didn't seem very loving to the child and treated it more like a business transaction. So, unless the police report has something really amazing in it, I'm afraid I'll probably end up right where the police ended up. Exactly nowhere."

"Actually, that could be helpful," Linc said, thinking it over. "I mean, how many grandmotherly types do you know who go around stealing babies?"

"True, but that woman could be anywhere now. For all I know, she was one of those deranged people who always wanted a kid, and now she and Daisy are living in some remote place together and will never be seen again."

Linc shook his head. "No. That doesn't sound right. You just said the lady told you that, while she might have looked like a grandmother, she didn't act like one. She told you she was very removed. Treated it like a business transaction."

"So…?"

"So, that kind of person doesn't sound very much like the type of person who has been pining away, looking for her chance at motherhood. My guess is that the baby isn't with her anymore."

Kylie reached over and squeezed his hand. "You're right.

But then, what did she…" Her jaw sagged as horror and something else—excitement?— crossed her expression. "Wait. You think it's part of a baby smuggling operation?"

He lifted a shoulder. "Maybe. I've heard a lot about child laundering rings. Most of them involve babies from overseas, but there have been plenty that involved babies from the States. The people who run them will take babies any way they can for their wealthy clients, usually to the tune of hundreds of thousands of dollars. It's a big business."

"Then if Elise's baby was taken, she's probably not the only one. Right?"

"Right, but this woman might work out of a large area to avoid detection. Usually, the criminals will target people who are young, poor, don't have much family…" He spotted the waitress at another table and lowered his voice even more. "Elise fits that profile. And it's a nasty business involving a ring of people, because one person couldn't pull this off on her own. The criminals were counting on the fact that Elise wouldn't have the resources to finance an in-depth investigation for her baby."

"But she did. And now she has me." Kylie rubbed her hands together. The remaining half of her sandwich forgotten, she grabbed her phone and started to jab something in, likely going down a research rabbit hole.

That was more like the old Kylie.

"What are you researching?" Linc asked.

"Adoption agencies and child welfare societies in Waynesville. They're the legal method of adoption, so I figure they'll be the best source of information on the *illegal* way, right? Plus, she said she was visited by child welfare, so they might have information on this particular case."

He nodded. It was a good idea. "Or the police. I'm sure Jacob could—"

"Here's one. Children's Hope in Waynesville. Hold on."

She put up a finger and tapped the screen to call the number. That was Kylie. Once she got an idea in her head, she didn't let it go. "Hello, I'm Kylie Hatfield, a private investigator with Coulter Confidential. I'd like to ask your director a few questions about a case I have." She winked at Linc. "An appointment? Yes, that would be great." She practically glowed as she scribbled something on her notepad. "This afternoon at four is perfect. Thanks." She hung up and clapped her hands together, then stopped when their eyes met. "What?"

He shrugged and stabbed a cucumber. "You said Kylie Hatfield. Not Coulter."

She smacked herself on the forehead. "Whoops. I keep doing that."

She keeps doing that, he repeated to himself, the knowledge affecting him more than it probably should.

He paid the check as she finished nibbling on her sandwich, and she didn't talk much at all, deep in thought. When they said goodbye to Elise and walked outside, Kylie was so deeply ingrained in this new lead that they broke apart and walked to their respective cars without so much as a "See you back at the house later on." He waited for her to turn around and remember him, but she never did.

Again, it affected him more than it should have.

He needed to stop worrying about it so much.

Maybe he should talk about his sudden insecurities with his PTSD therapist. He felt sure he was just overthinking everything, as usual.

Losing his entire team in Syria had left him vulnerable to feelings of abandonment, his therapist had told him. It pissed him off that she was right. He'd worked hard to seclude himself up on his mountain top, needing to worry about nothing but himself and his animals.

Then, Kylie had bounced into his life and karate-chopped

all his walls straight down. And he'd come to need her sparkle too much, he realized that.

He needed her laughter and fun. He needed the innate sexiness that drove him crazy.

And he needed her attention, which might make him a loser of the first degree, but there it was. She'd wormed her way into his life, and it scared him to think of losing her.

"Fucking loser," he cursed himself under his breath.

When he pulled out onto the highway, he groaned, realizing she was right behind him, and though it was drizzling, she didn't have her headlights on.

It wasn't wrong, looking out for her, was it? It was because he cared.

Caring was good. Right?

As he turned off the road, she honked her horn and blew him a kiss.

And just like that…he was smiling again.

Everything would be just fine.

10

D riving onto the highway, Kylie punched Children's Hope into her GPS. Another meeting. Hopefully, this one would get her somewhere. She desperately needed something to put her in a better mood.

She'd meant to be happy when she went out to lunch with Linc. Even though she'd resolved to be her old chipper self, she hadn't done a very good job. He and everything else just seemed to grate on her every last nerve lately. He'd made it seem like the business failing was her fault. He'd given her that disappointed look when he found out she was working on the Elise Kirby case.

And she felt awful about how she'd snapped at Elise. Elise was quiet and gentle and looked like a stiff wind would blow her over. Her face had crumpled when Kylie raised her voice. That was wrong.

It was the stress. And Linc wasn't helping things. Constantly looking at her like she was doing something wrong? Getting on her for visiting a freaking trailer park? He'd always been the overbearing, overprotective type, and god knew she sometimes needed it considering the sticky situations she'd been in…but Agnes Mott was about as harmless as a person could get. The world was not as big and bad as he made it out to be, with miscreants waiting around every corner, waiting to strike.

She swallowed as she drove, knowing that his need to protect her would probably only be magnified once he found out she was pregnant. He might not even let her leave the house. In fact, he might wrap her in bubble wrap, to save her from whatever dangers might lie *inside* their four walls.

It was amazing, she thought, that he'd even allowed her to go to Children's Hope on her own, since it was in Waynesville. Not that Waynesville was a dangerous town in the least, but if he'd been afraid of her meeting up with a blind, deaf old lady alone, who knew what other lengths he would go to?

She arrived at Children's Hope about twenty minutes before the appointment, so she pulled out her phone and checked her messages. As she'd hoped, the Haywood County Police had answered her request for a police report, emailing it to her.

Eagerly, she scrolled through the pages, but the report was markedly sparse. She scrolled down to the police officer's remarks and read: *Received call at 11:23 PM that mother Elise Kirby believed her child, Daisy Kirby, 2 months, to have been kidnapped. Arrived at caller's home in Luxury Acres at 11:35 PM and questioned Elise Kirby and babysitter, Agnes Mott, who stated that a wealthy, older woman claiming to be Kirby's aunt had taken the child away at approximately six PM in a late-model silver Mercedes.*

Luxury Acres is a busy park with numerous residences surrounding a courtyard. However, questioned neighbors did not see the woman arrive or depart. None had noticed the car parked in the lot. Fingerprints were taken in the residence of Mott but only Kirby's and Mott's were found.

Child was entered into the national missing persons database, however no leads were returned. Investigation into the mother found no evidence of foul play.

Well, that was great. And unhelpful. It seemed like there was so much more they could've done. What about scavenging the lot for tire tracks? Having a sketch artist recreate a picture of the woman based on Agnes's description and asking local businesses about a woman matching that description? Now, it was too late.

As far as Kylie was concerned, there was only one reason why they hadn't put everything into this case: To them, Elise was a nobody.

She looked at the name of the investigating officer: T. Stefak.

She still had a few moments before the appointment, so she quickly dialed the number for the police department. When someone answered, she said, "I'd like to speak to Officer Stefak, please."

The man on the other end said, "I'm sorry. Thomas Stefak hasn't been employed here in over a year."

Of course. "Do you have any idea where he might have gone?"

"Believe he moved his family to Florida," came the unenthusiastic response.

"Thank you."

She hung up and blew tendrils of dark hair out of her eyes. And now, that strange, uncontrolled feeling she'd gotten when she'd been talking to Elise was back. Worse than before. She felt like she was being backed against a wall, which frustrated her even more.

She shoved her phone in her purse and stepped out of her car, hoisting her bag on her shoulder as she looked up at the brick building. It was an office complex, with several different tenants, mostly doctors' offices, according to the directory at the front of the building. Children's Hope occupied the fourth, top floor.

Pressing the UP button on the elevator, she thought of poor Elise. *You're someone to me, Elise,* she thought to herself, and then felt even guiltier about snapping at the poor girl.

When she arrived at the top floor and the elevator doors slid open, she was greeted by a white wall with a giant Children's Hope logo—the "o" was a bright red heart. The lobby was furnished with comfortable chairs and the lighting was soft and welcoming. The receptionist smiled at her. "Are you Kylie Hatfield?"

"Um, actually, Kylie Coulter," she said, tapping the side of her head. "I just got married and I'm clearly having memory issues."

The woman laughed. "Oh, I understand. It happens to all of us."

Kylie was sure it did, but she wasn't quite sure it happened to people who'd been married for several months. If the wounded look Linc had given her at the diner was any indication, she probably should've gotten with the program by now. Wasn't it too early to have baby brain?

"Dr. Banks will be with you in a moment," the woman said, standing up and picking up her phone. "I'll let her know you're here. In the meantime, can I offer you any tea? Coffee? Water?"

"No thank you," she said, looking around. There was a wall of brochures near the reception stand, and Kylie gravitated to it. She read a couple of the titles: *Adoption and You; Making the Decision to Adopt; When Abortion is Not the Answer; So You Want to Adopt a Child; Becoming a Foster Parent.*

She picked up one of them and leafed through it as the woman behind her said, "You're a private investigator? That's exciting. Are you looking into a particular case?"

Kylie nodded and turned to face the woman. "As a matter

of fact, I am. A baby was kidnapped a couple years ago from a home around here."

The woman's face turned ashen. "Oh no, that's terrible."

Kylie rushed to comfort the woman. "It's not that anyone here is implicated." By now, Kylie knew how it looked whenever she showed her face anywhere. People always assumed that she was interviewing a suspect. "I just thought that a local adoption agency could provide me some insight into possible child laundering cases." She used Linc's words, *child laundering,* because it sounded more official.

"I see," the woman said, clearly still upset. "How awful for that mother. Looking for her lost child for years. As a mother, that's my worst nightmare."

Kylie's hand instinctively went to her stomach, and she began to feel queasy again. *Mine too.*

Just then, a door opened, and a woman swept in. "Hello!" she said loudly and brashly, grabbing on to Kylie's hand and shaking it so fast that she barely had a chance to process. "I'm Dr. Chastity Banks. Come right inside."

"Thank you," Kylie said, following the tornado of a woman with blonde hair that looked like a helmet. She had on an expensive looking flowery dress and too-high heeled sandals that her toes were falling out of and walked a little like a person trying to win a race. Kylie had a hard time keeping up with her.

When they reached her office, Dr. Banks offered her a seat, one of two blue plastic chairs. Kylie sat in one, glancing at the name placard on the enormous metal desk that said DR. CHASTITY BANKS, with a number of lettered designations that Kylie had never heard of. When Dr. Banks sat down, she rolled herself close to the desk and piled her hands in front of her, her bright pink fingernails a stark contrast to her pale skin. "How may I help you?"

Blonde. Long fingernails. Wealthy.

She wasn't exactly elderly, though. Nor was she young.

Kylie smiled. "I'm a private investigator, and I've been hired to look into the disappearance of Elise Kirby's infant daughter."

The woman's bright, lipstick-rimmed smile quickly faded. "Who?"

"Oh, you might have heard of it. It happened around here. In Luxury Acres about two years ago. I thought perhaps an agency like yours, which deals in the welfare of area children, would know of it."

The woman shook her head. "Perhaps, but it was a long time ago. I wasn't aware of it."

"Do you deal with the Haywood County Children's Protective Services?"

She nodded. "Yes. We work with a number of social workers who are part of the local and state units for child welfare. But our primary objective is in helping those who want to foster or adopt get through the process and pairing them with children we feel will thrive in their home environment."

"Are you aware of any child laundering cases from the area?"

Dr. Banks let out a bitter laugh. "I assure you that all of our adoptions are completely legal. I don't deal in the criminal nature of baby-trading, though I'm sure it must happen. Unfortunately, I'm not the person to ask about such cases."

She crossed her arms and stared her down, making Kylie feel small. "Okay, I understand that, but I'm just trying to determine if Elise's baby was part of some baby smuggling ring. Are there any resources you can point me to?"

She shrugged. "The county sheriff?"

"I've been in touch with the police. The mother had a caseworker that must've come from Haywood County's social services. She doesn't seem to remember what agency they worked for, but—"

"I'd check with the county's health and human services division."

Kylie wrote that down. "All right. Thank you," she said, standing. "I think that's all. I appreciate your help."

Dr. Banks sat back in her chair, and Kylie could feel her eyes burning into her back as she made it to the door. As she reached it, the woman stopped her.

"Wait. In fact, I do remember that case. Didn't come through us, unfortunately, so I can't help you."

Kylie's hand tightened on the doorknob. "Do you know—"

"There was some talk that the mother, who was not right in the head, might have murdered the baby, but the body was never found. A sad story, all around."

Kylie hadn't heard that one. It wasn't even mentioned in the police report. Besides, anyone who saw Elise Kirby would know she couldn't hurt a fly. "Thank you."

Well, that went over well, Kylie thought as she headed back to her car. The woman couldn't possibly be any more dismissive of her, even if she tried.

In fact, she'd gotten the feeling that just because she'd said she was an investigator, they'd been put off. Like they expected her to snoop around and create trouble, trying to air their dirty laundry. She was just trying to find out what happened to Elise's baby.

She climbed into her car and picked up her phone. She had a text from Linc: *Ok?*

He sent her that same text almost every hour when they weren't together. She knew he had a valid reason. If she hadn't been kidnapped, held at gunpoint, run off the road by a psycho, shot at...maybe he wouldn't be so concerned.

But yes, she had a way of finding trouble. She texted him: *Fine.* Then, biting her tongue: *Thanks.*

He'd certainly gotten better at texting since they first met. Before, he hardly used his phone at all. But now, he seemed to have it on his person at all times. And he texted more than she did. A moment later, he said: *Coming home soon?*

She wasn't sure. She felt like coming home now would be admitting defeat, and she wasn't ready to give up this easily.

She googled the health and human services division and went to visit them. When she was there, she asked about Elise Kirby and her baby, but interestingly enough, the division had absolutely no record of the case at all.

When Kylie asked where else the caseworker might have come from, the helpful young receptionist said, "Well, I don't know. We provide all the social workers for cases that come out of the hospital, but I'm not allowed to divulge that information to just anyone. I'm sorry."

Of course not. But that was part of Greg's training. He'd told Kylie once that there were ways of getting around tight-lipped information keepers. She decided to employ one of his ingenious tactics.

She doubled over, coughing. Patting her throat and gasping for air, feeling herself go red in the face.

The woman stood up immediately, alarmed, trying to see Kylie over the high counter. "Are you all right?"

"Yes," she said between loud coughs. "Actually, no. Can I trouble you for a glass of water?"

"Oh. Yes. Of course." The woman stood up and ran off.

Greg, sometimes you're brilliant, Kylie thought, straightening and scampering around to the front of the computer. *I'd like to thank the Academy, who made this performance possible.*

Jiggling the mouse, she found an entry for an E. Kirby. Where several names on the list had dozens of entries, there was just one small entry for Elise Kirby. She clicked and saw that Elise Kirby had originally been referred to social services by her doctor, but the referral had been cancelled.

Cancelled? By whom? That made no sense.

She looked at the date. It had been cancelled the day of the baby's birth.

But who would cancel the referral? And why? There was no doubt Elise needed the intervention of social services, being poor and jobless as she was. Had she simply fallen through the cracks? Had it simply been some mistake?

Elise probably wouldn't have cancelled it herself, knowing what dire straits she was in. Had someone done it for her? Someone who was part of an illegal operation? Someone who hoped to take the caseworker's place?

Kylie backed out of the entry on the computer and scooted back around to the side of the desk she belonged on, her mind racing through all the possibilities and questions. If this was a baby-smuggling operation, was it possible that someone could've cancelled the request and sent a false caseworker in the real one's place, someone who'd been able to scout out Elise's situation and figure out the best time for the "aunt" to make the grab.

The woman came back with a glass of water, and Kylie accepted it as graciously as she could, taking several sips. "Thank you so much. I bet there's still a lot of pollen in the air."

As if in commiseration, the woman sneezed, giving them both a good laugh before Kylie thanked her again and left. On the sidewalk, she decided that she needed to get more information on the child services and adoption process from someone who'd be a little more helpful than the people at Children's Hope.

First, she typed in a message to Linc: *Just a little longer. Don't hold dinner for me.*

Then she scrolled down the list under *Adoption Services* in the browser on her phone and found an agency in downtown Asheville. Southern Hills Child Welfare Society, which, from the address, wasn't too far from her mom's house.

When she called this time, though, she decided to take a different tactic. When the receptionist answered, she said, "Hello. I'm pregnant and not sure what I'm going to do. Can I meet with someone?"

SOUTHERN HILLS CHILD WELFARE wasn't much different than the other, although it was in its own building instead of part of an office complex. Once Kylie got inside, she had a strong feeling of déjà vu. Like Children's Hope, the reception area was made to look homey, with soft lighting and potted plants and photos on the walls of nature scenes. The same brochure rack that had been in the other office was here as well.

The big difference? The reception.

When she arrived, the woman at the front desk, a younger girl with bright red lipstick, came around and put an arm around her shoulders. Kylie was very touchy-feely, but even this seemed over the top. The girl was wearing such dangerously high heels that she towered over Kylie, making her feel like a midget. "You must be Kylie. So nice to meet you. I'm Cherry."

"Nice to meet you too." Kylie followed her into the back where she sat in a cramped office, across from a clean but beaten-looking wooden desk.

"Make yourself comfortable. Can I get you a drink? Don't be nervous. One of our social workers will be with you right away to discuss everything, all right?" The words tumbled out from the young girl's mouth a mile a minute.

"Yes. Thank you."

Another tiny woman with a round face, a short, hot pink

pixie cut, and a wide smile came in and gave Kylie a bear hug. Kylie cringed. "Hi, Kylie! So wonderful to see you! I'm Wanda, a social worker here. You have questions, and we have answers!"

Kylie shuffled in her seat, uncomfortable with the deception considering how nice everyone was being to her. "Hello. I'm not sure if I belong here."

"I understand. You're seriously not the first person to say that. It's a big decision to make. But just so you know," she drew a square in the air in front of her, "this here is a judgement-free zone. Whatever you choose, we're here to help you make the best decision for you and your family. All right? So, don't feel like there's anything you can't tell me in complete confidence. I will understand."

Kylie placed her hand on her stomach and whispered, "I'm leaning toward adoption."

God, she hoped her baby wasn't able to hear her say those words.

The woman leaned forward in her chair. "Well, we can certainly help with that. It's a great choice to make, helping another family who can't have children realize that dream. Right now, there are thousands of couples out there waiting to adopt." She cracked her knuckles before placing her fingertips on her keyboard. "I need to get a few details. Have you been to the doctor?"

Kylie shook her head.

"Well, we can help you get adequate prenatal care with our network of physicians and get you working on the forms in order to have the costs handled for you if you can't pay. If you choose adoption, the adoptive family will often cover all your medical costs. Sound good?"

"I'm not here to make any decisions right now," Kylie said quickly. "I have some time. I wanted more information about the options so that I can make an informed decision as I get closer to my delivery date."

Just then, the door opened, and the young assistant appeared with a small tray, setting it down on the desk. "I brought you some cookies and juice. I hope that's okay. We need to eat small meals throughout the day to keep our energy going."

We do, do we?

Kylie looked at the plate of cookies and smiled at the woman. She would've normally declined, but she was already getting hungry. She bit into a cookie as Wanda continued. "All right. Options are what we're here for! But you do need to see a doctor. That's most important. Do you know how far along you are?"

"Uh well, probably about six weeks?"

The woman wrote something down on a piece of paper. "All right. Since you seem to be leaning toward adoption, we'll start with that option first. You can seek an open or closed adoption, depending on whether you would like to be involved in the child's life?"

Kylie shrugged. "I'm not sure."

"All right." The smile never wavered. "You don't need to make the decision now. As I tell all my mothers, it's never too late to decide on adoption. You can do it at the hospital, or a year after you give birth, if you choose. There's no right or wrong time. The important thing is that you know we're here for you. We want to assist you and make sure you're comfortable with the option you choose."

"Okay," Kylie said through a throat clogged with emotion, wondering how mothers could make such a difficult decision. No wonder everyone was being so nice. The women who came through here must have been nervous wrecks.

"Please also know that you're not *giving up* your child.

Adoption is something mothers do out of love, to give their child the best shot at life."

Kylie's nose began to burn. Although she was sure she'd probably suck as a mother, she also knew she'd do her very best. She just wondered if her very best would be good enough.

"So, it'll generally work like this," Wanda continued. "When you decide on adoption, whenever that is, you'll fill out personal and medical history forms, which will help us get to know you and your baby and match you with the right prospective adoptive parents. Once we have your preferences of the type of family you'd like to place your baby with, we'll send you some profiles of families to choose from. We have a file of prospective parents, quite a large one, unfortunately, and they're all looking to add to their families."

"So…I get to pick who my baby goes with?" Kylie asked. "I didn't realize that."

"Yes. Considering you're only six weeks along, you'll have plenty of time to make the decision, but it's never too late. Or too early, for that matter. Like I said, there are so many families waiting to welcome your child. Then you can meet them to make sure they're the right fit. You'll also be able to discuss post-adoption contact preferences, if you so choose, should you want to watch your child grow up via pictures and letters."

"And do I just go to the hospital, give birth, and hand the baby over?"

Wanda shook her head. "Well, it's not as simple as that. You're in charge of how you want your birth to go, since it's your body. Your adoptive parents are not to interfere with your prenatal care. But after the birth, you will sign away your parental rights and the adoptive family will take custody of the baby. Then, you can remain in contact with the family as the child grows up, and you'll be provided free counseling from one of our adoption specialists as long as you need it."

She dug around in her drawer and pulled out a brochure, which she pushed across to Kylie. It was the same one she'd seen in the last office, but Wanda's card had been stapled to the top. Kylie glanced at the cover, gazing at a picture of a happy family having a picnic. Inside was almost everything Wanda had said, word-for-word.

"Thank you."

"Do you have any questions, Kylie?"

She thought of Elise. "What if I decide I want to give the baby up for adoption later on? Like, two months after the birth?"

Wanda's beaming smile beamed brighter. "That can be arranged. Like I said, it's never too late."

"And…you'll send someone to my house to take the baby away? Just like that?"

The smile faltered just a bit. "Well, like I said, there are forms, so it's not that easy, but essentially, yes. We need to make sure the parents are ready, but it can move quickly."

"What if I choose adoption, get to know the parents, but then I change my mind and decide to keep the baby?"

"You can always do that, as well. We try to keep this as low-pressure as possible, as we know it's a very stressful time you're going through."

"Thank you." Kylie set down her half-eaten cookie and stood up. She didn't want to be asked to fill out any forms, because if she did, she'd have to lie even more. "I appreciate the information. I'll think about it and let you know if I have any questions."

Wanda followed her out to reception. As they reached the front desk, Kylie saw the receptionist talking with a heavyset older woman with bright platinum hair. She turned to her as she approached.

"Oh, hello," the woman said brightly, and Kylie had to wonder if they gave these people happy pills. She took her hand and shook it brusquely.

Wanda said, "This is Kylie. She's considering adoption."

The woman patted the top of Kylie's hand with her smooth one. "It's wonderful to meet you, Kylie. I'm Leda Butler, director of this establishment. Whatever you choose, we're behind you. Please know that."

She said it so compassionately, with so much concern, that it almost drew a tear out of Kylie's eye. "Thank you."

Then she pulled her into an unexpected hug. "It's the least we can do. Please, please, please stay in touch."

The smell of the woman's perfume nearly overpowered her. It was strong. Too strong for Kylie's already heightened sense of smell. Her stomach roiled.

After ending the hug, the older woman reached into her pocket and pulled out one of her cards. "Here you go. Should you have any questions at all, don't hesitate."

As Leda handed the card to Kylie, Kylie had to admire her long, shiny pink fingernails. Then she hesitated, thinking once again of the description of Elise's "aunt" that Agnes Mott had given.

Kylie meant to say a thank you, but her mouth wouldn't seem to work.

Leda took her hand again. "Are you all right, dear?"

She blinked and forced a smile to her face, squeezing the woman's hand in return. "Oh. Yes."

As she left, she shook her head. She was being stupid. Leda Butler was probably pushing eighty. That sweet old grandma couldn't possibly be a baby smuggler.

Besides, what had she said before? There were plenty of women out there who fit Agnes' description. She'd already met one. It was likely just a coincidence.

I couldn't stop smiling.

Today was a good day. Meeting with adoptive parents. Women who were considering putting their children up for adoption. Making dreams come true, little by little.

And I'd just heard from K. The boy had been united with his new family, and they'd named him Forrest. They were absolutely delighted, and so thankful. K had thanked me so much for the support and told me he'd wired the money to my account.

Five-hundred thousand dollars.

Well, a chunk of it was already gone, thanks to that bastard Mark Lamb. But still…*cruise vacation, here I come*, I thought to myself as I deleted the email. *I'm going to drink cocktails in Bonaire this fall.*

But, of course, that's when the floor usually dropped out from under me.

As I walked back to my office, thinking just how wonderful everything was going, one of those wrenches got thrown into the works.

It came in the form of a voicemail on my cell phone. Chastity Banks from a county near the North Carolina-Tennessee border. She was a woman I'd worked with once. Only once, because the minute I met her, I could see how high-strung she was. I'd had an inkling she wouldn't be able to handle it and would crack under pressure.

Turned out, I was right.

I listened to her frantic message, her voice so screechy and on the verge of tears that I had to hold the phone away from my ear. "*Call me. Call me now. Please. I don't know what to do.*"

I frowned. She never knew what to do. It was remarkable she'd survived this long. Some people, like Mark, were pretty hands-off and understood this business. And then there were basket cases like Chastity Banks, who had somehow managed to become a doctor, and needed handholding at every step.

Going to my office, I closed the door, and locked it, should my assistant make the unwise decision of popping her head in again.

The phone barely rang before Chastity picked up. "Help," she croaked, as if someone had hands wrapped around her neck and was strangling her right then and there.

"Didn't I tell you not to call me? It's too dangerous."

"I know, but..." She started to sob quietly. "There was a woman here. A private investigator, and she was asking all sorts of questions."

"What kind of questions?"

"About Elise Kirby? The woman whose baby I let you know about? Remember?"

I rolled my eyes. I'd told this stupid woman never to mention that name to me again. Yes, I'd been involved. I'd contacted her, and she'd told me all about Elise Kirby, a girl who was mentally disabled due to fetal alcohol syndrome, yet high functioning. She was alone, poor, scared...the perfect candidate. She'd recently been discharged from the hospital, and Chastity's agency had a social worker assigned to the case.

Because Chastity was such a bonehead, though, I told her to call the caseworker off. Then I had one of my "caseworkers" scout the place out for me, finding when would be the best time to make the grab. They'd found out that Elise, not being as bright as most people, had an old, practically deaf woman watching her baby while she went to work.

It was so simple, it almost brought tears to my eyes, how well things fell into place. And then I went and picked up the child myself, dropped her at a clinic, and collected my fee.

But this was bad. If Chastity kept bawling and didn't get control of herself, she was going to blow the lid right off this thing. "Calm down. I told you people might come around asking questions. It's only natural. Granted, I didn't think it would take two years, but you've got to keep your cool. You understand?"

"Yes, but this woman said Elise Kirby had hired her, and I was so unnerved by the whole thing that I googled her."

"And?"

"And she might be young, but she's got a resume. She brought down the Spotlight Killer. She's not a slouch. I'm scared."

I leaned back in my chair and massaged my temples. "All right. But there's absolutely nothing to tie us to the Kirby case. I told you that. Just asking questions isn't going to get her anywhere. She has to. You're child services. So, you just need to refer her someplace else and send her on her way."

"That's what I tried to do. I told her I didn't know anything about it. If she somehow subpoenas our records, she won't find anything, but she seemed like she wasn't going to take no for an answer."

Dammit. I couldn't trust this woman as far as I could throw her. She was too jumpy. Too liable to give herself up under the first sign of tension. She'd take a wrong step somewhere, if we weren't careful. "What, exactly, did you say?"

"She asked about possible child laundering cases. I told her I didn't have any knowledge of such a thing and referred her to health and human services."

That was good. Amazingly, the good doctor had handled it well, for once. The state's bureaucratic red tape would make even the most seasoned investigator want to jump from the tallest bridge. "All right, then. She's digging, but she's not going to get far. Eventually she'll come up against a brick wall and stop."

"I hope." There was doubt in her voice.

"What's this private investigator's name?" I asked, pulling my laptop toward me so I could conduct my own search.

When she gave it to me, I had to admit, it sounded very familiar. I typed it in and it brought up the image of a young, dark-haired woman with a bright white smile. Kylie Coulter.

No wonder she sounded familiar.

Damn it all to hell, I thought, staring at the picture, then reading the woman's impressive professional resume. She'd made headlines for solving several high-profile cases in the Asheville area, and had recently started her own company, Coulter Confidential.

I hadn't stooped to murder to cover my tracks in a long time. But I'd decided long ago, when I was just starting my career, that if I had to, I wouldn't blink an eye. And I hadn't. Women like Patricia Hastings had just been part of the normal cost of doing business. A busybody who'd stepped in the wrong place. My career was at stake, as well as the careers of the dozens of other professionals who'd helped me.

And this Kylie, like Patricia, had clearly come too close.

11

Linc had always been the chef of the family since Kylie couldn't boil water, so he hadn't minded when she'd texted saying she would be late and that he should start on dinner without her. He decided to make something elaborate, since after fixing the dishwasher and putting the dogs through a nice hour-long workout outside, he had the time. After paging through his cookbook and checking the contents of the fridge, he settled on his famous beef short ribs with red wine gravy.

He knew it was one of Kylie's favorite meals, and after the busy day she'd had, she'd probably appreciate relaxing with a glass of red wine and enjoying a long, leisurely dinner.

But by six o'clock, when the food was ready, she still hadn't returned home.

He hated leaving the food to rest because it made the meat tough, but he had no choice. Going to the fridge, he popped open a craft beer and went outside to wait for her. As he did, he checked his phone.

No texts from Kylie, other than the last one, where she'd said she was fine. But that was three hours ago.

He sat down on the swing in front of the house, staring at the phone, willing it to give him some clue as to her whereabouts.

Not texting wasn't like her. And from their lunch at the diner, he got the distinct feeling something was really wrong. Her moods were becoming more and more erratic by the minute. Snapping at Elise like that? Getting riled after he told her he wanted to help with the financial situation? It totally wasn't like her.

Nothing was like her, nowadays. It was like she was transforming into a different person.

He hadn't bothered to ask her if she wanted his help at Children's Hope, because he knew the answer would have been a resounding no. He hadn't wanted to insert himself in the investigation because it was clear she wanted to be alone. Maybe they had been working too close together. Maybe she just needed her own space.

If this was what owning her own business was going to do to her, then it wasn't worth it. As much as she loved it, they couldn't continue with this. But how could he help if she was constantly pushing him away? He wanted the old Kylie back.

He'd nearly finished the entire beer by the time he heard a car coming up the gravel drive. He was glad, because he was starving.

But when he saw the police truck instead of Kylie's bright yellow Jeep, he cursed under his breath.

It wasn't that he wasn't glad to see Jacob, his best friend. He'd really been counting on someone else.

The second the truck pulled to a stop outside the house, the puppies swarmed it. Jacob jumped out and uttered weak commands like, "Heel" and "Sit," but for the most part, all of their training went out the window whenever they saw Jacob. Actually, whenever they saw anyone.

The burly, red-headed detective stood next to his truck with his hands up, looking at his friend like he was about to be overrun. "Little help?"

Linc whistled. Some of the pups listened, but for the others, it was just a free-for-all. He was still amazed that Kylie wanted to keep all of them. He shook his head as, eventually, the sea of dogs parted enough to let Jacob climb the stairs.

"You ever think of selling some of these guys off? Creating a little sanity here?"

Linc snorted. "Sanity is overrated." He shook his hand, then went inside and got his friend a beer. When he returned, the dogs were in danger of pouncing on him again. He ordered them to go off to the yard and play. Once Beatrice did, the rest followed. "So, what's new, buddy?"

"You know, the old grind." He took a swig and looked at the door. "What's up with you? Haven't seen you in a long time, man. Thought maybe you got eaten by your dogs. Kylie here?"

"No. She's out right now. She should be here soon, though."

Jacob set his bottle of beer on the porch floor and began to stroke Storm's muzzle. "Well, I do have some news. Hold on to your hat, because I think it's gonna shock the hell out of you."

Even knowing Jacob's cemented status as a playboy, Linc had a little bit of an idea of what it was. His intentions were made pretty clear when Jacob brought Faith to Linc's wedding. Where Jacob would normally dance with every single girl at the reception, that night, he'd only had eyes for one woman. "You've been chosen as Detective of the Year."

"Not quite. I asked Faith to marry me," he said with a big, shit-eating grin. "Amazingly, she said yes."

"Well, I'll be damned," Linc said in mock surprise,

extending his hand to shake again. "She must've gone insane; probably took too many hits in Quantico."

He laughed. "Probably. But it's working out for me in the end."

Truthfully, Linc couldn't have imagined anything better. Besides Kylie, Jacob was his favorite person in the world, and even with their history, he was fond of Faith. He'd once dated her in law school, which felt like a thousand years ago, until he dropped out of school and went off to basic training. "How's she doing with the FBI?"

"Well, it's been great since she's transferred to Raleigh from New York, but I'm still trying to get her to come a little farther so the two of us can be an unstoppable crime-fighting duo. Like Batman and Batgirl." He grinned. "So, from the man who knows, how's married life?"

Linc's grin fell away. Today wasn't the best time for Jacob to ask that question. Because right now, it seemed pretty damn shitty; the worst of it being that he wasn't sure how to fix it. Or did marriage involve ups and downs, even this soon? He wasn't sure.

"Great," he lied through his teeth. "You know, wedded bliss."

"Yeah? You look kind of tired. The dogs driving you insane?"

Linc jumped on the excuse. "Something like that. And Kylie's on another big case. You know how she gets when she's on her big cases."

Jacob dropped his head back and growled. "Oh, Jesus, do I ever. You might as well stand back. She on a tear?"

Linc nodded but didn't admit that he was worried that this one might be the worst ever. Because, this time, she had something to prove, a business to save. Now, she wasn't just eager. She had *attitude* as well.

"What's this one about?" Jacob asked.

He wasn't sure he wanted to talk about it, but since it would be a distraction from how Kylie'd been acting, he gave in. "You ever hear of the case involving Elise Kirby about two years back? Her two-month-old child was abducted from her trailer park."

He scratched the side of his face. "That rings a bell, yeah, but it was in another county, right? Over in Haywood, maybe? We didn't get involved in that." He took another gulp of beer. "How is Kylie getting involved in that, after all this time? Sounds like a massive lost cause. Kid's been gone a long time."

"The mother is an acquaintance of Kylie's. Saw her ad on a placemat at the diner and all but begged Kylie for help. And you know, Kylie being Kylie, she couldn't say no. So, she's god knows where now investigating, and not getting paid a damn cent."

Jacob whistled.

Linc hadn't meant to sound so exasperated, but when he saw Jacob's expression, he knew he'd said too much.

Jacob steepled his fingers together. "She needs to watch herself. Especially with Elise."

Exactly what he'd been telling her. But…Elise was harmless. Right?

"What do you mean?"

"From what I can remember, the rumors were that that woman wasn't right in the head. The case went cold because no one recalled seeing that aunt or relative anywhere and thought that maybe Agnes had made it up to protect Elise. A couple people said the girl was a liar of the first order."

"You mean, Elise might have—"

"Yeah. They thought maybe she'd killed the kid then gave it to her new boyfriend to bury somewhere because, a few days later, she moved out of that trailer and started living with the guy. And he was a real piece of work. The thought was that the boyfriend didn't want kids, so she removed the problem. Either that, or he did."

Linc stared straight ahead, remembering the kid who'd walked around the barn with him a couple days earlier. Was that the same boyfriend? Was the sweet woman who served him at the diner a psychopath of the first order?

And dammit. Had he given his favorite dog to a murderer?

"She seemed like a nice person. Slow, maybe, but not cruel. And hell. Why would she ask Kylie to look into it if she killed the kid?"

Jacob shrugged. "Good point, but you never know what people will do for attention or out of guilt. Well, it sounded to me like they did all they could, and the trail just went cold."

"I thought it could be a child laundering scheme."

Jacob shrugged. "That's a whole other can of worms."

"You don't think so?"

"Could be. I'd never say never. If it is, it's probably got lines reaching all over the place, so she'll end up getting tangled in a web of worthless research. But if it'll help Kylie, I'll pull a list of similar cases from the surrounding area."

"Yeah. That'll be good."

Jacob pulled out his phone and started tapping away with his thumbs. "I'll have it faxed to your office number, that okay? That fax is still good?"

"Yeah."

"My guess is, you'll find a bunch of different cases that *could* possibly be related, but there won't be anything to tie them together. That's the way it usually goes," he said, slipping his phone into his breast pocket. "And sent. I'm having an officer compile it for you from the missing persons database right now. Infant kidnappings, child never located, ages one year and under, from North Carolina and the surrounding states."

"Thanks, man."

He finished his beer and said, "Well, I was hoping to see your lovely wife and break the news to her also, because I know her heart will break now that I'm off the market. Tell her that she's always welcome to cry on my shoulder, if need be. But I did want to ask you both something."

Linc grinned. He already knew what this was. Jacob had been his best man, so it only made sense. "Of course I will. I'm honored to be asked."

Jacob looked like his face might split in two. "You think Kylie would like to be a bridesmaid?"

Linc nodded. Kylie lived to bridesmaid, she'd told him once. She had about twelve gowns in their closet upstairs to show for it. The woman had so many friends that he could barely keep track of them. She was a professional at that sort of thing. "She'd be honored to."

"Great. Faith wanted to ask herself, but she's in D.C. right now."

"Ah. When's the big day?"

"Soon. A month, six weeks at max. We're planning a big engagement shindig. Invite forthcoming."

Linc forced himself not to frown, wanting to ask why the rush. Was Faith pregnant? He mentally shrugged. If she was, his friend would tell him when he was ready.

"Sounds good. We'll be there. I'm sure Kylie will be just as thrilled as I am by the news."

They shook hands again, and he waved goodbye as Jacob got into his police truck and headed off. As he did, Linc searched down the driveway. Still no Kylie, and now the sun was starting to slip behind the trees, making their hilltop estate dark and shadowy.

He went inside as their old fax machine beeped. Going

over to it, he ripped off a sheet of paper and saw that it was from the sheriff's department. After that, the old machine started spitting out more pages. A lot more. He read through the file, finding the names of seven babies who'd disappeared in similar circumstances to the Kirby child within Buncombe and the neighboring counties. Then, there was a widened list that included Virginia, Tennessee, as well as all the neighboring states. That list went on forever. The first name on that list was a woman named Renee Best of Staunton, Virginia. She apparently died by suicide, and her weeks-old baby had never been found.

But that was from 1975, many years ago.

It would be ridiculous to try to connect the two cases, even if there were some similarities.

Yes, Renee was poor and lived in a trailer park in a small town. She had no support system, just like Elise. But other than that, Jacob was right.

There was no smoking gun connecting any of these cases.

He stopped leafing through the pages when he heard the sound of a car approaching outside. As the dogs barked, Linc followed them outside.

Finally. Kylie.

But when her Jeep rolled into the glow of the porch light, he realized she wasn't smiling. Her face looked not tired, not angry, not happy, not anything. Vacant.

His first thought was to rip into her for being late, but he tamped that urge down, knowing it'd just make everything worse. Instead, he smiled then went to open the door for her.

She didn't smile back. Yawning, she dragged herself out of the car. "Hi," she said, sounding tired to her core. "Sorry I'm so late."

"Tough meetings?"

Linc watched as she trudged up the stairs, not even bothering to pet the dogs as they swarmed her, wanting attention.

She muttered something under her breath that he couldn't make out.

He followed her inside, and she would've let the screen door slam in his face if he hadn't lunged forward to catch it and head in after her. "I made beef short ribs. Your favorite. I didn't eat because I wanted to wait for you. It's in the microwave, but I can just heat it up."

She stood there, about five steps inside the entry of the farmhouse, like a Kylie statue. After a minute, she startled and seemed surprised to see him standing there. "Hmm?"

"You hungry?" he tried again.

She wrinkled her nose. "No." Yawned again. "Tired. I need to sit down."

She went to the couch and didn't just sit. She collapsed, sprawling out on it. Since Vader had torn up the old sofa, they'd replaced it with this gigantic one. It was big enough that the two of them could usually lie together on it while watching a movie. But the way she was lying there, occupying most of it, it was clear she didn't want company. Actually, she looked like she was preparing for her final rest, lying on her back, her hands clasped over her stomach. She closed her eyes.

He sat on the coffee table across from her. "Did you make any breakthroughs in your case?"

A worry-crease appeared on her forehead, so he took it as a "no" even before she shook her head. "Wild goose chase. I feel like I've been hit by an eighteen-wheeler."

"Well, just rest. Maybe you've been pushing it too hard or picked up whatever bug I had. You should probably just stick around here and get some paperwork done tomorrow," he suggested.

She opened one eye and focused on him. "Can't. Have an appointment tomorrow."

"You want me to go with you?"

"No," she said, almost before he got the question out.

All right, then.

"How about I get you a glass of wine and some dinner? You need to eat something."

"No wine," she said quickly. Too quickly. She cleared her throat and smiled. "I'll never wake up. Water, please, and..." she cracked open one eye, "maybe some of your short ribs. I really do love them."

He went to the microwave and heated up the ribs, then poured her a glass of sparkling water. As he was doing that, he called to her, "Jacob stopped by."

"Oh?" The word ended on a yawn. "I'm sorry I missed him. How is he doing?"

"Great," he called as he took the steaming plate of ribs out of the microwave and set it on a tray. "He and Faith are getting married, believe it or not."

He lifted the tray and took it into the living room, setting it down on the coffee table.

"And he asked—"

He stopped.

Kylie was fast asleep, breathing heavily. Just short of a snore.

So much for a quiet dinner together.

He pulled the old afghan that had survived Vader's rampage from the back of the sofa over her, tucking her in. Then he took the tray back to the kitchen and covered her ribs up for leftovers. He sat down in the kitchen, eating the gourmet meal he'd made for two, all alone.

12

Kylie woke up with a start, after a dream that had doctors with probes reaching into her stomach and yanking her baby away from her. In it, the doctors had their faces covered with masks, and a bright light was shining down, practically blinding her. She'd managed to shove them away and rip off one of the masks, only to recognize the face as Linc's.

When she'd woken up, her heart was pounding in her chest.

She found herself down in the living room, covered with a blanket with six dog faces staring at her. She remembered leaving Southern Hills Child Welfare and getting into her car, going home, talking to Linc briefly, then…

Then…nothing. She must've fallen asleep.

Rubbing her head, she sat up, smelling fresh-brewed coffee and toast. It smelled kind of odd, almost rancid, but she'd noticed everything smelled differently now. As bad as it smelled, she still wanted coffee. She stood up, realizing she was still wearing yesterday's clothes, and as she straightened, felt a screaming pain rocket up the side of her back. Grabbing it, she massaged the muscles, but as she stood, she realized she couldn't fully straighten.

Was this that round ligament pain she'd read about on the *Babycenter* website? And if so, why was it coming so early? She thought it was supposed to happen later.

She walked like an old, hunched lady to the kitchen. "I pulled a muscle," she muttered to Linc, who was chewing on a piece of toast and paging through his phone.

"Yeah? I probably shouldn't have let you sleep on the couch," he said, studying her as she tried to stretch, wincing as she straightened a millimeter at a time. "I tried to get you to come up, but you were dead to the world."

Still rubbing her back, she poured herself a cup of coffee. Lifting it to her lips and blowing, she squinted to see the time on the microwave. Slowly, the blurred numbers came into focus. It was ten o'clock.

"Holy shit! Is that the time?"

Linc nodded.

She set her mug on the counter without ever having taken a sip. "Shit! My appointment is at eleven!"

Somehow the panic wound up overshadowing the pain in her back, because she flew up the stairs, took a quick shower, shaving her legs the best she could, and threw on a dress and sandals. She tied her wet hair up in a bun and ran for the door.

"Wait. Where are you—" Linc was saying as the screen door slammed behind her. She didn't wait around, because she knew anything she said to him would be a lie, and she'd much rather just avoid the question.

But Linc was on her tail. It was only when she got to the Jeep door that she realized she'd left her keys in the house. He followed her, holding them up.

"Is this for Elise's case?" he asked as she snatched them away.

She shook her head.

"Everything okay?"

Kylie nodded and blurted. "Of course. I'm just going to go and…have lunch with my mom. You know how crazy she gets when I'm late. She'll probably think I'm in a ditch somewhere." She felt herself blush at the lie.

"Oh. All right."

Like a good husband, he opened the door for her and kissed her cheek as she sat in the driver's seat. Then he slammed the door when she was settled and waved goodbye, wishing she had come up with a better lie. She went to lunch with her mom often, so it made sense, but he could easily call Rhonda and find out she wasn't where she said she'd be.

Miraculously, she managed to get to her OB-GYN's office in downtown Asheville five minutes before the scheduled appointment time. She walked into the busy waiting room, a little out of breath—she felt like she was always out of breath these days—and gave the receptionist her name. After finding an empty chair, she rubbed her sore back muscles as she settled in.

Finally having the chance to relax, she thought about yesterday. She'd only meant to devote a bit of time each day to her "hobby" case, and yet she could effectively say that yesterday, she'd socked every second of her time into finding Elise Kirby's baby.

That was bad. Work was probably piling up at home. She checked her work email and realized she had over two-hundred unanswered emails, most of them follow-up on worker's comp surveillance cases for Impact Insurance. Those were the cases Greg used to handle, but since she'd taken over the business, she'd come to dread them. She needed to attend to those, since they were the major source of the company's profits.

But god, they were dull. She yawned, just thinking of them.

She'd have to suck it up. She needed to ensure that Coulter Confidential was in the black this month. By any means necessary. Even if it bored her to death.

She silently made a pledge that, after her appointment, she'd go back home and get the paperwork and billing out of the way. That would help. Maybe she wouldn't feel that knot tightening in her chest so much after that.

Her eyes trailed across the waiting room, to a visibly pregnant woman, her hands cradled around her belly. A man sat next to her, his arm around her exhausted looking shoulders, nervously paging through his phone.

As she watched them, she wished with every fiber of her being that Linc was at her side. Maybe she should have told him.

No. Not yet.

She'd already determined that, while she was still trying to make a go of everything in the business, she couldn't. She needed to see to Elise's case first too. The second he knew that she was pregnant, he'd start insisting she cut down on the stress. Elise's case would probably be the first to go.

Not that she'd made much progress with it.

She thought of Leda Butler and the way she had smelled. Recalling the heavy scent, her empty stomach flip-flopped, and she nearly gagged.

Great. She hadn't had a thing to eat. And *Babycenter* said that was why morning sickness happened. Empty stomach.

Before she could lose what little was in her stomach, a woman next to her leaned over and handed her a small package of saltines.

Kylie took them, surprised. The woman was her age, maybe a bit older, and had a kind smile. She didn't look very pregnant at all, and was dressed fashionably, unlike Kylie, who'd just thrown on any old thing.

"Been there," she said to Kylie, patting her own belly. "This is my third."

Her third? Oh, Lord Jesus.

"How did you know?"

The woman laughed. "Your first, right? You look scared to death. I was the same my first time."

Did she look terrified? Probably. Blushing, Kylie ripped open the package and nibbled on a cracker, noticing the woman's husband on the other side of her.

In fact, as she looked around, she noticed that most of the pregnant women had their significant others with them. And here she was, alone. Why had she decided to do this alone, again?

"Kylie?"

Startled, Kylie looked up to see a woman in scrubs standing in an open doorway. "Come on back."

Thanking the kind woman again, she pushed to her feet, her heart galloping in her ears. The nurse led her to a small room where they weighed her—god, where had those extra pounds come from?—and took her blood pressure. Then she was herded to an examination room, where she was told to go into a bathroom and pee in a cup.

She was so nervous this time, she had no trouble peeing, almost overflowing the small container. She placed the cup in a little pass-through so that it could be tested as directed. Then, feeling like a cow being led to slaughter, she went into the exam room and changed into the hospital gown she was handed.

Dressed in the paper-thin moo-moo of a gown, she sat on the exam table and answered the approximately three thousand questions the nurse asked before enduring the blood pressure cuff attempting to squeeze her arm off.

"Everything looks good," the nurse said. "Dr. Ling will be with you shortly."

"Shortly" was a relative term when it came to doctor's offices, and Kylie had finished her saltines, flipped through a couple magazines, and was attempting to make an origami stork from the paper she was sitting on when a knock sounded on the door and Dr. Ling appeared.

"Hi, Kylie. We haven't seen you here in a while. I hear you have good news."

Was it?

Tears burned in her eyes as doubt and fear and joy and hope collided together into a soup of emotion she couldn't name.

"Well, I hope it is…" she said dumbly, then made a sound that was supposed to be a laugh. "It's a surprise, so…"

She didn't know how to finish, so she just closed her mouth before she burst into tears.

Dr. Ling tapped on the tablet in her hand. "Well, we checked your urine sample and there's a definite sign of increased pregnancy hormones, so let's do an examination, then we'll get an ultrasound and take a peek at your surprise."

Kylie stiffened. "So soon? I didn't know you'd…is everything all right?"

The doctor nodded. "Oh yes. It's perfectly normal in our practice. I like to do an ultrasound early in the pregnancy to ensure everything's as it should be and to get an accurate gestational age." She placed a stethoscope to Kylie's chest. "Take a deep breath."

Kylie inhaled the first deep breath she'd taken in what felt like days. It made her a little lightheaded, but it also cleared her mind.

She really, really wished that Linc was here.

Five minutes later, the exam was over, and Dr. Ling

smiled. "Everything looks good so far. Hold tight and an ultrasound tech will come get you."

Approximately a thousand years later, the tech knocked on her door. She led Kylie to a darkened room and asked her to lie down on a table. Dr. Ling appeared at the tech's side just as Kylie was about to ask why she had to put her feet in stirrups.

"We'll be doing a transvaginal ultrasound, Kylie, to confirm several important details, most notably the location of the baby in your uterus and a more definitive due date."

Kylie didn't know what that was until she saw the long, white wand that looked like a dildo. The ultrasound tech rolled a condom over the wand then slathered it with what looked like K-Y Jelly.

Now, she was very glad that Linc wasn't here.

The tech smiled. "I'm just going to insert this. It shouldn't hurt."

She took a deep breath as the foreign object slid inside, and she bit her lip, focusing on the screen to her left.

Dr. Ling stepped closer to the screen as the tech moved the wand about a bit, and then pressed a button on the keyboard as she studied the screen. Suddenly, the room was filled with a loud, squishy sound. It sounded vaguely alien.

"What is that?"

"It's your baby's heartbeat."

Kylie swallowed. It sounded so strong. So good. So amazing. There was a tiny living being inside her, growing and thriving. She held back tears as she listened to the sound of its life fill the air. It sounded sweeter than any sound she'd ever heard.

And she wished that Linc was there.

"I'd say you're six weeks along. And…ah, just as I thought," the doctor said as the tech pressed more buttons on the keyboard. "You had very high hormone levels, so I suspected that—"

Kylie met the doctor's grim face with alarm. "Suspected what? Is everything okay?"

"Oh, it's fine. But see these two shapes here? It means you're having twins."

The doctor brought up another picture, which looked like an empty, slightly bean-shaped bowl. At the very bottom of it, there were two very tiny round tadpoles.

Her babies.

"Oh," was all she could say. Two babies.

Twelve dogs. Two babies. One Kylie. One Linc. A failing business. And a partridge in a pear tree, in the smallest little madhouse on a hill.

And now Kylie really couldn't help it. She lifted her hand to her face and started to sob.

KYLIE SPENT the next few hours in a daze.

Twins.

Twins. Twins. Twins. Twins.

She repeated it to herself so much, the word started sounding funny and lost its meaning.

How had this happened? Didn't twins run in families? Linc didn't have twins in his family, did he? She didn't think her family had ever had any either. Double babies. How was her womb doing this to her?

One baby was frightening enough. But two? How could they manage all that? Her mother, Rhonda, had told her how difficult it'd been, just raising Kylie. And Kylie, of course, had been the sweetest little baby that'd ever existed. Yes, Kylie would have Linc, but she'd also have a number of other worries on her hands, including the business. How could she possibly handle all of it? She could barely handle herself.

And a husband.

And a farm.

And a multitude of dogs.

And a business. A dying business.

Heart still pounding in her chest, she found herself walking the downtown shops of Asheville, ending up at the Emporium, where crafters sold their wares. She knew she should probably be looking for practical things like baby booties and nightlights and nursery fixtures and things like that, but instead, she focused on a butterfly suncatcher. She purchased it as a split-second decision, then felt even worse for spending money she hadn't made herself.

She straightened her shoulders. She needed to stop feeling sorry for herself and actually do something practical before she landed herself and Linc in the poorhouse.

She needed to be positive. She needed to believe in herself and her abilities. She needed to believe that she and Linc were the perfect team who could make this all work.

It would be *great,* living on the farm with twins. And all the dogs.

Maybe they should put the puppies up for adoption. Let Linc train them as he'd planned, then let them go do good in the world.

She needed to stop thinking so crazy and use her head instead of her heart, at least some of the time.

By the time she got home, it was after three. She pulled up to the front of the house to find Linc working in the backyard, repairing the kennels, wearing gloves and shorts and hiking boots, swinging his hammer expertly at a nail.

He stopped for a minute to wave at her. She waved back, love filling her insides as he started swinging the hammer again.

He did work hard, what with all of his training seminars, rescues, and keeping up the farm. Yesterday was one of the first days in a long while that he'd had time to go to lunch with her and relax. How could she possibly ask him to work any harder?

She went to the fence and draped her arms over it, watching him. His bare chest was tan from all his work in the sun, and he had a baseball cap on that made him look like a teenager. Funny, he was looking better and younger every day, as if marriage really agreed with him. She hated the thought of what she might look like in another few months. Like an old enormous hag, most likely.

But...twins. Two babies. Two beautiful babies. As scared as that made her, she was also...excited. So excited, she almost shouted out the news to Linc.

Even as she opened her mouth to do just that, Vader jumped up on the side of the fence, his big tongue licking up her face.

Yuck. Was that her sign to keep her mouth shut for now, she wondered as she wiped her face with her sleeve. When she looked at her husband again, he was laughing.

"You were gone a long time," he called. "Everything okay?"

She nodded. "Yeah. Want me to start dinner?"

He lifted his hat up off his head, wiped the sweat from his brow with the back of his hand, and screwed it on tight. "Don't you have work to do?"

She scowled. Yes, she did, but she was trying to procrastinate on the dull Impact Insurance shit. Besides, she couldn't cook worth a damn. But the thought of doing those reports now, with all these other things on her mind...

Just the thought of the tedious work made her want to burst into tears.

Hormones were hell.

She straightened her shoulders, mentally pulled up her granny panties, and smiled. "Yes. I need to finish the Impact reports."

There.

It was the adult thing to do. The right thing to do. The keep-us-out-of-the-poorhouse thing to do.

He laughed again, probably at her expression. He knew how much she hated the tedious work. "Get 'er done. Have fun."

Instead of shooting him a middle finger, she blew him a kiss and headed to the house and her computer. Then... stared at the screen. She sat there, trying to churn out work, feeling the rush of a thousand warring emotions. He was right, she needed to...get this done.

But...twins!

Instinctively, her hands went to her belly, hovering over Bean One and Bean Two. What kind of madhouse would they be born into? One where dogs roamed free, and they were still trying to run a business?

Excitement flooded in. Twins! She wanted to shout it from the rooftops. She never could keep quiet about secrets, and this one was the biggest one of her life.

Linc came in a few minutes later, so she hunched forward, burying her face in her computer and pretended to be hard at work. She actually managed to get some work done while he banged around in the kitchen.

He poked his head around the doorframe. "Leftovers?"

She realized she still had her hands on her belly and dropped them to her sides. "Sounds good."

"Well, it won't be a repeat performance for you. You fell asleep before you could eat the short ribs I made last night."

That got her attention. Or, more like her stomach's attention. The two beans were obviously not vegetarians. "You made short ribs?"

He gave her a bemused look, tinged with worry. "Don't you remember?"

She scoured her memory. She didn't. "Oh, yeah. Thanks."

At least the fib wiped the worry from his expression. "And I opened that new red from the winery down the street. Not bad. Want a glass?"

She did. Desperately. She loved that funky little winery.

When they were first married, they'd go there for tastings almost every weekend, and always come back with a few bottles. But now she had to think about the beans. "No, thanks. Not tonight. I have a little headache."

That wasn't a lie. She'd had a perpetual headache for a couple weeks. Her back still hurt too. And all the things she could think of to numb the pain probably wouldn't be good for the tiny lives growing inside her.

The worry was back, but he played it off with a flippant, "Okay. Sparkling water it is." He went back to the kitchen, then reappeared a second later. "You fell asleep before I could tell you. Jacob came by last night. Says he and Faith are getting married."

She smiled, genuinely happy for the big, burly detective. "Really? That's great. It's about time he grew up, and Faith is a nice person."

Nice, other than the fact that she'd once upon a time slept with her husband. Of course, it was before Linc and Kylie had gotten together, but she sometimes wondered if he thought of Faith at all.

He leaned against the doorjamb. "Yeah. I'm happy for them too. He asked me to be his best man, and Faith wants you to be a bridesmaid. I told him that I was sure you'd say yes since you live for that sort of stuff."

Her spirits plummeted. "Um…"

He frowned. "You like Faith, right?"

"Of course I do, but..." she scrolled through her mental calendar, "when's the wedding?"

"They haven't settled on a date, but soon. They don't want to wait," he said, eyeing her cautiously. "Is that a problem?"

"No. It's fine," she said, thinking of what Dr. Ling had told her. Her due date was mid-April, but according to the doctor, multiples often came early. But not that early.

So...it was *great* that the wedding would be soon. If it was scheduled for sometime next spring, she'd be forced to show up at the wedding of her husband's gorgeous and sexy ex looking like a massive, ugly whale. That'd show her.

"And yeah. Engagement party. We'll probably get an invitation for it soon."

Well, that was nice. Maybe the attendees would get to know her before she became the Giant Whale that Ate Asheville.

A minute later, she could tell Linc was still studying her. Did she look different? Was *I'm pregnant* stamped on her forehead? *With twins?*

She gave him the best smile she could manage and nodded at the screen. "I better get back to work. Got to get the money rolling in."

He stood up. "Right. Oh. Speaking of that..." he leaned over his desk and pulled out a pile of papers, "this is for you. Jacob supplied it."

She studied it. It was a list of names of children from around the area. From the National Center of Missing and Exploited Children. "What is this?"

"It's a list of missing infants from around the surrounding states. I thought it could help you. You know, to see if anything fits the child laundering theory. To me, it looks like they're all over the place, but—"

"Why did you do this?"

He visibly stiffened. "What do you mean?"

"Well..." she lightened her voice, smiling at him again, "you don't want me working on this case, and then you go and give me more work to do. I don't get it."

"It's not that I don't want you working on it." He held up his hands. "Okay, okay. I didn't. But I know how much you want to, and that you'd probably do it with or without my blessing, so I thought I'd help you along. I know how busy you are."

She sucked in a breath, trying to control her emotions. She forced a smile and set the papers aside. "Thank you. Really." Tears clawed their way to her eyes, but she blinked them back. "I'll look into it after I get through all this."

She focused back on the computer screen, ready to answer an email, but when she looked up, she realized he was still looking at her, hands in his pockets, as if he was fishing for something else to say.

"Did you have a good time today?" he asked.

She very nearly burst into tears. He knew nothing about the stirrups or ultrasound or getting poked and prodded. He knew nothing about her sense of aloneness about being the only solo person in the waiting room of the doctor's office.

He was asking about her fake lunch with her mom. Her lie.

She just needed to tell him. Carrying this news on her shoulders was just too much. Lying to hide the truth just made everything that much worse.

Before she could say it, though, he said, "You were gone a long time."

"Well..." she cleared her throat, ready to come clean, "time flies when you're having fun. I told you I was going with Mom, but—"

"I spoke to Rhonda today. She told me she hasn't seen you in two weeks."

Kylie froze. The way he was looking at her made her insides go cold.

It only took a second for fear to morph into anger. Had he been checking up on her?

"Did you call her?"

"No, she called me. She wanted to let me know there's a sale at Macy's downtown, if you want to go shopping this weekend. I thought it was very odd, her calling me about that, considering you two were supposed to be together?"

Kylie closed her eyes. The last thing she wanted to do was go shopping. All her clothes already made her feel like a sausage bursting out of its casing, and she hadn't even begun to show yet.

The innocently curious expression was gone from his face. Now, he looked...wounded. "Why did you lie to me, Kylie?"

It wasn't a demand. He sounded hurt.

She opened her mouth, but nothing came out. She wanted to cry. Or punch something. Or pull out her hair. No, she wanted to do all of that at once.

"Kylie, is there somebody else?"

Oh, for god's sake. She almost burst out laughing for how ridiculous that idea was. Did he see her running around like a headless chicken? Not to mention the whole looking-like-a-sausage thing. Like she would have time for or interest in a rendezvous with another man?

But he was holding her gaze, accusing her. He really thought that little of her? After all she was doing, trying to hold it together and be a perfect wife and have the life of their dreams, that was seriously what he thought she was up to?

She didn't just feel angry. She felt insulted.

"Yes, that's right. There's someone else," she snapped defiantly, slamming the top of her laptop closed.

It wasn't a lie. In fact, there were two someones, each one barely the size of a sweet pea, and they were driving her insane from the inside out.

She pushed him aside and stomped up the staircase, slamming the door as forcefully as she could behind her.

And no, she didn't eat dinner with Linc again, for the second night in a row. Truthfully? At that moment, she wouldn't have minded never eating dinner with him again.

13

Sometimes, it was just a matter of spinning the rolodex and seeing where it landed.

Yes, I knew that the rolodex was a dinosaur of the office era, but I found mine to be quite useful.

For one, it kept all of my contacts so neatly, and it didn't call attention to itself. Two, the police never bothered with physical address books anymore—when they looked for evidence, they confiscated cell phones. One of my contacts had told me that, even if my trusty office companion was outdated, it was actually very smart. It could easily be destroyed, all evidence wiped away. Not so for your ordinary cell phone, which was why I very rarely communicated via it.

This time, I spun, and landed on Katy Valdez, a nurse in Athens, Georgia.

Hadn't dealt with her for a while, maybe five years ago, but from what I remembered, our last interaction had been smooth as churned butter. I liked that.

Without giving myself a chance to rethink it, I called her up and made the pitch. This time, we were looking for a girl with blue eyes and dark hair. Darker skin would be a plus, as well.

It was rare to get a second request from K like this, especially so soon after the last one. Usually, I did no more than three of these in a year, but K had told me the baby-business was booming. People wanted what I could offer them. Who was I to turn away good business? Who was I not to spare a child from poverty and place them in a home with all the love they could ever need?

I wouldn't have been able to live with myself had I told him no.

Katy was as professional as ever and told me that she would keep an eye out. As I hung up, I thought about calling another contact, but that could be dangerous. I'd just wait. That area of Georgia was an armpit. She'd find some good candidate soon. I was sure of it.

Sitting back in my chair, I decided that perhaps it would be fun to go on two cruises this year. I didn't like to get too flashy, or else it would call attention to myself, but two trips in one year wouldn't be too much. After all, if I pulled this off, I could definitely say I earned it.

Especially with a certain nosy parker poking around.

As I was forming a response to K that I'd put feelers out and would let him know the outcome by the end of the week, I got a call from Stephen.

That was interesting.

Stephen, my old buddy.

I'd had to get a new law enforcement official to work with after my last one had gotten arrested for domestic abuse, the moron. This one was good. He was ruthless and did the job, no-nonsense, no complaints. I asked, he delivered. He'd once been a cop in downtown Asheville until he'd been brought under investigation for harassing some of the female officers. Word on the street was that he was a real dick.

But he worked well for my purposes. And that was all that mattered.

"What's going on?" I asked him when I picked up the phone.

"Nice talking to you too, sweetheart," he said with a smarmy lilt in his voice. God, he was just like Mark Lamb, but nowhere near as attractive. "You're not one for small talk, are you?"

I sighed and rubbed my temple. I didn't have time for this. "Not when I think I might have a problem. Do I have a problem, Stephen?"

"Well, that's the big question. At this point, I can't tell."

"You have been following her? Closely? Like I said?"

I'd sent a picture of the subject to him yesterday and asked him to tail her, just to see what she was up to. People like her—those young, go-getting types—always made me nervous. And she seemed like she wasn't going to let a couple of little roadblocks stand in her way. I hated to feel this anxious.

"Yeah, since this morning. Bright and early."

"And?" It was difficult to eliminate the irritation from my voice, but I managed.

"And…she left her house around ten-thirty, kind of in a rush. At eleven, she went to the Asheville Women's Health Center, left there around twelve. From about twelve-thirty to two-thirty, she walked around to a couple of downtown shops, and then she went home, where she is right now, as far as I know."

I tapped a finger on my lips, thinking. I'd sourced a woman out of Asheville Women's Health once, but that was decades ago, and the nurse who'd helped me had long since retired. I was clean as far as that was concerned. "You think she was snooping?"

He snorted. "No. I think she had a legit appointment there, lady. For herself."

"What makes you so sure?"

"Hang on. I'll send you the pic and then you can draw your own conclusions."

I waited for a moment, and when my phone buzzed, I opened the text to view a photo of the same pretty, dark-haired Kylie Coulter walking out of the brick building. Her brow was wrinkled in concern, and she was holding on to a couple of tiny, white squares of paper in one hand and a "So you're going to be a mother?" bag in the other.

It could've been anything in her hands, but from the look on her face, I was pretty certain what it was. In fact, I knew exactly what it was.

She was holding ultrasound photographs and a bag filled with samples of things like prenatal vitamins. "She's pregnant?" I murmured.

"I think so. I don't know for certain, of course, but I'll keep on her."

"Good. Do that. And if she starts making any trouble, let me know right away. I can't let her get much closer than she's already gotten. She's making me nervous, and I don't like being nervous. Do you understand?"

"Yeah, I got it."

"If she starts doing anything weird, we'll have to nip it in the bud. Quickly."

"Understood."

I hung up, then pulled my keyboard closer and typed in *Kylie Coulter* again. I'd only looked into her enough to get Stephen the information he needed to tail her. But now, I started digging a little more.

I found that Coulter Confidential was a new business, but

that she'd gotten experience working for Starr Investigations before it closed earlier this year. I found that Kylie Coulter, nee Hatfield, had attended UNC for six years, majoring in a variety of different subjects, but had never received a degree. And I also learned that Kylie had recently gotten married earlier this year to a tall, strong, drop-dead gorgeous drink of water named Lincoln Coulter, some search and rescue guy who lived outside of town.

I stared at the picture of the dark-haired man with the chocolate brown eyes. A photo from his army days, he was wearing a uniform and holding the leash of a German Shepherd. Hmm. He was quite the catch. If I were her, I'd be jumping into bed with that often.

So, she very well could be expecting.

That was interesting.

But it wasn't my concern.

I was my concern. If she was snooping where she didn't belong, she would need to be eliminated. Just as I'd eliminated the cop in Virginia who'd gotten too close a few years ago.

I simply couldn't let her continue.

14

Linc slept in the spare bedroom for the fifth night in a row.

It wasn't nearly as comfortable as his big master bed. Now, he had bags under his eyes, aches all over, and because the dogs kept making noise on the floor beside him, he'd gotten a total of five hours of sleep the entire week.

Not to mention that he couldn't stop thinking about what Kylie had told him.

She'd admitted there was someone else.

And then, to make it worse, she'd stormed out of the room, went upstairs, and closed the door. Locked it, too, so there could be no discussion. No figuring out what he could do to make things better.

Had she been lying in a fit of anger? Or had she been telling the truth?

The not knowing ate at his insides.

He figured that eventually, she'd cave. Talkative Kylie couldn't keep quiet for longer than a few minutes.

But he was wrong.

He'd gotten nothing from her but deadly silence.

He'd tried extending an olive branch half a dozen times since then. He'd made her coffee. Stayed out of her way, though she'd mostly spent her time at her desk. He hadn't bugged her on the few times that she'd gone out. When one of the dogs had learned a new trick, he invited her out to see it. He'd have had better response from a wall.

Sometimes he wondered why he was even bothering. *He* wasn't the one who was cheating—maybe—after only a few months of marriage. He was still trying to make things work. But Kylie? He had no idea.

Now, as he lay flat on his back on the couch downstairs, with his feet hanging over the arm, he stared up at the ceiling as the first rays of morning sunlight filtered through the windows. He was wondering one thing: Who?

Who was he? Who was the man who might have romanced Kylie out from underneath him? They'd spent so much time together, he didn't think there was time to find anyone else. She'd gone on a few client appointments, she went shopping by herself, and sometimes she went to see her mom, but when had she had a chance to meet this asshole?

He didn't know who he was, but he hated him. He wanted to punch his fist through his head for touching his wife.

Maybe?

He stuffed his hands in his pockets so he wouldn't punch anything close.

Next to him, the dogs started to line up to go outside.

He let out a heavy sigh.

He couldn't live like this.

Maybe he should've told Jacob the truth. Marriage wasn't at all what he'd thought it would be. He thought tying the knot would bring him closer to Kylie. They'd have a family and grow old together. Now, it was like everything was falling apart.

A few minutes later, Linc heard the pipes creaking in the walls.

She was up, taking a shower in the upstairs bath.

He thought of how much she loved that bathroom the first time she'd seen it. She'd marveled at how cavernous the claw-foot tub was, remarked at how dainty and cute the farmhouse plaid curtains were.

It was his grandparents' house. His grandfather had built it board by board when he was only about twenty himself. But Linc had always helped out on the farm, so when they died, they'd left the place to him. He loved it. Loved every creak and moan the old house made.

But most of all, he loved the times he'd spent with Kylie. She was what had completed it for him. Those long summer nights they'd spent together, in that big tub, in the candle-light. The nights they'd spent playing chess by firelight, face to face in this very room, the board between them. He'd always beat her, say checkmate, and then she'd toss the board to the floor and tackle him.

He thought this was where he and Kylie would grow old together, just like his grandparents did. They'd talked about it before. Being an old couple, holding hands on the front porch.

Now, looking at the orange morning sunlight slashing over the walls, he wondered if she'd just been lying all this time.

Dammit it to hell.

He sat up, shaking the thoughts away. He had a lot to do to prepare for another seminar he was doing later this week, and he couldn't afford to slack right now.

Wiping his eyes, he adjusted his boxers as he stood and walked to the back door. He pushed it open, letting the menagerie of dogs tumble out.

In about five minutes, they'd all come back, expecting

breakfast. Linc went to get it from the big tub that he kept under one of the cabinets, but realized it was almost empty. Kylie had probably fed them last time and forgotten to remind him to refill it from the extra supply, which he kept in the outdoor shed.

Just great.

Yawning, he went to take the keys off the hook at the front of the house. He felt the peg with his hand, first one from the left, where he always kept them. No keys.

They were missing.

Kylie.

He knew it was her. She always did things like that. She'd never put the milk back in the same place she took it from in the fridge. She'd never close drawers all the way. Where Linc ran his home with the type of precision he'd learned in the army, she'd always ascribed to a more chaotic style of living.

He looked around, at a loss where to even start looking.

This day had only started, but already it just kept getting better and better. Really. What other wonders lay in store? For a moment, he considered going back to bed.

Then he went to their desks. His was perfectly arranged, with everything placed at exact angles to everything else. His stapler was a fraction of an inch crooked; he corrected that.

He looked over at Kylie's and a sick feeling came over him.

If their house was a bomb site, Kylie's desk was ground zero. In fact, it was hard to even tell there was a desk under it, so covered was the whole thing with papers. He went around to where her chair was and frowned at an empty Snickers wrapper lying crumpled about two feet away from a trash can. That was another Kylie-thing. She never threw anything away properly.

He moved stuff around gently, hoping she wouldn't

notice, and gradually uncovered a framed photograph of them on their wedding day.

He stopped to look at the picture, taken while they were dancing at their reception, under the big tent they'd erected right on the grounds of the property. They looked younger, somehow. Their smiles had been so bright. Hell, they'd been so happy. Was it possible that it had only been in May? A few months ago?

When he set it down, his eyes fell on something else.

He recognized it as the list that Jacob had given him; the one with all the missing children on it. But it was different now.

He pulled it out from under an avalanche of papers and discovered that in addition to a few coffee stains, there were also signs that she'd been looking into the names. And not casually, either. There were volumes of notes, written in different colors, things crossed out, lines connecting some of the names, question marks...

So, was that what she'd been doing for the past five days?

He knew she hated him being overprotective, but this was serious business. He wished she'd just stick to those boring cases for Impact. If she did enough digging on this, she could find herself in a hell of a lot of trouble.

But he couldn't tell her that now.

For a moment, he thought about hiding the list somewhere she couldn't find it. His eyes even darted around wildly, trying to locate a suitable hiding place.

But then they fell upon the staircase.

Where Kylie was standing, arms crossed, staring daggers at him.

She'd never scared him before. He was army, and she was a funny, clumsy, cute girl. But now, the sneer on her face? He felt like she'd transformed into the Hyde version of herself.

He was dangerously close to being scared of his wife. So he did the only thing he could do.

He dropped the papers and backed away from the desk.

As he did, he noticed the key he'd been looking for. He scooped it into his palm and said, "This was what I was looking for."

She clomped down the stairs, all dressed and ready to start the day, though her hair was still wet and hanging loose on her shoulders. She didn't look at him as she walked to the desk and snatched up the papers.

And she didn't say a word.

She grabbed her briefcase, the one she used for meetings, and piled the list and a few other things into it.

Then, still totally silent, she hoisted the bag onto her shoulder and went outside to her car. He heard the ignition start, and the sound of the Jeep driving away from the house.

Out back, the dogs were scratching and whimpering, waiting to be let in. He quickly rushed ahead and let them all in, then went and grabbed the last bit of food from the tub, filling their bowls as much as he could.

Then he ran upstairs, threw on some shorts, a t-shirt, and his work boots.

As he rushed back down the stairs, Storm was waiting for him. She knew something was up.

"Come on, girl," he said to her, opening the door. "Something's going on. Let's go check on Kylie."

15

From the time Kylie was a little child, her teachers had always said the same thing about her. They'd said it in different ways, some of them seeing it more as a virtue than others, but they'd all agreed more or less: Kylie had the gift of gab.

She befriended everyone. She spoke to strangers without hesitation. Sometimes, she'd go through her day talking to no one in particular.

So this? Being silent? Going through the day as if she had absolutely nothing to say?

It was the hardest thing Kylie had ever done.

Her tongue was practically bitten through from all the times she'd had to hold it. Somehow, she'd managed this for five whole days, which was far beyond her previous record of only a couple of hours.

But it wasn't just talking that she missed.

No. She missed Linc. So desperately that, at night, when she'd cuddle against a pillow in the big bed they shared, she'd find herself crying until she fell asleep. He may have been a bit of a helicopter husband, but he was also her best friend.

Every time she thought that she'd break her silence because she couldn't stand it anymore, she'd remember that, if she spoke to him, he'd likely try to put the shackles on her and stop her from investigating the Elise Kirby case. And she needed to. The more she dug, the more she felt like she couldn't give it up.

She had to admit that, though she hadn't wanted Linc trying to take over the case, his idea of getting that list from Jacob had been a godsend. It was, really, all the leads she had going for her now. She planned on going through the list, one by one, until she found some connection.

Today, she was heading out to meet one Allison Simmons, who lived in the Asheville area and believed her baby had been kidnapped back in the nineties. When Kylie had spoken to her over the phone, all the pieces had clicked. The woman had been poor and hadn't had any family. She'd given birth to a healthy baby but had been told later on that the baby had passed. She'd been so upset and hadn't known to ask the right questions. To Kylie, it seemed like a good option, even if the two cases had happened decades apart.

But as she drove farther and farther away from the farmhouse, she felt worse and worse. She was getting another headache, probably from all the crying she'd done last night. She'd managed to make a dent in all the work for Impact Insurance, and yet it had only served to show her how hopelessly far behind she was. It was probably a good thing she wasn't talking to Linc. It'd only put her even more behind the eight-ball if she had him to distract her.

She still missed him. As much as he annoyed her sometimes, right now, she longed for the distraction. She longed for him. The good Linc, which he was ninety-nine percent of the time. It was the bad Linc…the overbearing and suffocating part of his nature, that had her afraid of trusting him completely with the secrets she carried in her heart.

After she parked, she looked around, and an eerie feeling settled over her as she realized exactly what this place was. It was under new ownership, but she'd been here before. She'd gone to meet a potential witness in an art forgery and embezzlement case, but the witness had never shown up.

When Kylie had gone back to her car, she'd found the man slumped over the steering wheel of his car, shot in the back of the head.

Her teeth chattered as she stepped out of the car, and she clenched her jaw to keep them quiet. It was daylight, so the place was swarming with people, which should've made her feel safe. But as she walked to the front door, she still couldn't fight the strange feeling gripping her. She felt sickly, shivery, almost dizzy.

Then she opened the door and the smell of coffee hit her.

She was going to be sick.

Breathing shallowly, she went to the counter and ordered a Danish and a bottle of seltzer. Once she collected her breakfast, she decided she needed fresh air. Since it was a nice day, she went and found a small table outside on the sidewalk.

As she sat there, she took her file out of her bag and looked through it. Every time someone went into the café, she wondered if that person was Allison. She didn't have a picture but expected a woman in her late thirties, since she'd said she was a teen when she had the child. But no one seemed to fit that description.

Time slipped by, and the day got hotter. Kylie fanned her face as she studied the list, wondering which of the next few people she should contact. There was a woman not far away in East Tennessee, and another who lived close to Atlanta. It'd be a haul, but Kylie felt confident that one little detail connecting the cases might be all she needed to blow the case wide open.

Someone must know something. She needed to call them all. Start from the beginning.

As she continued to fan herself, she dialed up the first number from a case in Staunton, Virginia. The man, Alfred Hastings, had contacted the police because he thought the death of his wife might be related to the disappearance of a child she'd been a midwife for, a child belonging to a woman named Renee Best. The police had investigated and found no such connection, but poor Patricia Hastings had been shot, point blank, in the chest.

Had Patricia Hastings gotten too close to this kidnapping ring and someone had come after her? Maybe Linc was right, being concerned about Kylie's safety. After all, anyone willing to steal a baby probably wouldn't have any issue with murder to cover their tracks.

But the phone blared in her ear, coming up as disconnected.

Then she reread the file and realized that the case was from 1975. If Al Hastings was still alive, he'd be nearly ninety by now. And would he actually be able to remember something that happened so long ago?

Ending the call, she sighed. On to the next. She called a few more, all of them dead ends.

The next thing she knew, she looked at her phone and realized Allison was a half-hour late.

Now more than ever, the thought of that witness from the art embezzlement case hung in her mind. Had someone gotten to Allison, the way they'd gotten to him? She pictured the man, his body pressed up against the steering wheel, his dead eyes. Her stomach clenched at the thought. And now, here she was, a sitting target right here on the sidewalk.

Standing, she crept toward the edge of the brick building, feeling silly as a couple walked by, hand-in-hand, and eyed her curiously. The man threw a casual, "What's up?" at her as birds twittered in the tree above.

Kylie peered around the building, scanning the parking area. All she saw were cars, her own included, lined up, and a well-dressed man and a woman kissing each other goodbye.

She shook her head. She was being stupid. It was broad daylight. A killer would have to have a lot of nerve to attack her now.

She whirled and realized she'd left her phone on the table. As she picked it up, it buzzed with a message. It was from Allison. *Sorry for the late notice. Couldn't get out of work. Can we reschedule?*

Sighing with relief, she typed in: *Sure. Tomorrow?*

When she looked up from her phone, she spotted it across the street, just sitting there in a bank's parking lot.

A familiar pickup truck.

One that looked exactly like Linc's.

And she couldn't mistake the silhouette of the broad-shouldered man sitting in the driver's seat, wearing sunglasses and a baseball cap. Or the German Shepherd sitting patiently by his side.

"Damn him," she muttered under her breath.

So, even when they were fighting, he felt the need to follow her? Or did he really think he'd catch her having a rendezvous with some mysterious stranger? She knew she shouldn't have said that, that it would just throw his jealous streak into overdrive, but she'd been at her wit's end. Was this what he'd been doing all the time she thought he was giving her space? Following her at a safe distance and playing her shadow?

Grabbing her bag, she ran between two parked cars on the street, hurrying through the early morning traffic. She leapt onto the curb and came up close to his window, which was open. "Really?" she yelled. "What do you think you're doing? Following me?" After so long of not talking, it felt good to shout.

He looked around uncomfortably. Never one to make a scene. "Kylie, I—"

"Don't. I don't want to hear how I'm overreacting. This…" She waved at his truck. "This is what drives me crazy about you! You don't trust that I know how to take care of myself!"

He held up his hands. "Can we just go home and talk this—"

"No! I don't want to go anywhere with you! I want you to just leave me alone. Why are you here?"

He dragged a hand down his face. "Why am I here? Because I love you!" he said in a voice so loud Kylie took a step back, shocked. "Because whatever you're doing, I know it's my fault. I'm fouling things up, but I can't lose you. Tell me what I need to do, and I'll do it. If you want me to leave you alone and give you more space, I will. I promise. Just tell me you won't leave me. Okay?"

She stood there, stricken, her heart slowly thawing. He was normally so quiet, rarely emotional. And now he looked like he was truly going to have a breakdown. The devastation was so complete on his face, she'd never seen anything sadder.

She put her hands on the window.

"There isn't anyone else," she said softly. "Well, not in the way you're thinking."

His eyes snapped to her. "What does that mean?"

She let out a laugh, about to tell him the news. But the second she did, she felt a massive cramp in her abdomen and doubled over. As she clutched herself, there was a rush of warm fluid between her legs. Her heart started to pound as Linc's voice echoed in her ears. "What's wrong?"

She couldn't bring herself to speak, she was so afraid. She

was vaguely aware of the door of the truck opening and Linc's arm wrapping around her.

Around her, the world swirled and blurred. Everything in her vision went white. As he lifted her into his arms, she managed to get out one word, "Hospital."

16

Two hours after Linc brought Kylie into Asheville General Hospital, he sat in the waiting room, nursing his third cup of coffee and fidgeting. He'd managed to get Jacob to come and take care of Storm, so he wouldn't have to worry about her, but he still had plenty to worry about.

People rushed by purposefully, with things to do, but he had nothing to do but think.

He found himself running over her last words to him, again and again. *There isn't anyone else. Not in the way you're thinking.*

What did that mean?

He'd been thinking a hell of a lot. Everything bad. Especially when she'd pulled up to that old coffee shop. He was pretty sure it was the same one where the dead body had been found. Was she going there to meet her lover?

All Linc had known was that he needed to see the man. Maybe even confront him and beat the shit out of him. If he met any prick who'd laid a hand on her, he'd see red. Wouldn't be able to control himself.

But she'd been alone. No lover in sight.

And then, on the way to the hospital, she'd kept repeating over and over again that she was sorry. In typical Kylie fashion, she didn't let him get a word in. She rambled on that this was all her fault, that she was being stupid and should've been more careful, and he could see she wasn't angry anymore—more like scared to death. He didn't even have a chance to get in that *he* was sorry too.

She'd been clutching her stomach, and as he pulled into the hospital's U-shaped drive, she'd gone white as a sheet and passed out. The EMTs outside had laid her out on a stretcher and wheeled her in, telling him he needed to move his truck. When he came back, Kylie'd been wheeled off to the emergency room. He was told that his wife was being evaluated, and that he should take a seat.

That was two hours ago. An hour ago, a doctor had come out and said that she was stable and that her life was not in danger, but that they were in the midst of a number of tests. He hadn't said anything else or given him any indication of what the problem was. Maybe they didn't know.

He couldn't help thinking of his grandmother. She'd collapsed in a similar way, and it'd taken a battery of tests to determine that she had a tumor on her brain stem. Three days later, she was dead, and three weeks after that, his grandfather, who'd been previously healthy as an ox, went too, the victim of a broken heart.

Not Kylie. She was too young. They'd just started their lives together. God, he'd taken all the moments with her for granted.

He tried to scroll through his phone, but nothing interested him. All he could think about was his wife.

Finally, the doors opened and another doctor appeared. "Mr. Coulter?" he said.

Linc nodded and stood up. "How's Kylie?"

"She's stable. We did some tests, and she's resting right now."

"Is everything all right?"

"Yes. She's just been under a lot of stress, so we're recommending bed rest for the foreseeable future, until she gets herself on more solid footing. But the babies are all right."

Linc nodded along, until the words really sank in. He froze. "Babies?"

"Uh, yes," the doctor said, shifting uncomfortably. "Did your wife not tell you? I suppose that's understandable as she's only a few weeks along."

"Babies?" Linc repeated.

He nodded. "Yes. Twins." He motioned to the double doors. "I won't delay you. I'm sure you're anxious to see her."

He followed the doctor, in a daze.

Twins.

Twins.

There isn't someone else. Not in the way you're thinking.

Holy fuck. She was pregnant. That's who the other someone else was. Her babies.

His babies.

Their babies.

Twins.

Two of them. At one time.

Through the daze, the pieces started to fall into place. Why she'd been tired. Why she'd been moody. Why she'd given him the cold shoulder. No wonder. She was completely stressed out because she was trying to get this business off the ground. Add in a pregnancy?

Suddenly, it all made sense.

And he felt fan-fucking-tastic. Relieved, excited, dazed, a little scared, but so incredibly thankful that he wanted to drop to his knees and praise God.

He found her in the hospital room, a sheet pulled up over her chest, her eyes closed. When he walked in and sat on the edge of the bed next to her, he took her hand and kissed the back of it.

She opened her eyes. "Oh. Hi."

"Hi, Lee. Hi, sweetheart. How are you feeling?"

"Tired."

"Well, that makes sense. Considering."

"I'm sorry I didn't tell you." Her voice sounded so weak, he had to lean forward in order to hear her clearly. "I wanted to. I actually tried to a few times but—"

He smiled. "I know why you didn't. Because I'm one crazy son of a bitch."

She drew her bottom lip under her top teeth, holding on to his hand tighter. "Are you happy?"

"Happy?" He leaned forward and took her other hand too. "Baby, I'm *thrilled*. A few minutes ago, I thought you were dying. And a few minutes before *that*, I thought you wanted to get divorced. So all in all, it was a pretty shitty day, up until right now."

She shook her head slightly, her eyes still glazed. "I love you. I don't ever want to leave you. I just know how hard it's going to be. Things are already so crazy."

"Nah. They're not so bad."

"They want me to be on bed rest for the rest of the trimester, Linc. That's six weeks. How can I—"

"Don't worry about that." He straightened and put his hand over the creases that had begun to line her forehead. "We'll figure it out. When are the babies coming?"

"April. April thirteenth, to be exact."

Amazing how this one little answer explained all of her weird behavior over the past couple of days. And it was such a good answer. A great answer. The best answer. A freaking miracle. He was going to be a dad. "Wow. I can't believe it."

Tears shone in her eyes. "You are happy, right?"

"Hell yes. Beyond happy. I think you just made me the happiest guy on the planet. I can't wait, Kylie. But I want you to be well, first. That's most important. These kids need a healthy mom."

"I'm trying."

"Hey. Relax. Don't try. Just take it easy, and it'll happen on its own. All right?"

"They said it's a good thing you got me here when you did. Something about my progesterone and…" she furrowed her brow, "a threatened miscarriage because of some bleeding."

He patted her hand gently. Nothing was going to happen to these kids on his watch. "But you're okay now. The babies will be okay. We'll just do every single thing the doctors tell us to do. Okay?"

She nodded. "I don't want to tell anyone yet. Not until we're sure I'm out of the woods."

He understood. His parents would be beyond excited, considering they'd always thought of him as the permanent bachelor. Kylie's mother, Rhonda, would probably buy out all the baby clothes in the Asheville area.

Holy shit. Yeah, there was so much to think about, but it was all good stuff. Unlike all the shit they'd been dealing with for the past few weeks, this was so, so good.

"Yeah. Of course, but everything will be fine." He leaned over and kissed her. "You just need to take it easy."

"But I don't know how I'm going to get everything done."

He laughed. "Remember? There's two of us Coulters in Coulter Confidential. I can do your dirty work while you're on bed rest. Just tell me what you need."

"But you're already so busy."

"I'm not *that* busy. And I get it. I'm sorry if I contributed to your stress, Lee. That's not what I wanted. I wasn't trying to be your warden. I just want to help. You can use me to help. Anything you need. All right?"

Kylie laughed, and he knew it was because he was rambling, which was very rare for him. He pressed his lips together to keep from promising her the moon.

She laced her fingers through his. "I have a lot of paperwork and billing that needs to be done. I guess I can concentrate on that and let you focus on the outside stuff for now. You know, the investigative stuff. Impact has a slew of work waiting for me."

He knew it'd be hell for her. She never sat still in one spot for long. Of course, if he took over the Impact assignments, she would be in heaven, so this could be a win-win for them both.

"Yeah. It *will* be good. You'll see. It'll all work out." He stood up and kissed her forehead again. "Now, just get some rest. All right?"

She closed her eyes. "I love you, Linc," she said, her hands moving to her stomach, covering the tiny lives they'd come so close to losing.

He smiled and sat back on the faux leather chair, watching her as her breathing slowed, the monitor on her heart quieted, and the worried creases on her forehead slowly faded away. Then, he got up and walked down the hallway.

Not too far, though. Just enough to get himself some exercise and work off all the nervous energy he felt pulsing through his veins.

He needed to be there when she woke up.

17

"Shit!" Kylie screamed as she poked her finger with the sharp end of a knitting needle for the third time in five minutes.

Looking at the haphazard pattern she'd created with the mint green yarn—she thought green would be safe since they didn't yet know the sex of the babies—she sighed. The sock would fit just fine, if the baby's foot was about the size of a regular human's foot.

She'd forgotten to make a turn somewhere, maybe.

Lifting her knees slightly, she adjusted her cell phone so that she had a better view of the YouTube video entitled *Even an Idiot can Knit These Baby Booties!*

She'd been so encouraged by how simple the instructor had made it look that she'd ordered Linc to go out and get her the materials at the hobby store downtown, right away. After all, after a week of sitting in bed with her laptop, she'd not only managed to file away all the paperwork and billing for Impact Insurance, she'd also revamped the billing system to make it easier and pre-created all of their invoices for all the work in progress.

So, even though she was happy that she'd finally gotten a handle on the accounting end of her business, she now had something else to worry about.

She couldn't freaking knit worth a damn.

Would that make her a bad mother? Was that a prerequisite for having kids?

Groaning, she threw the whole thing, needles and all, onto the floor and petted Vader, who was lounging on his side beside her, hoping her dog's love would give her some sorely needed calm.

Breathe in, breathe out.

She had to relax.

Above all, that was what needed to happen. Doctor's orders.

She'd never been so scared in her life as she'd been a week ago. It was only when she'd felt that gush of fluid between her legs while she was outside the coffee shop that she'd realized something: She wanted these babies.

Like, really, *really* wanted them.

No, they weren't a hindrance. An annoyance. Not even a problem. How could she have even thought that? They were a blessed gift from God.

On the ride to the hospital, she'd kept her eyes closed, saying quiet prayers, telling herself that if everything came out all right, she'd never take these children for granted again.

Sucking in a deep breath and slowly letting it out, she stroked her stomach. So, the babies would have store-bought booties. Big deal. They wouldn't mind. They'd be too busy with other, more important things, like trying to find their thumbs to suck. Kylie had never cared much about shoes, either. These kids would buck fashion trends and looking cool. They'd go their own way.

A couple of moments later, Linc poked his head through

the door. "Everything okay? I thought I heard…" He looked at the pile of yarn and needles on the floor. "Problem?"

She shook her head, then held up her red pointer finger. "I've just decided to give up knitting."

He came in with a tray for her. Her lunch, a grilled cheese sandwich and tomato soup. He was such a good nursemaid, almost too good, but she figured she'd earned it because she'd tended to him after he'd injured his shoulder.

He set it down on the bed beside her, lifted her finger, and kissed it very gently. "Rule number one: If a hobby makes you bleed more than it makes you smile, it isn't worth it."

She smiled.

"I was thinking…for the nursery, my grandparents never threw anything away, so I think the old crib my parents used is in the back shed somewhere. I bet I could refinish it."

"Yeah, but we need two," she reminded him.

"Okay. But I could probably build the other one."

She had no doubt. He was good with tools, a very handy guy. But every time Linc opened his mouth, it was something about the babies. Which of the two remaining upstairs rooms —the guest room or the storage room—should be used as the nursery. Whether it made sense to paint the whole house now, or if that would be bad for the babies. Since there were so many things they'd need, whether they should register for baby stuff somewhere, and if so, when.

She wanted to be happy about his excitement. She really did. But his mind was so occupied by thoughts of the kids that it seemed he'd forgotten one thing: He'd promised to be her go-fer when it came to all things Coulter Confidential.

Oh, he was helping out. He was extremely helpful on her getting a handle on the Impact Insurance worker's comp surveillance cases. He'd gone from one of those to the next like a busy little beaver, watching and documenting the activities of various insureds on worker's comp and bringing home the details for Kylie to enter into the electronic reports she filed for Impact.

The dull stuff, Linc excelled at.

But it was the kinds of cases that made Kylie's heart race that he'd been decidedly…removed from. And yes, okay, they were maybe the slightest bit dangerous, but that was what made them exciting.

For example, Elise Kirby's.

Well, it made sense that he was avoiding that one. That had been her "hobby" case, after all, and it wasn't bringing them in any money. She'd called Allison Simmons, the mother she'd arranged to meet at the café, to tell her what had happened and told her that her husband would be out to talk to her in a few days. But Linc kept putting off the appointment.

Granted, he was more of a loner and wasn't great with people. Interviewing, he probably wouldn't be great at. Still, the more time that went by, the more Kylie began to believe he was avoiding the case entirely.

"Did you call Allison yet?" she blurted as he went to fluff her pillows.

"Uh. Not yet. Probably tomorrow." He scratched the side of his jaw. "I finished the last of the Impact cases on the docket this morning. Now I've got to get the pups to the vet for their check-up. I was going to leave in a few minutes."

Sure. He was more interested in the pups than in solving this case. Or maybe he just didn't think there *was* a case. Whatever it was, it was clear he wasn't as invested in it as she was.

He reached into the pockets of his cargo shorts for his keys. "Will you be all right here for the afternoon if I leave for a few hours? I might not be back until dinnertime, but I can pick up some KFC if you're interested?"

KFC? If it was food, she was interested. Lately, mention of food of any kind made her ravenous. She lifted up her sandwich and took a bite. "Yes, I can manage, and yes, would you think I'm a pig if I asked for an entire bucket for myself?"

"Nah. You're eating for three. What are you going to do, if not knitting?"

She pointed to her laptop. "I have a few more reports to finish up."

"All right." He leaned over and kissed her. "Now, remember, I don't even want you taking the stairs. The doctor said you had to take it super, super easy."

She rolled her eyes. That was why he'd been carrying her everywhere, like some legless creature. For the past week, she'd been confined up in her bedroom, except for one brief moment when she made the mistake of trying to go down the stairs. The dogs had gotten all excited to finally see her again, since they apparently thought she'd fallen into a hole and died. Linc rushed past them, scooped her up, and delivered her back to the bed before she could say *Escape,* with a severe warning not to ever do that again.

"Fine."

"Bean One and Bean Two, did you hear that?" he called, using her nicknames for the little spuds. "Stay put and don't give your mom trouble."

"They heard. Now go."

He lifted his cell phone. "All right. If you need anything at all, just call. My phone's on."

She waved him away. Like she'd make him drop everything to drive a half-hour back up the hill so he could get her a new roll of toilet paper. "I'll be fine."

Linc seriously didn't even want her getting out of bed, except to pee, and it surprised her that she hadn't developed bed sores. She had to think that getting no exercise whatsoever had to be bad for the babies too.

As soon as she heard the door slam, she climbed out of bed and went to the bay window, where she saw Linc trying to herd the puppies into the truck. It was like a fun tornado at his feet. *Good luck with that.*

But even though the puppies were a handful, he had more of a way with them than most people would've. Eventually, he got them inside the kennel he kept in the back seat of the truck and closed the door. She watched him pull away, then went and grabbed her phone, quickly putting in a call to Greg.

"Hey," she said when he answered.

"Well, to what do I owe the pleasure, short stuff?" he said in his typical surly way. Wait…it was barely noon. Was he drunk again?

"I'm having a bit of a crisis," she said to him, sitting down on the bay window's ledge and soaking in the sunshine. "I thought you could give me your guidance, oh brilliant one."

"Maybe. Is this about that child kidnapping again?"

"Well…it's more of a general question about the business. Surveillance cases aside, how much do you think you could've gotten done on some of your biggest cases if you were say, confined to your bed for two months?"

"Uh-oh. What did you do?"

"It's just a hypothetical!" she protested.

"Sure it is. Well, I was confined to my bed for three weeks after a hernia operation, and…not much."

She gritted her teeth. That was not the answer she wanted.

"Oh."

"But luckily, that's why there's two of you. You and that hunky hubs of yours."

Right, she thought, sighing, drumming her fingers on the glass pane. God, she missed the outdoors. She slid the window open and pressed her face against the screen, sucking in the fresh air, like some poor prisoner who hadn't seen daylight in ages.

"What? He ain't holding up his end of the bargain, kid?"

"No. It's not that. He's really helpful, but he's not exactly one of those sharks, you know? The type who can dig deep and ask the right questions from witnesses to get results. Actually…I think he may be putting it off. Especially the hard, investigative stuff."

"Okay…so now that we've established that this *is* about you, and you're confined to a bed…you mind telling me what's broken?"

"Nothing!"

"Come on. I hear the desperation in your voice. What's going on?"

"Nothing's broken," she said with a sigh while picking at a loose thread on her tank top. Well, he was like the father she never had, and he was too far away to spill the news to anyone else, so… "I'm pregnant."

Unlike her mom, Greg wasn't one to get all crazy about her announcements. He'd barely blinked an eye when she got engaged. "Well, congrats."

"But it's strictly on the down-low. I'm not even two months in and I'm on bed rest because I nearly had a miscarriage."

"Jesus. Well, you do need to stop stressing out, short stuff. I know you. You're about as high-strung when it comes to these cases as a person can get."

She sighed. "I know, I know. But I really feel bad for Elise. I really want to find her daughter for her. I guess I'm all hormonal too. Anyway, I just want to help her. And Linc's just not able to ask the questions and feel out the witnesses the way I'd want to."

"Yeah. Well, that always was your big strength, kid. You

can draw the shit out of people. I don't even know how you do it."

"Well, thanks. But there's not much I can do from my bed."

There was a pause. "No…now, wait. Maybe you don't have to go anywhere. You ever think of asking your witnesses to come to you?"

Well, she had thought of that, but she didn't want to inconvenience them. Then again, Allison had been very interested in telling her story. During her googling session, Kylie had learned that Allison was a high-ranking advertising executive at a prestigious agency downtown. Since her baby had disappeared, she'd certainly made a name for herself and seemed important and busy. Even so, Allison had almost volunteered to drop everything and come to her the first time she'd called, but Kylie had been too worried about Linc getting in the way. That's why she'd made the first meeting at the café.

So, maybe Allison would come to her.

Greg continued, "And…that reminds me. After we got off the phone last time, I got to thinking. I remember a case that was similar to the one you described. Where the baby was kidnapped from the mom's house. Police thought it was the father, but when they tracked him down in Mexico, he didn't have the kid. There was talk he might have ditched the kid, but he insisted he never had anything to do with it. Name of the mother was Hanson, I think. It's in the files."

Kylie's heart whirred. "Really? That's great. I'll—"

"Wait. Hold on. You should take it easy. Knowing you, you won't, but can you *try* at least? Let that man of yours do most or all of the heavy lifting? You got a baby to think of."

"I know, I know. Two, actually."

"Shit. Twins? Really?"

"Mmm-hmmm. Double the fun."

"And double the reason to just relax your little ass."

Kylie made an affirmative noise, but right then, she couldn't. She did her best to pretend she was calm, asking him how his retirement was going and listening to his latest fishing story, but inside, that tornado had begun brewing again.

By the time she hung up with him, she'd already formulated her plan of action. One: Call Allison and ask her to come over right away. Two: Go through the file cabinets downstairs and look for the Hanson case.

Perfect. It was so nice to have a plan, and one that she could actually carry out, even on bed rest.

Without waiting another second, she called Allison's number. "Allison Simmons speaking."

"Hi, Allison, this is Kylie, the private investigator.

"Oh. Yes. Hello. I'm so very sorry for bailing on you last week."

"It's completely okay, and I'm hoping we can reschedule. The problem is, I'm on doctor's ordered bed rest because, well, I'm expecting, which is why I haven't been able to connect with you. So, I'm wondering if you might have time to come over to my house today?"

"Well, congratulations! And yes, today actually works for me. My schedule's pretty open until three. Why don't you text me your address, and I'll come right over."

Kylie's spirits lifted. "Sounds great, but just so you know, my house is a little out of the way. It's north of Asheville in the mountains. Is that okay?"

"Fine. I could stand to get out of the city for a little bit."

After rattling off the address, she hung up, smiling, then looked down at herself. She'd showered…sometime. A long time ago. Actually, it had been a bath, which had been lorded over by Linc, who'd insisted on helping her wash all the difficult-to-reach places, and even some of the not-so-difficult ones. He'd washed her hair, lifted her out of the tub like a princess, and dried her with a pile of fluffy towels.

Overboard? Completely. She'd felt like freaking Cleopatra.

She went to the bathroom and quickly ran a washcloth over herself, sprayed some dry shampoo in her hair, and put on deodorant. Good enough. Then she threw a cardigan over her tank top and boxers.

Lovely.

She donned some sweats, which weren't exactly nice-looking, but were better than boxers.

But as she crept to the door, she reminded herself that all would be fine, and what Linc didn't know wouldn't hurt him.

Vader looked at her as if she was doing something wrong as she opened the bedroom door and stood at the top of the staircase in her bare feet. She glowered at him. "I *am* taking it easy. It's just twelve steps down, twelve steps up. And I'll go slow."

He still looked doubtful.

"The doc never said I couldn't climb steps. That was Linc."

It didn't help her case any. His expression remained unchanged.

One hand on the railing, one hand on her stomach, she descended the staircase in search of the Hanson file.

18

Allison Simmons was, as usual, running late.

That's what happened when a person had over one-hundred employees to manage in a busy but unpredictable industry. Advertising was like that. There was always some deadline looming or some fire to put out.

This was the latter. Their social media ads for their biggest client, one of the country's biggest suppliers of running shoes and apparel, had performed dismally with test audiences, and they were due to deliver them to the client later that day.

As soon as she'd hung up with Kylie Coulter—a peppy, sweet girl who sounded more like a college cheerleader than a private investigator—she'd found herself face-to-face with two of her senior account managers, who'd broken the news.

Dammit, she'd thought, but only for a second. It was her can-do attitude that had gotten her through a lot worse in her lifetime. She broke into action, doling out orders, telling them exactly what they needed to do to keep the client happy, *and* keep them from being an ex-client.

When she was done, they thanked her, relieved, as if they wouldn't have known what to do without her help.

That was why she was at the helm of The Creation, Asheville's best and most innovative ad agency. She'd never had any formal schooling beyond a GED, just hard work and determination. She'd worked her way up to President and Senior Account Executive by the skin of her teeth, starting as a receptionist when she was seventeen years old.

She'd had to.

After she'd given birth, there was no way she was going back to high school. She'd had SLUT painted on her locker enough while she was walking around with a growing baby belly to know she didn't need the drama from those immature, college-bound losers.

Besides, all of her friends who'd offered support had gradually dropped off the face of the earth after the baby died a few hours after birth.

She didn't need them, anyway. Just like she hadn't needed the father, an old boyfriend who'd pretended she didn't exist the moment she told him she was pregnant.

She'd wanted that baby. Planned for the baby. Was excited about being a mom.

When the worst happened, she could've crawled into herself and died.

Crib death. SIDS. That's what they'd told her. No explanation. It had happened while the baby rested in the nursery on only her second day of life.

Instead, she channeled that grief into something good. The day her baby died, her life took a turn, and she went barreling off on a new trajectory. She got her GED, started working at The Creation, got her B.A. and then her Masters, and kept rising in the ranks. She put family on hold, indefinitely.

But she never stopped thinking of what her life would

have been like had that baby survived. Two completely divergent paths, stemming from one pivotal incident. An incident she'd never be able to forget as long as she lived.

When she finished putting out that latest fire, she snapped her laptop closed and stood up in her corner penthouse office. She checked the time. She'd be late, but that was okay. She was happy when Kylie had invited her to her house outside of town. After all, Allison was a fixture downtown; everyone knew her. It was better than meeting in the coffeehouse with the off-chance one of her employee's friends might overhear something.

Quickly, she packed her things into her briefcase and set out, closing her door and telling her receptionist that she'd be back for her three o'clock appointment.

Then she headed for the elevators and took one down to the attached parking garage.

As she did, she thought of Kylie's call.

It was funny. Some days, she didn't think of the baby at all, and yet every once in a while, something would happen and make it hurt worse than before. When her baby had been born, the nurses had all exclaimed about how beautiful she was. She certainly looked healthy, and her Apgar score had been strong.

And then, just like that…she was gone. Complications, they'd said. Mysterious crib death, which had no actual cause.

Had she been older and less naïve, Allison might have thought to question exactly what complications they'd been talking about. She had a death notice that said something about a heart defect, but nothing else.

A couple years later, she'd read an article in the newspaper about something called child laundering and called the police, asking if it was possible her child had been involved. They assured her that no, no other children from the area had been taken in that way. Then, almost ten years to the day that she gave birth, she saw a little girl playing on the street that looked almost exactly like pictures of herself at that age.

It made her ache.

It made her wonder.

It sometimes felt that, no matter how many years passed, she'd still never feel at peace with what had happened. When Kylie called with questions about child laundering, Allison had felt compelled to speak to her.

The elevator doors slid open on the garage floor, just as Allison was typing in a message to Kylie: *Running a little late. Leaving now.*

As she entered the garage, she waved to a security guard stationed there. There'd been a few bomb threats made earlier in the year, so it was good to see they were beefing up security. It was someone she didn't recognize, but he clearly recognized her because he said, "Ms. Simmons, where are you headed to? You usually don't leave until a lot later."

She laughed. It was true. She was fond of burning the midnight oil in her office, but that was how she'd gotten where she was. "Well, it's a crazy job," she said with a shrug. "I have a meeting outside of Asheville for a change, but I should be back before three."

He smiled and gave her a little salute before she continued on to her BMW convertible.

Something made her pause, though. She hadn't realized how empty the garage was in the middle of the day. All the cars were here, but people usually walked during lunch. There were no people.

A shiver climbed the length of her spine as she reached her car. When she turned around, with the elevator still in view, she realized the security guard was gone. The elevator doors must have reopened without her noticing, and he'd stepped inside.

Now, she was really alone.

As she hurried to the convertible, her heels clicking on the concrete, the feeling that something was wrong wouldn't go away. She saw it before she heard it. Actually, she didn't hear much at all. It was a battery-operated car, and it was so silent that she had no idea that it was heading straight for her.

But it was.

Fast.

Too fast.

She didn't have time to move out of the way. She barely had time to think of anything, except that the man behind the wheel looked an awful lot like the guard she'd just seen only moments before.

"No!"

She closed her eyes and braced for impact, and even as the single word vibrated around her, the back of her head slammed against the pavement.

19

I was just sitting down to a nice cup of coffee and a scone, my afternoon snack, when the call came in from Stephen.

"You're lucky," he said before I could even say hello.

"Let me be the judge of that," I said, not liking the tone of his voice. "What happened?"

"Well, you told me we'd have to nip it in the bud if your subject ever stirred up some shit. And she did. I tapped into their conversation while I was monitoring the little investigator. Allison was on her way to meet with her, but I took care of her for you. With my car. Lights out."

I stiffened, pressing the phone even harder against my ear. "You hit her with your car?"

"Not my car, of course. I ain't stupid." He seemed so proud of himself.

"Did anyone see you?"

"Nope."

I didn't like the sound of this one bit. There was very little a person like Allison Simmons could do twenty years after her baby had disappeared. So what if she'd gotten to talk to

Kylie Coulter? Maybe they'd make a connection, but her kid was long gone by now.

But people like the private investigator? They were the real threat.

Trying to choose my words carefully, I reached over and adjusted a photograph of myself with the mayor, taken when I'd received an award a few years back for my humanitarian work.

"Listen to me and listen good. I don't give a rat's ass about Allison or any of the other mothers. What I care about is that little witch who's meddling in my affairs. Do you understand?"

He sputtered. "Well, I—"

"I'm not paying you to create a little trail of blood that will lead the police right to my front door, Stephen," I said, trying to keep my voice calm. "I want the real problem gone."

"Yeah, but...I don't know. It doesn't—"

"I'm not paying you to be soft, Stephen."

"But ma'am. I heard her husband talking while I was tailing him in the hardware store. He was looking for enough wood to build some cribs. Two of 'em. Your girl's pregnant. With twins."

I sighed. Sometimes fertility was wasted on the wrong people. It was a shame, how much money that little womb of hers could be worth. But it didn't matter. "I don't care. She's too close and needs to go. And soon."

"But she hasn't—"

"She was going to meet with Allison, wasn't she? That means she's getting close. If she meets with enough of the mothers, she might start making connections. It's too dangerous."

"She never leaves the house," he put in, seemingly looking for any reason to spare the bitch. He was getting on my nerves.

"Then you'll know where to find her. Wait until she's alone so you can't be followed and *take her out.* Do you hear me?"

"Yeah," he grumbled. "I hear you."

He didn't seem very happy about it, but the moment I knew it was done, you could bet your ass I was going to celebrate. Good and long.

Maybe I'd book myself another cruise.

20

Driving down the hill and back with ten puppies and a kennel with a faulty latch wasn't the best of ideas.

Linc had handled it, though. He'd only had to pull over three times to get the dogs back into their rightful spots.

Once he did that, he tried bracing the broken lock with different things he had lying around the cab of his truck, but each time, the little rascals were too smart for whatever solution he'd devised. One minute, he was driving sixty down the highway, headed for Asheville Veterinary. And the next? He had a lap full of fur, doing everything they could to tear his eyes from the road.

Two of them, especially. Roxy and Zita, two little girls, were exactly like Vader. They were black puffballs with the most mischievous side. They had none of their mother, Storm, in them at all. He'd barely get one under control when the other would go off in the opposite direction.

He'd been thinking about going to the hardware store and picking up that lumber he'd ordered to build the cribs. But after he'd gotten done getting the puppies' clean bill of health from the vet, he was, in a word, exhausted.

Not to mention, he was sure wrestling with the creatures on the way back up the hill would take a lot more out of him.

And he missed Kylie. Even though she was just sitting at home, he wanted to make sure she was okay.

As she'd probably expected, which was why he figured she hadn't told him, he'd gotten all the more protective of her since he'd gotten the news. He couldn't not be. He tried to be cool about it, but those three were his whole family. If anything happened to Kylie now, he might never recover.

As he refastened the latch, he climbed into the truck and lifted out his phone. He started to type in a *You ok?* to Kylie but erased it.

She'd probably come back with some snide remark. After all, she was at the farmhouse with Vader and Storm. What was the worst that could happen?

His mind started to wander to a dozen unlikely—but possible—scenarios. She could fall out of bed. She could hear the phone ringing and run to get it and trip down the stairs. She could have tried to take a bath and slipped in the tub...

He quickly typed in: *You ok?*

A moment later: *I'm trapped under a large piece of furniture. Send help.*

And there it was. The snide remark. *Superdad on the way.*

He chuckled and put his phone in the cup holder, then pulled out of the vet parking lot. After making it about a mile down the street, a pile of fur did a free fall over his shoulder, landing in his lap.

Roxy.

He groaned. "What part of *stay in the kennel* don't you understand?" he said, stroking her ears.

He nudged her to the passenger seat, but she put her front paws on the elbow rest and started to lick at the window. What was that all about? Did that actually taste good?

He reached for her, pushing her away from the glass. "If I

want that done, I'll go to a car wash," he told the pup, pulling over to the shoulder of the road just as Zita followed her partner-in-crime over to the dark side. Now the window was coated in swirls of thick dog saliva.

He opened the kennel and got the dogs back in, shaking his head.

As he did, he thought about how they'd manage two car seats in a truck like his. Two car seats, and a sea of dogs. No, it wasn't possible. His brothers had no more than two kids each, and their family had graduated to massive three-row SUVs. Was that what they would have to do? Maybe buy a minivan? A tour bus?

And how would they all live in the farmhouse together—and carry out a business there too? Talk about Grand Central Station.

He got into the truck again, thinking how strange it was that, though their entire world was about to be flipped on its head, Kylie hadn't mentioned much about it. She didn't seem keen to talk about their plans for the future. He chalked that up to nervousness, wanting to make sure that the babies were all right before she got too excited.

And maybe that's what he should've been doing too. Waiting for the go-ahead from the doctors that everything was okay.

But he couldn't. He was too excited.

So, he'd done little things. Nothing too crazy. He'd put up a wipe-off board in the kitchen, where they could write potential baby names they liked. He'd started to clean out the spare bedroom, which they used for storage. He paid more attention to ads for things like dance studios and baseball leagues and summer camps in the area, even clipping out a couple he'd seen in the free newspaper they got on Wednesdays. Just for future reference.

But Kylie? She hadn't mentioned any of that. When he'd

mentioned doing an announcement or gender reveal via the Facebook she loved so much or some crazy YouTube stunt to let all the family know they were expecting, Kylie, who'd normally be all in to that, just shrugged and said, "We'll see."

It was a strange thing, considering Kylie was usually the fly-by-the-seat-of-her-pants kind of person. She usually threw caution to the wind and followed her heart with little concern for her safety.

Now, though, she had someone else's safety to think about.

Maybe this new caution was a good thing. It was good that she was finally starting to live a little more in his world, where what-ifs dominated and anything could go wrong.

As promised, he stopped at KFC on the way back up to the house, getting a bucket of chicken and the fixings. He hoped she hadn't been serious about eating it all herself, but just in case, he ordered a few extra drumsticks.

Before he went up the drive, he stopped at the mailbox and unloaded its contents. Among the piles of wedding planning postcards and brochures—why were they still getting those?—he noticed a handwritten card with a familiar Asheville address and tore it open. It was the invitation to Faith and Jacob's engagement party, at one of Jacob's casual barbecue places, though the invitation was printed in a flowy script that was probably the more formal Faith's idea.

He had to laugh. The differences were what made it interesting. Good thing they were compromising.

Pulling the truck farther up the drive, he stopped in his normal spot in front of the barn and let the puppies free to do their bidding in the fenced-in yard. Yipping happily, they headed off in all directions like a stack of Pick-up Sticks.

Shaking his head, he took the pile of mail and climbed the stairs. He pushed open the door and looked around.

No Kylie. Good.

"Kylie?" he called up the stairs. "I'm home."

"Hey, honey," she called back. "I'm just up here…skydiving."

"Ha, ha," he said, scanning the room as he put his truck keys on the hook. "Got your chicken."

"Thank you. I'm starving."

He walked to the kitchen and started the coffee maker, looking up at the room's one new addition—the board where he'd told Kylie they could write name ideas, so that when the time came, they'd know. They'd talked it over and decided not to find out the sex of the babies, so they had both boy and girl names in mind.

He'd put on a total of five names, two of which had special meaning to him. His grandfather's name, Gavin, and his grandmother's name, Margaret. Other than that, he'd jotted down nice-sounding names he'd heard, since now, any time anyone was introduced to him, he ran over the name in his mind for its potential. But lately, he'd been putting names down just to see if it would get her attention.

Granted, she wasn't down here very often. But he did bring her down once or twice a day to sit out on the porch or to eat dinner in front of the fire. She hadn't remarked on his choices of Aravis or Corin from one of his favorite books growing up, C.S. Lewis's *The Horse and His Boy.* Neither had she added any of her own to the mix.

He poured himself the coffee before yelling, "Anything special I can bring you up there?"

"A million dollars."

He grinned. "Want to come down and eat on the porch? It's nice outside."

"You mean I can have my freedom, master?"

As he was climbing the stairs, though, he noticed it. The filing cabinet was open a sliver, and a corner of one file was sticking out. Things like that drove him batshit. He couldn't let it go.

With a groan, he went over, opened the drawer, and started to right it before curiosity got the better of him. He pulled the file out and read the tab. Hanson, a name which meant nothing to him, and the folder was a bit older, which made him think it wasn't a recent case. He also realized it was a part of the "unsolved cases" section of the cabinet.

He opened it up and found himself staring into the face of a tiny naked baby, crying in a hospital bassinette, a photo which must've been taken only moments after it had been born. Underneath the photo was written *Jewel Marie Hanson, 12-1-07.*

He paged through to a police report and found that Jewel Marie Hanson was born to an unwed, poor woman named April Hanson from Sylva, North Carolina, and that the baby had disappeared too. The police probably never put much work into finding the baby since April Hanson had admitted to being strung out on drugs and couldn't remember what happened.

It appeared that, years later, she'd contacted Greg Starr for help, but by then, Greg hadn't been able to do much. Originally, April had thought the father might have taken the baby, but when Greg tracked him down in Mexico, he admitted he never saw the kid. The file showed that after that, Greg had contacted various possible witnesses in the apartment building where April lived, but most hadn't seen anything. There was one who thought he saw a well-dressed, elderly blonde women leaving the place with the baby, but he, too, was a heavy drug user.

Closing the file, Linc replaced it in the filing cabinet and looked up the stairs. No doubt about it. She'd been down here. And she was still researching the Kirby case.

He took a couple of calming breaths. It was all right. The

doc had said she could get "light exercise," which probably meant going up and down stairs, but he hadn't wanted to take any chances, insisting that "bed rest" meant just that.

And the Kirby case? Well, what damage could she do from here?

At least, he hoped.

He decided not to mention it as he climbed the stairs. When he got there, she was sitting up in bed, staring at her phone. She looked a little flushed. He hoped that didn't mean she'd run all the way upstairs when she heard him coming. "All good?"

She yawned so wide he could see her tonsils. "Just bored."

He noticed that the front window was open a little, the gauzy curtain pushed all the way back despite the hot sun streaming in. He waved a hand in front of his face. "Hot in here." Then he noticed she had put on a little lip gloss and brushed her hair. "Were you waiting for someone to come?"

She bobbed her eyebrows at him. "Yes, my lover," she deadpanned. "We were going to have some really hot, non-doctor-approved sex." Then she grinned, tossing a pillow in his direction. "No, I was waiting for *you* and my chicken, Dumbo."

Damned she was adorable when she was sarcastic.

"Okay." Enough with the suspicion. He easily lifted her up into his arms as she cradled her laptop and cell phone on her stomach, and he carried her down the stairs, sitting her on the big porch swing outside. "This good?"

She rubbed her hands together as he set the bucket of KFC next to her. "Thank you."

"There's mashed potatoes, coleslaw, biscuits, and of course, lots and lots of fried chicken. Lemonade?"

She smiled, licking her lips as she peeked into the bucket. "Yes, please. Thank you very much."

He went and poured her a glass, and when he returned,

she was hugging the bucket of KFC to her chest, devouring a drumstick like it was her first meal in days. As she ripped the crispy coating off, she made noises of gratitude. "Dis is guh," she said, absently checking her phone.

So, maybe she had been serious about all that chicken being for her.

He grabbed the bag and pulled out the extra drumsticks and the coleslaw, which he knew Kylie never ate. He'd deal. "We got the invitation to Jacob and Faith's engagement party," he said, passing it over to her.

She looked at it and sighed. "It's only two weeks from now. I guess you'll be going alone? I can't go like this." She licked her lips. "Mmm. And it's a barbecue. Talk about cruel and unusual."

"I can bring you back a plate. Or...two, even."

"Three. Since there's three of me." She nodded and took another bite, patting her stomach. "It's crazy. I'm ravenous like, all the time. Well, when I'm not puking."

"The doctor said that's a good thing. You were losing weight before, with the morning sickness, so you need to put on weight now." He shrugged, tearing into his own drumstick as he watched her check her phone again. This was the third time since he put her out here five minutes ago. "Expecting a call?"

She tucked the phone under her thigh. "Oh. Yeah. Just waiting for some business stuff."

"Business stuff?"

"All right, all right. I was expecting Allison Simmons to get in contact with me. She said she would. But she hasn't."

"Allison...oh." He scowled at his drumstick. "Is this because I wasn't working fast enough for your liking?"

Kylie picked at her chicken, pulling off a piece of the extra crispy crust. "I'm sorry. The woman clearly had a story to tell regarding the baby she lost. She's eager to get it out. She even agreed to come meet me here."

Linc scratched the side of his jaw. "She's going to come here?"

Kylie nodded, observing his face. He hadn't said anything, but his expression must've done some weird, completely involuntary contortion because she sighed. "Don't give me that. You were dragging your feet because you're not comfortable with it."

"It's not that. I—"

"Yes, it was. Admit it."

All right, it was.

It was one of those things he would've gotten to eventually, but so many other tasks were competing for his attention. He conceded the point with a shrug. "Okay. I hate doing that shit. So…you're still looking into this case?"

Her face transformed into a half scowl, half pout. "Barely, but I want to try."

"And I guess that was you, going through the Hanson file downstairs?"

Her guilty expression gave her away before she admitted the truth. "Yes. Fine." The word was more like a growl. "I should've known you'd find out. Did you install motion sensors I wasn't aware of?"

He bobbed his eyebrows in a *maybe* gesture before admitting, "No, but you're a slob. You left the cabinet partway open."

"The horror." She tossed a chicken bone back in the bucket. "Okay. Greg told me about an old case that sounded similar, so I was just looking into it. I swear, I took it easy. I just went down…very, very slowly…and right back up again."

She was starting to sound a lot like Rapunzel, locked in her tower.

"I'm probably going overboard with the safety stuff," he

admitted, "but I know you're just as concerned about the babies as I am."

She placed a hand on her stomach, a small smile playing at her lips. "I am, but I'm even more worried that my being nervous about it is going to make it worse. They tell me to relax, but how can I relax when I know that I'm solely responsible for whether these kids make it? It's a lot of pressure."

But even as she was speaking, her eyes drifted down to her phone.

"So, this woman blew you off?" he asked her.

"Unfortunately. Which is so weird because she really seemed like she wanted to talk. I mean, she volunteered to come all the way up here."

"You think her case and the case of Elise Kirby are connected?"

She blew out a breath that made her lips flutter. "Well... here's the interesting thing. I did find a little bit of a connection. It's a thread. Not even a thread. A strand. Maybe not even that. But I have a description from Agnes Mott of the 'aunt' who took the baby."

Linc held up a finger. "An elderly blonde woman who smelled like perfume and had claw-like nails."

Kylie gave him an impressed look. "Exactly. And just now, reading the file on the Hanson case, one of the witnesses mentioned a similar elderly blonde woman. Coincidence?"

Linc rubbed his jaw. "Could be."

"So, I was really hoping Allison might be able to add to that. I'm wondering if she or anyone else she knew might have been aware of such a woman."

Kylie's eyes were all lit up, the way they only got when she was working on a juicy case. He shouldn't have expected her to be happy knitting booties all day. He should've known she'd be miserable, not using her newly honed detecting skills.

He stabbed a spork into his coleslaw. "Interesting."

"I know. And here's the really weird thing. A few weeks ago, when I went to one of the adoption agencies, I actually met a woman who fits Agnes's description of the aunt almost to the letter, right down to the claws and the perfume. She's the *director* of the agency."

He took this all in, staring at his wife. "Seriously?"

Kylie nodded.

"So, if you met her, she knows you're investigating," he went on, a sick feeling growing in his stomach.

Kylie waved a drumstick at him. "Relax. She doesn't. I told her I was pregnant and simply looking for options for my pregnancy. That was all."

He eyed her doubtfully. She'd told him to relax before, and that was usually when the floor dropped out. "I wasn't saying anything."

"You were looking constipated," she said as she dug into the new piece of chicken, smacking his foot with her own. "And that says it all. But I'm fine. I'm up here in the middle of nowhere with a slew of dogs to protect me."

It wouldn't be the first time Kylie brought danger home. He thought of Storm and her career-ending injury. How he'd almost lost his beloved furry friend down in Georgia.

He mentally shuddered. "That sounds like the beginning of a horror movie, you know."

21

Kylie sat in bed, stroking Vader's fur while listening to her mother blabber on about the weekly gossip and her eternal bliss with her new husband.

They'd already been on the phone for two hours, and Kylie had no intention of shutting her mother up. Kylie was a social being. She needed to socialize, something Linc didn't fully understand. It was like fuel for her body.

She was happy her mother had found true love with the handsome and charming Dr. Jerry, who treated Rhonda Hatfield Phillips like a princess. After all, Rhonda hadn't had the best luck when it came to men.

Kylie's own dad had been a definite dud who'd left them when Kylie was only days old, and Rhonda had rarely dated until she met Jerry, quite literally by accident.

Rhonda's wedding to Kylie's father had been a boring justice of the peace kind of deal. Jerry's first wife had passed away, so he'd done all the frills before, but understanding that Rhonda had never had the fairy-tale wedding, he had been more than happy to make his second wife-to-be's every dream come true. He'd rented The Venue, one of downtown Asheville's most expensive wedding spots, for the event.

They'd gotten married in March, and Rhonda had been floating on a cloud since then.

To Kylie's surprise, Faith had enlisted Kylie's mother to help decorate for her upcoming wedding to Jacob. Rhonda was in decorating heaven and was already talking about opening up her own decorating business.

Kylie was happy for her.

"And you're going to die when you see the centerpieces," Rhonda went on. "Simply die! They're marble and glass and probably the most beautiful thing I've ever seen. And the spray of irises? Divine!"

"Sounds nice, Mom," Kylie said, forcing warmth into her voice. "Can't wait to see."

"You're going to love it. Now…about getting you a brides-maid dress."

"Oh, right. Sale at Macy's."

Or Mother's Warehouse.

"Oh, honey, that was weeks ago, and you missed it," Rhonda said with a tsking tone. "I'm sure there will be another sale, or you can shop online, if you want. I've had luck with buying a bunch of sizes and returning everything I don't like."

Kylie lifted up her knees and highlighted another name on Jacob's list. A woman in Knoxville, Tennessee, which wasn't too far away. She'd put in a couple calls to her before, but they'd gone unanswered. She'd try to contact her again later.

"Oooh. I just found a new ad for Macy's. Summer clearance this weekend. You need a dress, sweetheart. It is really nice of Faith to let you choose the perfect one."

"Eh," Kylie muttered. Right about now, she had to start loading up on maternity clothes. Plus, money was tight, and she was nervous about what she'd find when she did the next round of Coulter Confidential financials. "I have a little black dress I could wear."

Her mother sounded less than thrilled at that option. "So, you're going to look like you're attending a funeral. Is that it?"

"No," Kylie insisted, even though she did feel a certain amount of dread about the occasion. She loved weddings. Normally, she'd have been so excited about this, but she had to think about the babies. And though the wedding was technically well after her first trimester, and she should be fine by then, she couldn't guarantee it. She was already missing Faith and Jacob's engagement party. What if she was kept on bed rest for the rest of the pregnancy? "I'm just not really in the mood for shopping."

"What happened to you? You used to be so excited to shop. But then, getting your wedding dress was like pulling teeth. And now?" She tutted. "Busy with the job, is that it?"

"Yeah. And I'm gaining weight."

"That's because that husband of yours is an excellent cook. Those short ribs are divine."

"Yes, and other things..." she admitted, then stopped herself before she just blurted it out.

The secret was burning a hole in her soul.

"Well, I'm losing weight. I've been doing a nutrition shake I saw advertised on the internet. I've lost twelve pounds since April. Maybe you should—"

"No. Probably not."

"Really, honey. You don't seem as excited about the wedding as I'd hoped. Are you sure you want to be a bridesmaid? I'm sure Faith would understand if you bowed out. After all, she'd only want women who were supportive in that role."

Kylie felt the slap of the words and promised to do better.

"I'm just tired. Sorry for not sounded overly excited."

"Then…what is going on? Don't try to fool your mother. I can tell something's up. Is it because your wedding's over? Are you feeling let down? I read in a magazine that that's a very real condition. It's called the Post-Wedding Blues. Maybe you need an antidepressant."

Kylie pressed the heel of her hand into her eye. "No, Mom, that's not it. I love Linc. I love my job. I love everything. Love is in the freaking air up here. And I most definitely do *not* feel bad that my wedding's over." How could her mother suggest such a thing? And an antidepressant? Well… that actually didn't sound like such a bad idea.

Kylie shook her head and rubbed her belly.

"All right, then…what is it?" Rhonda prodded, and Kylie felt she was at that hopeless moment of the conversation where her mother would not stop until she got her answer.

She took a deep breath and blurted, "I'm pregnant."

There was a pause.

Then it was like the eruption of a very large volcano. "What? Oh my gooooodnesssss!"

"Mom…calm down," Kylie attempted, but her voice was drowned out by hysterical wailing on the other end of the phone.

"When did this happen? How did this happen?! I thought you were going to wait! You told me! OH MY GOD! Are you serious? Oh my GOSH! KYLIE! Oh…I need air."

Alarmed, Kylie sat up. "Mom? Are you okay?"

"Yes. Fine. Just threw open a window." Great. Now all of downtown Asheville would know the news. "Are you serious? You two must come over here to celebrate!"

"Yes, but Mom," she said carefully, flattening the sheet over her stomach. "I'm early still, and I was just in the hospital because I nearly had a miscarriage. That's why I haven't been down to see you. I'm on bed rest."

Another pause. This one longer.

"Are you okay, honey?"

"Yes. I just have to take it easy for a few weeks."

Kylie could feel the relief in her mother's voice. "We can bring the party to you. Wait until I tell Jerry. He'll be thrilled!"

"Mom, I'm not telling anyone. At least not until I'm out of the woods. You're the only one we've told." She wasn't going to bring up telling Greg because that would open up a whole can of worms—why she'd told her boss before she told the dear mother "who'd sacrificed everything to bring her into the world."

"Oh. Oh my goodness." Another long pause. "I still need air. I'm going to be a grandmother."

"Breathe, Mom. You sure you're going to be fine?"

"Kylie…you just made my day! Be sure to rest well. Take your prenatals. Don't overexert yourself. And for goodness' sake, don't take on any dangerous jobs!"

She stifled a moan. The last thing she needed was another Linc on her case. "Mom, I've got it covered."

"Well, I'm still coming over there. Let me bring you lunch. How does that sound?"

"Not today, but tomorrow would be great."

"All right. It's a date," she said excitedly. "Right now, I'm going shopping! To the baby store!"

As much as she loved the enthusiasm, she was uneasy that planning too ahead would jinx things. "Mom, um—"

"What is it? Do you know? A boy or a girl?"

"I don't know yet. But, Mom…" She took a deep breath. "Are you sitting down?"

"Why?"

"Because I'm not sure how you're going to take this after this last bit of news, and I don't want you passing out from lack of oxygen."

"What, there's more? Is the baby the mailman's or something?"

Kylie sighed. Was her own mother seriously insinuating that she'd cheat on Linc? "No...but it's not *a* baby."

"Wh-what?" Rhonda sputtered. "What does that even mean? Are you have an...*alien*?"

Kylie laughed. "No. It's *babies*. Plural. Twins."

This time, when her mother screamed, Kylie knew all of downtown Hatfield had to have heard it. Rhonda Hatfield Phillips, a more effective and less expensive form of announcement than Hallmark.

22

The following Saturday, Linc hesitated in the doorway of the farmhouse, wearing his best polo shirt and shorts. He had the card for his friends with a gift card to their favorite restaurant, a bottle of wine as a gift, and a whole boatload of reservations.

"I don't have to go," he said to Kylie as she lay on the couch, deeply engrossed in an episode of *Stranger Things.*

"Hmm-mmm," she said, popping a piece of popcorn into her mouth. "Have fun."

She clearly wasn't listening.

He pressed his lips together before grabbing the remote, pausing the show. "Did you hear what I said?"

"I did. And I also want to see what happens to Steve right now. He's in a crisis," she said, waving a hand at the television. "I think the Demogorgon wants his blood."

Linc didn't move. "I have no freaking idea what you're talking about."

Kylie sighed a sigh of the eternally damned. "Go to the party, and don't worry. I'm fine. The only danger I'm in is that of killing myself from boredom."

"Do you have enough to do?"

"I have enough Netflix to watch," she murmured, patting her laptop. "And I might just do some work if I feel like it."

"Don't tire yourself out."

"I won't. I have to do last month's financials. I've been putting them off."

"What about the dogs?"

"They probably can't help me much. Their paws are too big to get the right buttons on the calculator."

He tilted his head at her. "Did your pregnancy make you funnier and more sarcastic, or is it just me?"

She grinned. The dogs were usually trouble, but in anticipation of his being away, Linc had taken them on his favorite hike through the mountains, which happened to be nearly sixteen miles of hellishness.

Kylie had attempted it once, in the earlier days of their relationship when she was eager to show him what a "good sport" she could be and...never again. She'd had blisters for a month. Right now, the dogs were feeling it too, because they were lying together, a pile of snoring fur.

"I think I'm good. If they get restless, I'll just let them run in the yard. I can handle that."

He knew she could. He was actually more worried for himself than for her, for once.

Parties. He hated these damn things.

Get-togethers of any kind usually gave him hives, and it'd been a hell of a long time since he'd gone to one without Kylie by his side. Kylie was like his suit of armor, the added bit of protection that made him feel safe. She excelled at small talk and didn't do awkward silences.

Which was directly opposite of Linc's *modus operandi* at these things—grabbing a beer and melting into the wallpaper. Counting the moments until the end of the night.

Even though Jacob was his best friend and he knew every

person who'd be in attendance, it would still be awkward. Add to that that he and Faith had once, while they were in law school, seriously considered marriage themselves… Well, all he wanted to do was put in his couple of hours and then do his typical Irish Goodbye and beg off for the night.

"All right, then," he said, handing her the remote and petting the very few dogs who seemed to care that he was leaving. "I guess I'll be going."

She hit the play button and mumbled, "Have a great time. Don't forget the barbecue. Bring me a plate. A big one. And…limes."

"Limes?"

"I really just want a lime. To suck on."

He laughed. She had a one-track mind for food that was quickly becoming an obsession. Yesterday, he'd brought home a carton of chocolate chip cookie dough ice cream, only to find the whole thing gone by the afternoon. And that night, to his horror, he'd caught her eating Cheetos, but dipping them in strawberry yogurt.

"It's a good thing you're pregnant," he'd said to her as she polished off the entire bag and licked her fingers. "Or else I'd think there was something seriously wrong with you."

Outside, the sun was still bright, but the late summer days were starting to shorten. Even so, it was balls hot. He'd taken a shower right before, but his back felt sticky with sweat as he slid into his truck and headed out.

He pulled into a packed parking lot of the Rusty Nail and barely found a space. The place wasn't any classier than when he and Jacob used to hang out there in college. Linc wasn't sure how Jacob had managed to convince Faith to go for a place like the Rusty Nail, since this definitely wasn't her style. She must really love him, he decided as he went inside.

"Well, look who's here," Jacob greeted him the second he walked in, clapping him on the back and simultaneously shaking his hand. "The best man makes an appearance. Where's Kylie?"

"Ah. She's home. She wasn't feeling well."

Jacob snapped his fingers. "Dammit. Are you sure everything's okay with you two? Because I've seen her maybe once since the wedding. She isn't driving you so crazy that you have her tied up in the barn?"

He shook his head, laughing, though if Kylie was here, she'd probably remark that he wasn't far off.

"Hey, Linc!" a blonde, statuesque woman shouted, parting the crowd. She was dressed to kill, as usual, in an elegant black sheath. Linc had to say that whatever she and Jacob were up to, it agreed with her. She'd looked a little run-down when she'd been working for the FBI up in New York, trying to bring down the mob ring Kylie's father had been involved in. But now, she looked great.

"Hi, Faith." She wrapped her arms around him and hugged him tight, kissing his cheek. She smelled like the Chanel she always used to spritz behind her ears while she got ready. Some women never went anywhere with lipstick, but Faith never went anywhere without scent.

She took his hand and squeezed it, and he felt the size of the engagement ring. Jacob had gone all out. "Can you believe it? Me, getting married?"

He dug his hands into the pockets of his shorts and shrugged. "Crazy."

It was especially crazy since the times he was away on his first overseas tour, he'd written to her while she was in her second year at law school, saying he wanted to marry her. And how did she respond? The standard Dear John letter.

They could laugh about it now, but it really did prove that things happened for a reason. If she'd have stuck with him, he never would've met Kylie.

Kylie, who, as crazy as she could sometimes be, was absolutely the right fit for him. As he listened to Faith going on about how Jacob had proposed, he thought of his wife. His wife, his babies, his family. He smiled contentedly. It didn't get much better than what he had.

Just then, a tall, thin waif of a woman hooked her arm through Faith's. Faith gasped in surprise, then threw her arms around the younger woman, immediately bursting into tears.

"You made it! I'm so glad."

They hugged some more, tears spilling down both women's faces. Faith turned to Linc. "Let me introduce you to my favorite cousin. Sky Stryker, meet Linc Coulter. Sky lives in upstate New York but has big plans to move to the Big Apple very soon."

Linc winced. He couldn't think of anything he'd want to do least.

They shook, and Linc liked Faith's cousin immediately. She exuded warmth. He knew Kylie would especially love her.

"It's so nice to finally meet you," Sky said with a bright smile. "I hope to meet your wife soon."

Linc raised an eyebrow. "Oh?"

Faith jumped in. "My dear cousin is a writer, and she especially loves to investigate true crime."

Linc immediately understood. "And you want to interview Kylie for one of your books?"

Sky nodded vigorously. "Yes. For such a young private investigator, she's handled some pretty hairy cases, and I'd love to get a glimpse inside of her mind, better understand what she was thinking at the time."

Linc snorted. "Good luck with that. But sure..." He dug into his wallet and gave the girl one of the Coulter Confidential business cards. "Ring her up. But warning, my wife has a gift of gab, so be sure to plan to stay all day."

Sky beamed at him. "I sure will."

After that, he made the rounds through the crowded restaurant, shaking hands with acquaintances, doing his best to keep up with small talk, which mostly involved how he was enjoying married life. Then, of course, there were the gentle ribs, when people remembered that he and Faith used to be an item. By the time he made it to the bar, he felt like he'd earned his beer.

Though it was probably Jacob's duty to circulate, he must've sensed Linc's unease, because he sat down on a stool beside him and made himself comfortable. "So, how did Kylie react to the news that I'm off the market?"

"Heartbroken," he deadpanned, drinking from his glass of draft beer. "I think that's probably why she's so sick."

"Yeah. I know. The whole female demographic of Asheville weeps tonight," he said. "She good with the bridesmaid thing?"

"Oh. Sure. She's in," he said. They'd talked about it and agreed that she would do her best to be there. "She's excited."

"But I'm telling you…Faith is going a little nuts with this wedding planning. She wants it to be a replica of Meghan and Harry's royal wedding…right down to the dress. I told her we should do a carnival theme. Like, have a Ferris wheel and shit."

Linc winced at the idea. "I think you should just let Faith have her way. It's good practice because you're going to be letting her have her way until death do you part. Trust me."

Jacob groaned and banged his head down on the bar slowly, deliberately. "Yeah? Fuck me. That's what I thought you'd say. My father said the same thing. Is it really that bad? Does marriage steal your entire soul?"

Linc shrugged. "You'll get used to not having a soul. Life's a lot less complicated that way, anyhow. Souls are overrated."

"Shit," Jacob moaned into his beer. "I'd better have one hell of a bachelor party, that's all I'm saying."

"Sure. We'll have chicks and guns and fire trucks and hookers and drugs and booze..." Linc said, quoting one of their favorite movies, *Bachelor Party.*

Jacob laughed. "Yeah, all the things that make life worth living."

Linc patted his best friend on the back. "Just so you know, I'm taking you golfing."

"Yeah. That'll be good." He seemed a little dejected, but then he cleared up. "So how's the new business venture going?"

"Oh, you know. It's going."

"Kylie still working on that Elise Kirby case?"

He nodded.

"Getting anywhere?"

He shook his head.

"Well, that reminds me." He reached into his pocket and pulled out a piece of paper, unfolding it. "This could help her. It's a new case of a missing baby. It's not my jurisdiction because it's from way down south, but it looks like something similar."

Linc studied it, both the similarities and the differences. It was a case down in Mississippi where a young, single mother had given birth, and her baby had died. The mother, Avery Boone, filed a police report because she hadn't gotten to see the baby before it was cremated without, she said, her consent. She was livid. She thought for sure that she had been the victim of malpractice because her baby had been perfect at its birth, and she blamed a male nurse for being suspicious, saying he'd messed with her IV twice, making her sick before her child went missing.

Hmm. Whether this case was connected to Elise or not,

Kylie would be interested. "Thanks man," he said, folding and pocketing the article.

"So, other than that, how are things with you two working together? You want to rip each other's hair out, or what?"

"Well…" He could grin about it now. Now, it was a lot better than it had been a few weeks ago. They were getting along great, now that all the stupid misconceptions and miscommunications were out of the way. "Kylie runs a tight ship. She wants things to go a certain way, and if they don't, she gets up in arms. She already has at least a dozen people on her shit list for not doing her bidding. Me included."

"Yeah? I'd hate to be on your wife's shit list. What did these poor unfortunate souls do?"

"A bunch of things. For example, this one woman was supposed to meet her a few days ago, but never did. Didn't call or text to say she'd be late, and when Kylie called her, she didn't answer. Kylie was pissed. And to be honest, more than a bit worried."

"Jesus," Jacob said on an exhalation of air.

"Yeah. Right now, Allison Simmons is number one on Kylie's shit list. But that's subject to change, and often." Linc looked at his friend, who had frozen with his pint glass almost touching his lips. "What's wrong?"

Very slowly, Jacob lowered the glass. "Did you say Allison Simmons?"

Linc nodded. "Yeah. Why? You know her? Ad exec, I think."

Jacob's face had grown ashen. "When were they supposed to meet? A couple of days ago?"

"Yeah. Why?"

He pulled out his phone and began to scroll. "Well, Allison Simmons, who is an ad exec from downtown Asheville, was struck by a hit-and-run driver a few days ago after leaving her office building in the middle of the day. She was killed."

Linc's eyes snapped to Jacob's. He had to make sure he wasn't joking. Not that Jacob would ever joke about something like this, but...hell. "Are you serious?"

"Very. We have closed caption video of the incident from the garage's security cameras and it looked pretty deliberate. We haven't been able to find the car, and all of the victim's co-workers said it was odd for her to leave in the middle of the day."

Dammit to hell, Linc thought. *Here we go again.*

"She was coming to the house to meet Kylie. It's related to the Elise Kirby case. She had a baby in the nineties that died, but from what I understand, the circumstances were suspicious and—"

"I know about that. The report was in her file. She'd actually made two reports. The last one, she thought she saw a kid who looked like her on the street. It was actually one of my first cases. I went all over the place looking for that kid. I think I was assigned it because my supervisors knew it was a wild goose chase. We had a valid death certificate for the kid, and at the time, it was thought Allison Simmons might be a little looney because she was on bipolar meds. You think it has something to do with that case?"

Linc stood up. "I don't know. If it does, and that woman was mowed down because someone didn't want her to talk to Kylie, then that means..."

Fuck.

"Calm down," Jacob said, grabbing his arm. "It might have been deliberate, but it doesn't mean that it has anything to do with Kylie."

Yeah, he knew that, and yet it didn't make him feel any better. Not with Kylie's track record of attracting trouble.

Sure, it could've been nothing.

A coincidence.

But coincidence or not, he didn't want Kylie alone. Especially if people surrounding this Kirby case were now dying.

Ripping his phone out of his pocket, he jabbed in a text to her.

It looked like he would have to make his Irish Goodbye a little earlier than he'd planned.

23

The creepy eighties synthesizer music blared, signaling the end of the last season.

Kylie switched off the television and stretched, then looked around the darkened house, lit only by moonlight streaming in through the open windows.

Damn, that *Stranger Things* sure was a good binge-watch.

It was a little freaky too.

She reached over and flipped on the light, startling some of the dogs. "Sorry, guys," she said, "but Momma's gotta work."

Also, and she hated to admit this, but the show had given her a big case of the willies. The Demogorgon...shiver. As excited as she'd been to get free of Linc the Hoverer and just spend some time in peace and quiet, she was a total wuss when it came to anything scary. Maybe she shouldn't have taken her friend's recommendation to watch that show? Maybe she should've watched some good ol' *Steel Magnolias* instead?

She switched on her laptop and tried to concentrate. She still hadn't touched those financials. She'd been afraid to because she didn't want to find out that they were in the red for yet another month.

Opening up the Excel spreadsheet, she began to work on a few of the entries when her eyes caught on Jacob's list on the coffee table beside her. A lot of the cases were so old that she couldn't find the people involved, but there were a few that were very good prospects. She checked her email and voicemail again, hoping to find some responses from the people she'd contacted.

But there was nothing.

Maybe it was a lost cause. Kylie understood why these parents wouldn't want to talk after all this time. They'd likely moved on and getting involved would only open up old wounds. Allison had been one of the few local cases from the list who'd been eager to discuss her story with Kylie, but she must have backed out at the last minute. Kylie had called and texted her numerous times since the missed appointment, but she'd gotten no response.

Lifting up the list, she looked at another case that was in Southern Virginia. Well, it wasn't *that* far away, and it'd happened only a few years ago. She could broaden her search. Maybe that would help.

Closing down the Excel file, she opened up a search for a mother named Uma Ness, finding her email. She fired off a message to the woman, telling her she was looking into a possible child laundering ring, and asked to talk via phone briefly to answer a few questions.

Then she put away the list and fished out the information she'd collected on the Hanson case, Greg's old case. It wasn't much. She'd discovered the one witness who'd described the older blonde woman making off with the baby, had died three years ago from a drug overdose.

So…another dead end.

She shoved it away and opened up the spreadsheet again. Financials. She had to get them done.

She was about halfway through the long list of accounts, going back and forth between the billing files and her spreadsheet, when her phone buzzed. What she thought would be a text from Linc, asking if she was surviving, ended up being a call from Elise.

She answered right away. "Hey, Elise. It's so good to hear from you! I've been meaning to call you."

"Have you?" she asked in her slow, lilting voice. "Did you find any new stuff about my case?"

Kylie sighed. "Well, not as much as I'd have hoped, honestly. It's been a little crazy here. I've learned that I'm pregnant."

Shit! She hadn't meant to blurt that out. This woman had lost her baby, and now Kylie was bragging about having one…two…of her own. She wanted to slap her own face.

Elise didn't seem affected. "Oh…you are? Congratulations!"

"Thank you, but I'm only telling you that because I've been put on bed rest after a miscarriage scare. I promise, though, that I'm trying to work through as much as I can from my home base. I'm having a hard time racking up witnesses and other people who've lost their babies that are willing to share their stories. But I'm trying."

"Yeah. Oh. Okay," Elise said. "Thanks for tryin', Kylie. It means a lot."

"Not a problem." As she smiled, she heard a loud cracking noise somewhere upstairs. Just the house settling, probably, but it nearly made her jump to the sky.

Chill out, dumbass. You're acting like you've never been alone before!

She tried to remind herself that, pre-Linc, she'd happily lived alone in an apartment on the UNC-Asheville campus and never had been quite so jumpy. Maybe it was her history. Or maybe she'd just gotten used to depending on Linc.

"Oh, which reminds me. I wanted to ask you. When you first found out you were pregnant and were looking into your options, did you visit any clinics, Planned Parenthood, counselors…anything like that?"

"Well…yeah. I visited one, I think. My friend took me. Somewhere downtown, I think. An adoption agency. But that was before I decided I wanted to keep Daisy."

The hair on the back of Kylie's neck stirred, her spidey senses going to work.

"Okay, this is important. Do you remember the name of the agency?"

"Ummm…" She was quiet for a long time. "No. Darn it. I can't."

Kylie closed her eyes but forced her voice to remain calm. "That's okay."

It was probably Children's Hope, which was closest to her house.

It didn't prove anything, just that if Elise had filled out any paperwork, there would be a record that she was pregnant. People would have known about the baby, and that she was having second thoughts on it, she was scared, and she was poor. She really was the perfect target for this kind of thing.

"How's Britt?"

"He's so cute!" Elise squealed like a child. "I really love him. Tell your husband that Cody and I took him to the vet. He got his shots. Didn't like them one bit. But no one likes shots, I guess."

"That's great, Elise," Kylie said. She still got the feeling Linc was a little sore over losing the puppy. At least she could report to him that Britt was being well taken care of.

"Tell your husband thanks for lettin' us have him."

"I will. We're both glad you're enjoying him and that he has such wonderful parents."

Elise giggled, making Kylie smile. "Yes, we do treat him like he's our baby. Cody cuddles him more than he cuddles me now. I'm gettin' to be the jealous one."

"Aw, I'm sorry. That's too bad," Kylie said with a laugh. "Well, I'll be sure to keep you updated on any developments. And if you do think—"

"I meant to talk to you about somethin' else," Elise broke in, speaking more quickly than usual. "Somethin' a little weird."

"Okay..."

"A couple weeks ago, a man came into the diner. He was kind of old, nothin' much to look at, like a million other guys I wait on. They try to flirt with me all the time, and I'm just my normal nice self."

"What happened?" Kylie prompted.

"Well, I never seen this guy before, but he was nice. Flirty like. Ordered a lot of food and gimme a good tip. And then he was gone, and I thought nothin' of it."

"All right," Kylie said as Vader picked up his head and put it on her lap for a pet. She stroked his ears, the way he liked. "And...?"

"And well...a couple days ago, I got off a late shift. I was goin' to my car, and then I look up as I get inside, and there the same man is, just sittin' in his car, smokin' a cigarette. Watchin' me."

Kylie pressed her fingers to her lips, unsure what to think or how to react. Elise was pretty and not very bright...an easy target for all the asshole men of the world. Or...something sinister could be at play.

"You were all alone, at night, in the parking lot?"

"Yeah. The lights and such ain't much good, either."

"Elise, listen to me. The next time something like that happens, you should call the police. When did this happen?"

"Well, that's the thing. It happened two days ago. And then it happened again, last night."

"Elise!"

"But I got smart last night. I asked Gary, our big, scary dishwasher, to walk me to my car. Guy in the car took one look at him and sped away right quick like."

Kylie shook her head. Poor Elise was probably so discouraged by the last case she'd contacted the police about, she didn't trust them. "I know you might not trust the police now, Elise, but really, the next time you see that man, you contact them. I'm a private investigator, and I'm just as well equipped to handle that as you are. Meaning that I'm not. You're lucky he didn't follow you home. You always make sure you have someone with you, do you hear me?"

Geez. She was already sounding like a mother.

"Yeah. Okay. Thanks, Kylie. I am really happy for you. And that baby of yours."

Kylie smiled. Well, she'd already spilled one secret. Might as well spill the other. "It's two, actually."

"Twins. Oh. That's so nice, Kylie. You'll make a good momma. Your house will be so full of love. All those puppies and two sweet babies."

Well, that was the plan. A madhouse, and yet a wonderful, loving, happy one.

Kylie wished Elise good night and ended the call, wondering if it was the pregnancy hormones that had her slipping into a maternal role with the young woman. Elise wasn't much younger than she was, but Kylie felt so protective of her. Only a few short years ago, Kylie hadn't thought she had a nurturing, motherly bone in her body.

She went back to finishing up the financials, and a few

minutes later, she stared in disbelief at the bottom line of the spreadsheet.

They were thirty whole dollars in the *black*.

Kylie's mouth dropped open, and she started to do some wild sofa dance, pumping her arms and getting as crazy as she could for a person on bed rest. As she did, her phone buzzed with an incoming call from Linc.

There it was, the expected check-in. Officer Linc Coulter, reporting. Oh-nine-hundred hours.

Grabbing it, she answered with a whoop. "Guess what? You'll never—"

"Kylie, listen to me," he demanded, talking over her. "I want you to go around and make sure all the windows and the doors of the house are locked."

It wasn't so much the concern in his voice than it was the fact that he actually wanted her to rise and be on her feet. As she stood, Vader and Storm looked around in concern, raising their heads from their respective dog beds. They could probably hear Linc's authoritative voice blasting through the speaker.

"Why? What's—"

"Do it, Kylie." He was gruff, barking. "Then sit tight. I'm coming home right now."

Talk about overkill. She hated to close out the heavenly mountain breeze that was blowing through the windows, rustling the curtains, and making everything delightfully cool and comfortable after such a stagnant day.

But all right.

"Are you sure you're just not using me as an excuse because you're sick of the social scene?"

"No, this is serious. Do as I say."

She closed the two windows behind her, then went to the door and sealed that too, turning both of the heavy-duty locks that Linc had installed despite the fact that they rarely ever got visitors up here. Then she went to the kitchen and closed the window over the sink. It immediately felt stuffy.

"All right. I did it, but I don't like it," she said, grabbing the smallest cannister on the counter. As long as she was up, she might as well make herself a cup of decaffeinated peach tea.

"Listen. That woman that you were supposed to meet? Allison? She's dead. She was mowed down by a hit-and-run driver right before she was supposed to come meet with you."

Kylie's breath caught in her throat. "What? Oh my god. Really? She's dead?"

"Yeah. They think it was deliberate."

Deliberate? Kylie thought of her conversation with Elise. What were the chances the man spying on Elise was the same one who'd gone after Allison?

That was ridiculous. Why would someone be after those people just because they were trying to tell their story?

Unless…unless they were getting too close to the truth. And if they were getting too close, it was only because Kylie, herself, was headed in the right direction.

She stood there, feeling dazed, holding the tea cannister in her hands. Suddenly, her stomach hurt.

"I'm coming home," Linc said quickly. "I'll be there in half an hour. Don't panic."

She snorted. Who was the one panicking?

"I'm fine. Just enjoy yourself, my love. And also, know that if you come home without my three plates of barbecue, you're a dead man."

"Kylie, I really should—"

"Stop."

"But—"

She tapped her toe on the floor. "Seriously. Stop. I'm okay, and you can't bail on your best friend's party."

"All right." He heaved out a long breath. "I'll only be gone a little while more."

"Great. I'd say for you to stay until you turn into a pumpkin, but I really want that barbecue." She hoped her attempt at humor would settle him.

"I know. Just be safe. Kylie, I don't know if this is the best…"

She opened the top of the tea kettle and started to fill it with water at the sink. "Come on, Linc. It's all good. The doors are locked. The windows are closed. I'm safe, and I promise you there is no one out on top of this mountain but me and this herd of Newshephardlands. So just relax and—"

Crack!

The window in front of her shattered, and she dropped the kettle and fell to the floor as shards of glass rained down upon her like a relentless hailstorm.

24

All Linc heard was the breaking of glass and Kylie's high-pitched shriek.

Then the phone went dead.

"Shit." He tried calling back but there was no answer.

He looked up at Jacob, who was eying him with concern. "What's up, man?"

Linc didn't say a word, just headed toward the door. The only thing on his mind was getting to his wife. "I don't know. There was screaming, and now the line's dead. I've got to get there."

Jacob grabbed his arm, hauling him to a stop. "What happened?"

In a blink, Faith was at Jacob's side, her cousin practically on her hip. "What's wrong?"

Linc yanked his arm away. "I've got to go. Something bad—"

Jacob pulled out his keys. "Come on, let's take my truck." He looked at his fiancée, giving her a sorry smile, but she waved him away.

Beside her, Sky said, "I'm going with you!"

Faith pulled at the girl's arm. "No, you're not."

"But—"

"No!"

They were still arguing as Linc slammed into the door with both hands and rushed out into the night. Jacob's truck was parked close to the entrance, and as he climbed into the passenger seat, Linc was glad to have his best friend at his side. His hands shook as he kept dialing Kylie's number as Jacob turned on the sirens and lights of the unmarked vehicle.

"Still not answering?" he asked as they slid around a curve.

"No. Right to voicemail. Fuck." Linc's breathing was out of control as he fisted his hands on his lap, willing the car to go faster. Jacob was already breaching ninety in a sixty, but even that didn't seem fast enough.

"Okay. Calm down, bro. What exactly was she saying to you?"

He let out a bitter, ironic laugh. "She was telling me what she always tells me. That I was overreacting and going overboard with concern." He raked his hands through his hair. "And then I heard the sound of glass breaking and shrieking and the dogs going crazy. Then it cut out."

"All right, well…" This was the part of the conversation where Jacob would offer some reasonable explanation. But there was no reasonable explanation for what he'd just heard. And why wasn't she answering her phone? "Just take it easy. She'll be okay."

But Jacob didn't know the half of it. It wasn't just Kylie he was worried about. "Kylie's pregnant," he said through gritted teeth.

Jacob glanced his way. "What? Are you serious, man?"

"She's on bed rest. That's why she couldn't come to the

engagement party. She's pregnant with twins, and she almost had a miscarriage, which is why my concern is in overdrive."

"Jesus. Well…now I guess that explains a lot of things," he said, upshifting. "Don't worry, man. We'll get there and they'll be all right. Storm and Vader are there too, aren't they?"

Linc nodded.

"They'll take care of her."

"Yeah," he muttered, knowing that Jacob was just trying to make him feel better.

Yeah, the dogs would stay with her. They'd comfort her if she was hurting. They'd even go after an asshole who attacked her. But there wasn't much more that they could do. If she was bleeding, they couldn't give her medical attention. She was in trouble. She needed him.

"Let me ask you. Do you think that whoever killed Allison might be after Kylie too?"

Jacob was quiet for a moment. "You think Kylie might be getting too close to something they don't want her to get close to?"

"Yeah."

"Could be. All the more reason for her to be careful. She should let us handle it."

Linc knew that. That's exactly what he'd told her, again and again. Let someone else handle it. But he knew Kylie too well. "Since when did she ever listen to that kind of reason?"

Jacob nodded. "Shit. Now that I think about that Allison woman, it's kind of sad. Yeah, she was on meds for her bipolar episodes, but there was something else about her. She was adamant that someone had taken her baby. We thought it was just trauma, and she was holding on to those last threads of hope. Even when we showed her the death certificate, she insisted that something sinister had happened. She called it a mother's intuition."

Linc leaned his head back against the headrest as the car barreled up the hill, lights flashing. Maybe Kylie was having that same intuition herself. "And…?"

"And well." He cursed a long string of foul words. "A police officer's life is full of regrets. If only I'd gotten there sooner. If only I'd known that that was going to happen." He shot another quick look at Linc. "Man, I don't want to be regretting this one."

Linc understood. If they'd taken Allison a little more seriously, the woman might not be dead. And maybe Kylie wouldn't be in trouble right now.

The tires squealed as Jacob took a hard turn into the farmhouse's gravel drive, nearly colliding with the mailbox. He surged up the hill, through the trees, until the farmhouse came in sight. The porch light was on, as well as another interior light, but all seemed just as he'd left it.

He threw off his seat belt and jumped out of the car before it even came to a full stop. Taking the stairs two at a time, he reached the door and tried to push it open. Finding it locked, he rummaged for the keys in his pockets and finally managed to explode inside to a chaos of dogs barking and crowding around him.

The first thing he saw was the glass shattered on the kitchen floor. Moving closer, he found her phone amidst the rubble near the sink. But no Kylie.

"Kylie!" he shouted as the dogs began barking again.

Storm approached him, giving him an urgent look.

He crouched down. "Where is she, girl?"

The German Shepherd whimpered and led him up the stairs. Wishing he had his gun, he climbed, following the dog, holding his breath the entire way. He was afraid of what he'd find. Storm stopped and planted herself in front of the bedroom door, wagging her tail.

Linc threw open the door and stepped inside, scanning the room for his wife. "Kylie?"

A second later, a pale hand peeked out from under the bed. "Did you find him?"

Find who? Unfortunately, Linc had been so focused on finding her that the sky could've been turning rainbow colors and he wouldn't have noticed.

"No, but you're safe. I'm here. You can come out now." He crouched down and she crawled out from under there, her face red, her hair crackling with static. When she looked up, a vacant expression on her face, he noticed the blood. "What happened?"

"Someone…someone shot at me," she said. "Through the window. Just like you said."

He shook his head as he piled her into his arms, taking her face into his hands. Other than the small, bloody scratches on her face which must've been from the glass, she looked all right. Stunned, but it could've been so much worse. "I didn't know this would happen."

"But you did," she said, her voice breathy and faraway. "You warned me, and as usual, you were right."

He hugged her to his broad chest. "But you're all right? Nothing hurts?"

"No. I guess I'm fine. I was just making tea. When the window shattered, I was so scared that I ran upstairs and hid under the bed." She tucked a renegade strand of hair behind her ear and flinched a moment later when Jacob came rushing into the room.

"Everything okay?"

Linc nodded. "Someone shot out the kitchen window, I think."

Jacob nodded. "I just came from out there. Saw a bunch of cigarette butts but that's about it. Whoever he was, he's gone now."

"He's probably the same person who's been following Elise."

"Wait." Linc closed his eyes. "Someone's been following Elise? Why didn't you tell me?"

"I just found out about it tonight. She told me some man's been hanging outside the diner, watching her."

Linc glanced at Jacob, who was already on his phone. He lifted his mouth from the receiver and said, "We're looking into it."

Linc helped Kylie to her feet and sat her down on the bed. Her skin was covered in perspiration and she was still trembling. "Just lay here and relax, all right?"

She glanced at the open windows. "Can you close those?"

He went over to them, slid them shut, and closed the curtains tight. "Better?"

She nodded.

He kissed her forehead. "I'm going to go talk to Jacob. I think if they're looking into it, that's good. But I think we need to reconsider your involvement in this case too."

She shook her head, gripping onto his pillow with white knuckles. "I don't need to reconsider anything. I'm calling Elise tomorrow and telling her I can't continue with the case," she said, her voice hollow.

He almost asked her to repeat herself. "Are you serious?"

"Yeah. It's not worth it."

He'd thought for sure they'd end up fighting on this point. He hadn't expected her to capitulate quite so easily. In fact, she hadn't even capitulated. It was like she'd laid down, dead. Like she'd given up completely.

That wasn't like Kylie. She wasn't one to turn her back on a case like this.

But then again, Kylie had never been pregnant before. And maybe now she saw that some risks really weren't worth the price.

25

Kylie made a little knot, snipped the threads, and set down her knitting needles, gazing at her creation proudly. "Yes...yes...yes," she said, turning it over in her hands.

Linc walked into the bedroom and gave her a look. "Hey. You going to get ready?"

"And you said it couldn't be done." She slammed her green yarn creation on the quilt in front of her. "BAM! Done!"

He picked it up and studied it. "First of all, I never said you couldn't do it. Second of all...impressive. That actually almost looks like something one would put on a baby's foot."

She lifted it and admired it some more. Sure, there were some missed stitches and weird knots all over the place, but it actually resembled a bootie now. She'd finally buckled down and made that *Knitting for Idiots* YouTuber her bitch. "I bet I can finish the match in another month. Then, two more to go. Then I bet I can do a blanket!"

He held up his hands. "Whoa. Aren't you getting ahead of yourself?"

She agreed, she probably was. A blanket was probably a big undertaking. But as dull as it had been, she'd eventually gotten into a kind of groove. The more she did it, the more relaxing she found it to be, especially since the stress could sometimes have things slipping her mind. When she knitted, she didn't really have to worry. She could just sit there and let her baby-brain wander and find her zen.

It'd been a month since the shooting. Since then, she'd totally forfeited all of her files and research over to Jacob and his men. Jacob had also put two officers at her house to guard her. She'd called Elise and apologized for leaving the case, but explained that, after what happened, she needed to take it easy. She'd tried not to pay attention to it, but she'd overheard Linc asking Jacob about it. Supposedly, the leads from the file went nowhere, and they were never able to find the man who stalked Elise, ran down Allison, or shot at Kylie.

And yes, sometimes Kylie felt bad. She'd had to have been close, or else she wouldn't have been in danger. She realized that the man had probably wanted to scare her into suspending her investigation, and she'd played right into his hands. But every time she got that urge to dig again, she reminded herself how close she'd been to getting shot. She'd almost had her babies killed, because of her snooping.

And she was determined not to ever put them in danger like that again.

Even though she was trying to take it easy, she did still have the business to think of, though she'd made a concentrated effort to decline anything that sounded too difficult. So, the majority of her work had been Impact Insurance surveillance.

It worked well while she was on bed rest. Linc would go out and assemble the footage, and Kylie would compile his chicken scratch into a legible report. They'd done so well that Impact had been praising them at their monthly check-in meetings and funneling them even more work.

Nice. Stable. Well-paying.

And yes, boring as hell.

But she'd learned to grin and bear it. After all, she'd finished her financials for the last month, and they'd actually turned a profit. Nothing that would allow them to buy a villa in France, but enough that she could actually think of starting a 529 for the kids' education. That was what mattered. The company was doing well, the babies were doing well, and Linc was happy she wasn't out killing herself.

"I can do it," she told him with a gleam in her eye. "I want to knit new blankets for both of them. I am going to be a knittin' fool."

He sat down on the edge of the bed, near her feet, and slipped on his hiking boots. "How about this? How about you get your ass up and get ready for your doctor appointment?"

"Right!"

She jumped out of bed. She was excited for this appointment. For the first time, Linc would be going with her, and he'd get a chance to meet the little nuggets. Plus, since she was now in her second trimester, she was hoping the doc would give her the green light to go off bed rest.

She was feeling much better too—more energetic, and the morning sickness had definitely tapered off. She'd read in the *What to Expect When You're Expecting* Linc had bought that this was the honeymoon trimester of pregnancy, and it definitely felt like one. She and Linc were getting along a lot better too.

After she showered, she put on her new maternity shorts. She didn't truly need them, but they were more comfortable on her slightly protruding belly. She topped that off with a flowy pink maternity blouse she'd ordered online.

With her new outfit, she felt officially pregnant.

Linc grinned when he saw her and patted her stomach. He kept telling her it was the cutest, sexiest thing. She was embracing pregnancy now, like he always wanted. Of course he was thrilled.

She was thrilled too.

As long as she didn't think too much about the things she was giving up, she was fine. This was good. Perfect. Better than ever.

They got into the truck and drove as Kylie went on and on, babbling about the last ultrasound and what they might be able to see this time. She read him a little passage from the baby book, telling him that the babies were the size of a peach and that they might be able to suck their thumbs. Linc listened, rapt.

"After we get the all-clear today, you think we can make the official announcement?" he asked.

"I just hope we get the all-clear. But if we do, yes," Kylie said. "I'll post it on Facebook."

Up until now, it'd been on a need-to-know basis. Most people who were close to them had already found out, so the announcement was really a formality. Linc's family was thrilled, but no one was more excited than Rhonda, who kept bringing gifts for the nursery over each week. The nursery was now more packed with stuff than it had been when it was a storage room.

"You know people are going to want to know the sex."

She looked at him. "Do you want to know?"

He shrugged. "Not unless you do. It doesn't matter to me."

"Yeah. That's the way I feel. Though it would be helpful with picking a name," she sighed. "You really think Corin is a contender? The first time I saw it, I thought it was Corn. I'm not going to name my baby after a vegetable."

"Well, it's Cor for short."

She wrinkled her nose. "I did like Aravis, if it's a girl. What do you think of a boy named Donovan?"

"Uh. No. I don't like Don for short."

"Hmm. Eric?"

He shook his head.

"Cole?"

"Nah."

She sighed. Naming ten puppies had been way easier than this. They'd just picked words out of thin air and assigned them to the pups randomly. "This might be awful. But what about Trey? When I was growing up, I had an imaginary boyfriend named Trey."

He shrugged. "Could work."

"Wow. That's the first name I suggested that you didn't shoot down completely. What's wrong with you today?"

He reached over and grabbed her hand, kissing her knuckles. "I'm just in a good mood. Also, I have a feeling they're girls, so I might as well not argue, because it won't matter."

She nudged him. "Oh, you're so funny. I actually think they're boys."

"Fine. If they're boys, we name them Trey and Donovan. If they're girls, Aravis and Maggie. Done."

She raised an eyebrow. "Maggie?"

"Short for Margaret. My grandmother. No?"

She rolled it over in her mind, then smiled. "Actually, I like it. Put it on the short list."

It was actually one of Kylie's favorite things about now— planning for the future of their babies, now that she felt they'd have a future. And the farther she stepped away from the hopelessness of never having a juicy case again, the more hopeful for the future she became.

But she also wondered…once the babies were born and all the excitement of becoming new parents died down, would she be able to handle working on those boring surveillance cases for the rest of her life. Or would she always be yearning for more?

She forced herself not to think about that. Negative thoughts were bad for the babies. And she needed to get off bed rest. As she rode in the passenger's seat, she crossed her fingers at her side and prayed that the docs would say everything was okay.

"What are you thinking?" he asked her suddenly, dipping his sunglasses.

She smiled and patted the little pooch under her seat belt. "Nothing. Why?"

"You just looked a little worried there for a moment. You thinking about whether the doc will give you a pass?"

"I'm not nervous," she said, looking out the window. It was more like *uncertainty*, not straight-up nervousness. "Everything's fine."

"You excited? If the doc clears you maybe you can start doing some fieldwork again."

She swung her head to look at him, eyes wide in surprise. "You'd be okay with that?"

"Yeah. Why wouldn't I?"

Oh, now she understood. He was talking about the surveillance cases. Those were pretty cut-and-dry. All they entailed was sitting in a car, taking photos of the subject whenever he or she left the house. He didn't mean cases like Elise's, or the Spotlight Killer's, or the real dangerous ones.

And truthfully, as much as she loved working those cases, she couldn't go back. Not now. She had her kids to think of. "I might take a few surveillance cases off your hands, but I think I need to concentrate on working from the house."

He gave her a doubtful look. "You're not serious."

"Yeah, I am." She met his look with one of her own. "We need to face the facts, Linc. Soon I'm going to have two babies here. And you're sure as hell not going to breastfeed them, are you?"

"No, but—"

"You were right. My job, first and foremost, is being a mom. Nothing else matters. I've got to think of them. They need me."

He didn't have time to argue. Right then, they pulled into the lot for Kylie's OB-GYN. What a difference it was from the last time she'd been there. This time, Kylie jumped out and proudly walked into the office, her head up high, with Linc on her arm.

She gave her name at reception but this time, as she looked around, she noticed quite a few single pregnant ladies, all sitting by themselves. They all seemed a lot braver than she had been.

Linc stood fidgeting in the middle of the room, like he wasn't sure if husbands were allowed to sit. Kylie grabbed his arm, took him to an empty pair of chairs, and handed him a copy of *Outdoors* magazine that she found in a rack.

Instead, Linc seemed mesmerized by a large poster on the wall, indicating the size of dilation. Kylie grimaced at how big ten centimeters was, grabbed a copy of *Allure,* and studied the Fall Fashion Guide, which included a number of lovely and fashionable pieces that Kylie sure as hell wouldn't be wearing that season. *And look. Skinny jeans are in this fall. Go me.*

She closed the magazine in a huff and stroked her belly.

Again, she reminded herself: Losing her figure, giving up the things she loved about her job, being confined to the bed for the next six months—all of it would be worthwhile, because it was for their babies.

It's all worth it, she told herself, looking up at that picture of the ten-centimeter dilation. *All worth it.*

The door to the offices opened, and a nurse came out. "Kylie? Come on back."

Linc hesitated, but she took his hand and led him with her. "Hi. This is my husband, Linc," she said, introducing him to the nurse as she took her blood pressure and weight. Kylie tried not to concentrate on the numbers, even though she was definitely heavier. Almost to the tune of ten pounds heavier. *It's all worth it.*

It was all the same as the last time, and Kylie felt so much more comfortable. "Now," the nurse said, reading over her file. "You've already had your initial ultrasound."

She nodded. "Yes, but my husband wasn't there for that. So this is the first one he gets to see."

The blonde nurse with the fair, ruddy complexion smiled at him. "You're in for a treat," she said, handing Kylie her gown. "You know the drill. The doctor will be in in a moment."

Kylie did as she'd done before, changing in the bathroom and providing her urine sample, then hopped up on the exam table. Linc shifted in his chair like a lost puppy, scanning everything as if he'd never been in a doctor's exam room before. "How long you been coming to this place?"

"Since my mom put me on birth control when I was sixteen," she said casually.

"Oh, yeah? Sixteen? And why did you do that?" He leaned forward, interested.

"Forget it. My periods were all over the place, so I used birth control to regulate them. The end." She grinned. "You were hoping for a hot and heavy story about my first boyfriend?"

He hitched a shoulder. "Not really."

"Good. Because there isn't one." That wasn't a lie. Kylie had always had a strong personality that frightened guys off, according to Rhonda. Even just a few years ago, she'd wondered if she would ever meet any guy who wouldn't be intimidated by her, let alone *the one.* Looking at her stomach now, it was hard to believe that was not so long ago. She felt like she'd known Linc forever. "Besides, what does any of that matter?"

"It doesn't. I have been wondering, though. If you were on birth control, how did you end up pregnant?"

It was a good question.

"In a word…antibiotics. Remember how we were supposed to use a secondary form of birth control after I got sick a few months ago?"

He stared at her blankly. "You were?"

Oops. Kylie scanned her brain. Had she even told him? God, was this all her fault?

As she was mentally berating herself, Linc shrugged, grinning. "Just because you're having kids doesn't mean you need to sacrifice any of what makes you, you."

Was he quoting her now? Was he making fun of her? She got the feeling that he would take the pregnancy in whatever way it had happened, like he'd been wanting kids a lot more than he'd let on.

Before she could ask about that, Dr. Ling came in, a big smile on her face. "That's true! Wise man!" She extended her hand for him to shake, and Kylie introduced them. "It's important not to lose our identities because of our kids. Sometimes we think we need to shut off a certain part of our lives to avoid hurting our children, but that's not the case."

Kylie's eyes narrowed. "What do you mean?"

"Well, a mother who quits her job to be a stay at home mother. There's nothing wrong with doing that, but some mothers are very fulfilled in their jobs and need to get out of the house. There's nothing wrong with not spending every waking moment with your child, and it might actually be good for them because when a mother's at her best, doing what she loves most, a child senses that."

"Oh," Kylie said.

"We were just discussing whether Kylie should return back to her regular job once she gets cleared off bed rest," Linc put in.

"Well, that depends. Do you love it?"

"I do, but it's kind of dangerous," she told the doctor. "And well, I guess I should first see if I'm cleared before I'm even worried about that."

"Right." The doctor snapped on a pair of gloves and sat on a chair, wheeling herself close to Kylie. She performed the exam, every once in a while nodding that everything was all right, and then it was time for the ultrasound. "Scoot on over here, Dad, so you can have a front row seat."

Linc stood up and moved to the other side of the table, scooping up Kylie's hand as the ultrasound tech squirted the warm gel on Kylie's stomach. Then, she gently put the paddle up against Kylie's abdomen, moving it along her side. Kylie squirmed a little, watching as the image slowly appeared. She gasped. "Is that…oh my gosh, they're so much bigger. They actually look like humans now."

Dr. Ling laughed and went through everything they were seeing. The babys' heads, an arm, a few feet, confirming that everything was on schedule and developing normally. No problems. Once that was determined, Kylie kept her eyes on Linc. He was completely rapt, and at one time she thought she saw him blink a tear out of his eye.

After Kylie had sat up and wiped the goo off her stomach, the doctor looked over her chart and smiled. "I think you should be able to go ahead and take yourself off bed rest. Light exercise. Not too much stress. There's no reason to believe you can't have a normal pregnancy from here on out."

Kylie and Linc smiled at each other. "Great," Kylie said. "That means I can go to my friend's wedding? Dance a little?"

Dr. Ling nodded. "Sure. When is it?"

"In about a month."

"That should be okay. Just like with everything, take it easy. Don't overdo it, and you should be fine."

Linc laughed. "No breakdancing."

Kylie snapped her fingers. "Darn."

He leaned over and whispered, "See? Everything's going to be great for them. I'm telling you."

She would do everything possible to make sure that everything was good for them. That was her job. But just how much of her identity would she have to give up in order to do that?

She didn't know.

And she didn't know if it mattered anymore, anyway.

She gazed at the ultrasound picture the tech handed her.

Bean One and Bean Two were certainly bigger. Growing stronger day by day.

Whatever I have to do, it's worth it.

26

Linc sat, dressed in his best suit, next to Kylie, at Rhonda and Jerry's six-month anniversary party. They'd gone all out and rented out an enormous, screened, outdoor gazebo. He kept pulling on his collar, wishing he could go home and shed his jacket and tie. The late September heat was unbearable.

"Is your suit all right?" Kylie asked him.

"I'm wearing it, so no." He hated wearing a suit. The last time he had was for Jacob and Faith's wedding, and before that, his own wedding, and he'd been so mesmerized by his wife at each event that the discomfort he felt hadn't registered in the least.

Kylie, though? Tonight, she was glistening. Glowing. She was wearing an older dress he'd seen on her before, but she looked simply stunning, with her long dark hair falling down her back. For the past few months, other than wearing a bridesmaid dress for Faith, she'd been wearing nothing but pajamas, her hair up in a ponytail, so he'd almost forgotten how magazine-cover gorgeous she could be.

She had the tiniest little round baby belly, and he couldn't stop wanting to pat it and caress it and the rest of her. And she was smiling, completely in her element, socializing with every person she came in contact with.

If the heat was bothering her, one wouldn't know it.

The only indication was when she fanned her face with her napkin and checked her phone. "It's hot, and I'm starving."

Linc laughed. At least some things never changed.

No sooner had she finished her sentence than piano music began to play, and waiters and waitresses came out carrying trays of food. They served the honored couple first, and Jerry looked at his bride the same way he'd looked at her on their wedding day.

Rhonda was smiling, looking just as in love. It seemed as though all the Hatfield women were glowing tonight, because Kylie's mother looked more beautiful than ever. She was wearing a pale pink lace dress, her blonde hair done up with loose tendrils that floated around her face as her husband of six months got up to make a toast.

"At my age, I have to take every opportunity to celebrate," he said, and the guests tittered at this explanation for the elaborate party, before he went on to describe how much he loved his wonderful wife.

Next to him, Kylie began to sob quietly. "Pregnancy hormones," she explained.

Linc took her hand. "It's all right. You don't have to explain. You go ahead and cry. It's nice to see your mom so happy."

"Can you believe it! Six months went by in a flash," Rhonda said after the meal was done, rubbing Kylie's tummy. "How are my grandkids?"

"They're good. Mom, you look as beautiful today as you did on your wedding day."

Her mother stood, gazing at Kylie's growing belly.

Kylie looked behind her at the guests. Rhonda had invited more people than Linc and Kylie had invited to their wedding; a *lot* more. In fact, Linc had no idea who most of these people were.

She shifted uncomfortably. "Uh. Mom? You should probably greet the other guests, don't you think?"

"Oh! Right!"

A million years later, Rhonda picked up a glass and tapped it with a spoon to get the attention of the guests. "If you don't mind," she said to everyone. "I'd like to take a few minutes to say a couple words."

Kylie leaned over to Linc and said, "She has never said just a couple words in her life."

Linc smiled. The same could be true of Kylie. Since the shooting ordeal, Kylie had gotten a little bit of that spirit back. She'd focused herself entirely on the babies, because that bullet that narrowly missed her was a wake-up call to her that she needed to.

But for the past few weeks, he'd been wondering if she had been going overboard. She was dutifully grinning and bearing all that boring surveillance work and background checks, but he could see the life go out of her eyes every time she sat down at the computer. He had to wonder whether once all the excitement of babies and weddings was over, she'd be left feeling unfulfilled? Would he and the babies be enough for her?

Rhonda said, "I would like to thank each one of you for coming to our anniversary party and making our second special day even more special. We're beyond happy that all of you could be here with us. Six months ago, I made my dreams come true by marrying the love of my life. Not only did I become a wife to the most wonderful man, I'm also going to become a grandmother next year, as my lovely daughter is expecting twins!"

Rhonda presented Kylie, who was sitting across the table, sipping water. She swallowed it in a gulp as everyone gasped and applauded for her. She nodded and mouthed the words, "Thank you," then looked at Linc and rolled her eyes. "Oh, my god. So embarrassing."

He laughed. It was probably just as embarrassing as when Linc's family took them out to his father's Asheville Legal Association's annual dinner at the country club last week. Linda, who adored her daughter-in law, couldn't stop touching Kylie's belly with great excitement. His father, who was chair of the ALA, had gotten up to give a speech to the lawyers present, and had somehow managed to squeeze in words about how his "lovely family members and family members-to-be were present." Then he'd gone on to say that his youngest son and daughter-in-law were expecting twins, garnering more applause than the rest of his, rather dull, speech.

Kylie had blushed but was absolutely pleased. Linc and his father had never seen eye to eye, and Jonathan Coulter had never been one to praise his son. That was about the closest he'd ever come to it.

When the speech ended, Kylie grabbed Linc's hand and led him to the dance floor. "Come on," she said. "I need to trip the light fantastic and shake off the embarrassment."

As they made their way around the tables, people stopped and congratulated them. At the dance floor, a slow song was playing. She wrapped her arms around his neck and said, "Figures. She tries to make an event that's supposed to be all about her, all about me, and of course, it's when I look like a sack full of potatoes. Lumps everywhere."

"You make a very attractive sack of potatoes," he said, nuzzling her ear. As he did, it was no longer her breasts pressing against his chest, but her belly against his lower abdomen. When her head fell to rest against him, he whispered, "You really do look beautiful."

She tightened her arms around him and sighed.

He wasn't sure if it was a sigh of contentment, or boredom.

"Are you happy?" he asked her.

She looked up at him. "Of course. Why?"

He shrugged. "Because I'm worried about my wife. I want her to be happy."

"Well, I am."

"I don't know about that. I see you when you're working. You're not as...*Kylie* as you used to be. Yeah, you look happy, but I can't help thinking you're missing something."

She eyed him suspiciously. "I have everything I need."

"Yeah. But what about the things you *want*?"

She shrugged. "They're the same."

He spun her on the dance floor. "I don't know about that," he said. "What about your job?"

"I like my job."

"No you don't. Not anymore."

She frowned. "Why do you say that?"

"It used to be something you lived to do. Now, I don't know what it is. You look at the computer day in and day out, like you want to kill it. And if that's the case, why do it? I can make enough money for both of us. I'll just pick up more seminars."

"Is that what you want me to do? Give up my job?"

"No. But I don't know if it's something that will keep you happy five, ten, twenty years from now."

"I'm happy, Linc. And not everyone loves their job. I'm fine."

He wanted her to. He loved the way her eyes lit up in a way they only did when she was on a big case. They were on their way to an argument, and he didn't want to ruin this perfect night, so he let it go.

They danced for a couple more slow songs, and by then, dessert was being served. As they made their way off the dance floor, Kylie looked up and nudged him. "Now, it's nice to see him, but I know *he* wasn't invited."

Linc followed her line of sight to the open doors, where Jacob was standing, face grim, holding his hat in front of him and searching the crowd. "Shit. You think it's bad news?"

Kylie nodded. "Why else would he be here? But all my family's here. I hope nothing happened to your family?"

He sat her down at their table and went to meet his best friend. Jacob waved as he approached. "There you are. Sorry to bother you here. I called you a couple times but then I remembered you said you'd be here."

"Everything okay? My family all right?"

He rubbed the back of his neck. "Sure, sure. This has nothing to do with them. But I just wanted to let you know that we were called to the scene of the Sunset Diner about an hour ago. Seems that Elise went out back to have a cigarette and someone shot her."

"What? Is she okay?"

"She's at the hospital right now. Critical. But after Kylie's involvement in the case, I thought I'd let you know."

Linc's eyes drifted across the dance floor to Kylie, who was sitting in her chair, watching them intently. He turned his back on her so she wouldn't see the worry on his face. "Let me guess. The guy got away."

Jacob nodded. "And from what I hear, no one saw anything."

"Jesus. Why would the guy go after her? Why now?"

"At this point, we don't know anything. Whether it's a random shooting or what."

Linc eyed him suspiciously. "You really think it's random? Kylie said a guy was following her."

"I know. And Kylie might've pulled herself off the case, but I can't say the same for Elise. Turns out, she started contacting other PI's, doing her own research based on what Kylie had already started. I'm officially putting more men on the case. It looks like someone is going to a lot of trouble to make sure we don't find something out, and in my guess, it's all interconnected and has to do with a child laundering ring. Elise was probably just a very small part of it, but maybe she went too far."

"What? Is Elise okay?" a voice said behind them.

Linc turned. Kylie was standing there, pale. With the pounding of the band playing "Oh What a Night" nearby, he hadn't heard her approach. He held his breath, not sure how to break this to her so he pulled the band-aid off quick. "She was shot in back of the diner. She's at the hospital."

"What? Oh, my god." Kylie covered her mouth with both hands. "It's because of the child smuggling, isn't it? I knew it."

Jacob held up a hand. "Now, we don't know that. It could be a coincidence."

Kylie snorted. "I don't believe that. She was being stalked. Why was no one watching her?"

"We had police on her for two weeks after the last incident. Then we took them off. Same as we did for you. We don't have unlimited resources," Jacob said. "We're doing the best we can."

"Well. I'm happy to help. Do you want my most recent notes?" Kylie asked, springing to action. "What can I do?"

"Whoa. Hold your horses," Jacob said. "Yes, I'll take your notes, sure, and any other information you can provide. But you don't have to get them to me now. I just wanted to let you know what happened, because you were involved."

Kylie crossed her arms. "But don't you want to go after this guy?"

"Yes. We are. We're going to talk to Elise when she wakes up and get her side of the story. That's what we're focused on right now. You just sit yourself back down and enjoy your mom's party. Tell the happy couple congrats for me."

He turned to leave, and Kylie stared after him. Linc saw it all in a couple of seconds. The excitement on her face when she thought she could get back in the game, and the disappointment that flashed across it seconds later, when he told her to relax and enjoy the party.

Enjoy the party? Looking at Kylie's face now, Linc didn't think that was possible.

They walked back to the table, and Rhonda said, "Is everything all right? I saw the police arriving and thought they were going to escort someone out in handcuffs!" She tittered nervously.

"No, Mom, that's Jacob. Linc's best friend, remember?" Kylie said absently, her eyes still trained on the doors. "Everything's all right."

Kylie put her hands in her lap and sighed.

"What's wrong?" Linc asked her gently.

She gave him a sideways glance. "I'm fine. Why do you think something's wrong?"

"Because you look like a kicked puppy." He took a sip of his beer. "It's the job, isn't it? I saw the way you looked at Jacob. You want to get back into it."

"No," she said weakly, picking up her glass of sparkling juice.

"Right. Liar. Admit it."

She sighed at him. "Okay. Fine. Maybe a little. But what I really want to do now is see Elise in the hospital. She's got no one other than Cody, and he's kind of a prick to her."

"You want me to give you a ride over there?"

She blinked. "You'd do that? But what about..." she gripped her napkin on her glass and scanned the room for her mother. "Wouldn't it be rude?"

He followed her gaze to find Rhonda and Jerry on the dance floor, dancing to a slow song and gazing into each other's eyes as if they were the only people on earth. "Actually, I don't even think your mom will know."

She smiled. "All right then." She downed her drink. "Let's go."

KYLIE DASHED into the sliding doors of the hospital with Linc following behind her. She gave Elise's name to the receptionist, who told them that Elise was on the sixth floor. After going to the gift shop and grabbing a balloon bouquet with a stuffed dog that looked a little like Britt, they took the elevator up.

As they did, Linc said, "You should be prepared if they won't let you see her."

Kylie studied her reflection in the shiny metal doors. The giant stuffed dog wasn't enough to hide her growing belly. "What do you mean?"

"I mean that it's probably family only."

"Well. At least we can drop this off and let her know we're thinking of her," she said, shifting her eyes up to the floor number. "I feel bad, especially that she doesn't have parents to dote on her."

The bell above them dinged, and the doors slid open to the ICU. Kylie stepped out and craned her neck around the bouquet to find the nurse on duty. "Hi. We're here to see Elise Kirby?"

The woman shook her head. "I'm sorry. Visiting hours are—"

"Hell, what are you guys doing? Following me?"

They turned to find Jacob striding toward them. Linc explained, "Kylie felt so bad about Elise, she wanted to come see her herself."

"She doesn't have much family," Kylie added.

He motioned them into the back. "All right, come on. Good timing. She was just waking up a minute ago. I was going to ask her those questions. You can join me."

Kylie's eyes lit up. Jacob usually tried to keep her from his investigations. He'd never actively included her. Maybe she should've finished up her criminal justice degree and become a police officer, because she loved this part of the job. Loved it. She suddenly felt her blood rushing through her veins.

And as she followed Jacob, she knew Linc was right. If she went her whole life just doing surveillance, she'd probably go insane.

"*But*," Jacob said, turning on her suddenly. "Let me do my job. No interfering, okay?"

She gave him a mock-hurt look. "Me? Never."

He eyed her, stroking his chin. "I know you. You can't shut up."

She made like she was zipping her lips and throwing away the key.

They walked down a long corridor with numerous doors, but it was obvious which one was Elise's. There was a bored-looking guard standing in front of one of them. He jumped to attention as Jacob approached.

Jacob stopped at the door and allowed her to go in first. Elise was sitting up in bed, her gown rumpled and pulled down over one shoulder to reveal a large bandage on her upper arm. Her eyes, half-closed, blinked open. "Oh, Kylie," she said breathlessly, smiling big.

Kylie smiled at her, set the balloons down in a corner, and lifted the stuffed animal up to her. "I figured they wouldn't allow Britt in to see you, so I brought you the next best thing."

She grabbed it and cuddled it like a child. "It's so cute! It looks just like him! I'll call him Britt Two."

Kylie laughed. "All right." She sat down on the chair across from her. "So, what happened to you?"

"I got shot," she mumbled, touching her bandage. "It really hurts. Or it did, til they gave me drugs. Now I'm high as a kite."

Kylie looked over at Linc and Jacob. "That's awful. We want to know more about it so we can catch the guy. Was it the same guy who you said was following you?"

She shook her head. "Don't know. Didn't get a good look at him."

Jacob cleared his throat.

Oh, right. She had a way of overstepping her bounds where the police were concerned. She never meant to. It just happened, because she got so excited. Promising she wouldn't interfere again, she said, "This police officer has some questions to ask you. Is that okay?"

She nodded.

Kylie backed away and smiled at Jacob as if to say, *All yours.*

"Thank you," Jacob said to her, sitting on a chair and pulling out his pad. "All right, Elise. Just tell me in your own words, exactly what happened."

Still clutching the stuffed dog in her lap, she looked over at Kylie for a moment, as if asking for permission. Kylie nodded encouragingly.

"It was nearing the end of the dinner rush, and when that happens, I usually go out for a cigarette out back of the diner, next to the dumpsters. So like, eight o'clock or a little after, I goes outside and told the others I'd be back in five. I'd just lit up a ciggy and was puttin' my lighter back into my pocket when I heard a loud bang behind me and felt somethin' hit me from behind. I dropped my cigarette and fell over, and it was only when I saw all the blood and heard the car's tires squealin' that I realized I was shot. Then Gary, the dishwasher, came outside, found me, and called for help."

"Did you see anyone else out there in the alley?"

She shook her head.

"And did you perhaps wait on someone new, who took an unusual interest in you? Did you see anyone while you were reporting in to work?"

She shook her head. "And I'm extra careful now, because I'd been followed before."

"Right." He flipped back in his pad and scratched his jaw. "You told me that man was short with dark hair. Kind of square-faced. Maybe late forties, early fifties. Unshaven, with a scar on his chin."

"That's right. I bet it's him," she said, looking over at Kylie. "I've been lookin' into Daisy's disappearance more. I went to a place called Southern Hills, but I was thrown out. The director didn't even want to see me. She told her receptionist she'd have the police escort me out if I didn't leave. And I wasn't doing nothin'. Just asking questions."

Kylie's ears perked up. "Southern Hills Child Welfare Society?"

Elise nodded.

Kylie stood up. "Did you get a chance to see Leda Butler? The director?"

Elise shook her head. "She wouldn't let me talk to her. She's the one who had me kicked out."

"But—"

Jacob cleared his throat. "Um, Kylie. Let me—"

"Wait," she said, standing up. "Don't you see? *I* met with Leda Butler, too, right before all this stuff started happening. And Agnes Mott, the woman who was babysitting when

Elise's baby was taken, said the woman who took her was blonde, and older, and smelled like strong perfume. That's exactly what Leda Butler looks like."

Linc and Jacob just stared at her.

"And not only that, Jacob, there's the Hanson case from Sylva. The only witness said he saw an older, well-dressed, blonde woman, leaving the scene. That's Leda Butler. I'm sure of it."

"All right, but—"

"No buts, Jacob. She's our man. I got a weird vibe from her, too, like she was trying too hard to be friendly. At least just check her out."

He raised his radio to his mouth. "You said Southern Hills?"

She nodded.

He spoke into the mouthpiece. "Hey, Harper? Can you check in with me on a Leda Butler, who works for Southern Hills? Get me an address and whatever info you can find."

Kylie grinned at Linc.

Her heart was thumping in her chest now. Just the act of working this through, detecting, it thrilled her like nothing else. The doctor had said to take it easy, but with all the adrenaline pumping through her veins, she felt like she could run a marathon.

The radio crackled with static. "Jacob. I've got a residential address for you." Jacob wrote as the dispatcher rattled it off.

"That's right downtown, near the hardware store," Linc said.

Jacob fastened his hat on his head and looked at Linc. "You want to come with?"

He looked at Kylie, who nodded. She waved them on. What could happen here in the hospital? They had a guard watching them too. "Just go! We'll be fine!"

Linc leaned over and kissed her forehead, then the two of them headed out. She was so excited, she wanted to go with them. But poor Elise was all alone. When they left, she patted the dog's fake fur along with Elise and said, "Where's Cody?"

She sniffed, her eyes growing glassy with tears. "We broke up."

"You did? Oh no! Where are you living?"

"Well, we're still living in the same place for now. It's kind of recent. I'm lookin' for a place but there ain't nothin' either of us can afford by ourselves. So, I guess we're just room-mates right now."

Kylie didn't like the sound of that. Maybe she shouldn't have let them have Britt since their family life was so unstable. "Well, don't you think he'd want to know about what happened?"

She shrugged. "I don't know. That's the reason we fought in the first place. He thought I was gettin' too carried away by the Daisy thing. He got sick of me wastin' so much of my time and thinkin' on her. I guess he's right. But I had to. If he's gonna make me have to choose between the two of them, I choose her."

"Oh, honey," Kylie said, leaning over and giving Elise a hug. "I don't blame you. I would too. Every time."

27

How did this happen?

I thought I had everything under control. That snooping private eye, Kylie Coulter, had backed off, enough so that I'd almost entertained the idea of opening business back up again. I'd been in Code X—meaning that I was to have no contact with K, nor he with me—ever since Kylie had shown up at my office, asking questions. I'd gone through the contents of my office and removed anything that could cast suspicion on me. I'd covered my tracks.

Then that little dim-witted bitch came after me.

I'd had enough. I told Cherry not to admit her, that I didn't have time to deal with any more of these ridiculous questions. I'd smiled at Cherry and convinced her everything was all right. I didn't like that my own people were starting to get suspicious of me now.

I'd needed to stop this in its tracks, once and for all.

And what did Stephen do?

He fucking shot her in the arm. He didn't kill her, the moron.

"Are you absolutely serious?" I cried into the phone

when he told me the news. "You are a hit man, aren't you? Or did I hire a hurt-man? Because you know what, Stephen? You should probably consider a new line of employment."

He'd stumbled over his words, trying to explain, but I'd had enough.

"What hospital did they take her to?"

"Asheville General."

"Great. Thanks for nothing." I wished I had one of those old phones that I could slam down so hard that the bell inside rang. Slamming down a cell phone was liable to break it.

I'd been making myself a TV dinner and looking forward to a night of watching Lawrence Welk on PBS while drifting off to sleep.

This threw a wrench in those plans.

I quickly got changed into a pair of scrubs, put my own gun and a few necessities into my purse, and hurried to my car. I was glad it was Asheville General. I had a lot of friends there. I used to work as a nurse, back in the day, before I got my master's in social work, and I worked with nurses all the time. I knew my way around a hospital, especially Asheville General.

I'd rather not have had to do it at all, but I'd take care of it. It would be fairly simple. It wouldn't be the first time that I'd been in a jam. After over fifty years in the business, I knew a thing or two.

I smiled as I drove toward the hospital. I'd be seventy-five next May, but this job kept me young, I always said. People always asked me why I didn't retire. I'd received award after award for my humanitarian work, but it wasn't the accolades that kept me active. No, I didn't retire because this was in my blood. Uniting families and giving them the best chance of life was just a privilege to me.

Of course, I did love going on my cruises, too, something I probably wouldn't have been able to afford on retirement.

Parking in the lot outside the hospital, I grabbed the identification badge and affixed it to my collar. Having intimate knowledge of the hospitals in the southeastern part of the country, I had fake credentials for nearly every one of them. Patting my hair down and checking my face in the rearview mirror, I pushed open the door and stepped outside.

I was tempted to wear a wig, but then the staff wouldn't know me. It was a risk to present myself as me, but I could do it.

I'd done it before.

That was the great thing about Asheville General. It was so big, no one even batted an eyelash when I strode through the sliding doors. It also helped that I had the face of an angel. No one ever suspected the grandmotherly type. I waved at the front desk and security guard and went walking right on with authority toward the elevators.

I glanced at the list of departments, even though I knew the ICU was on the sixth floor.

If they knew what was good for her, they'd probably have a guard watching, a wet-behind-the-ears newbie who could easily be avoided.

When the doors opened, I walked out into the ICU and smiled at the one nurse who looked up. "How is your day?" I asked.

She barely looked at me before muttering, "Same old."

Oh, this was almost too easy.

I peeked down the hallway and...bingo. There was the guard, hunched over in a chair and yawning. It was almost a positive thing for me that he was there—it saved me from having to peek in every open door. I walked right on over to the door, smiling at the officer. Just a kid.

A kid who was about to have a worse day than I was having.

"Let's check on this patient," I said and pretended to look at my tablet while reaching for the needle in my pocket.

He shrugged and started to yawn again.

As he did, I struck, injecting the liquid into the flesh of his neck. He reached over to touch it, but before he could, he'd already slumped over. Gone.

I loved how quickly this stuff worked.

Making sure he only looked as if he was sleeping, I peered down the hall, then inside to make sure I wasn't observed. No.

I took another step inside. It was a surprise to see she wasn't alone.

In fact, a very nice surprise. She was there with Kylie Hatfield Coulter.

My day just got better. I suppose this was what you would call killing two birds with one stone.

28

The drive to Leda Butler's house was a tense one.

They took Jacob's police truck, and he kept the lights going. As they drove, Linc pulled up information on Leda Butler on his phone. He frowned as he read.

"Listen to this. Leda Butler has been a staple in the Asheville area children's welfare community for over half a century. She has been decorated with numerous honors and has won multiple awards for her tireless championing of children's rights in Western North Carolina and the surrounding areas." He looked up at Jacob. "How can this be the right woman?"

"Well, we'll see," he said as Linc continued to scroll through the search results.

There was a picture of Leda Butler receiving some award from the mayor of Asheville. She was small and portly, with chipmunk cheeks. Yes, she looked like anyone's loving grandmother. But she did have almost white-blonde hair, and she was well-dressed.

Could this woman be a baby-smuggler? And if so, how had she been doing it so long without having been caught?

"This doesn't seem right," he said to Jacob when they reached the house, a small, brick row home with bright blue violets in the windows. Jacob parallel parked on the street in front as Linc looked up at the door, which had a "Welcome Friends" plaque on the front. The curtains in the front windows were some kind of lace, and there was a cat peering out at them from one of the ledges. "It doesn't seem like the house of a baby smuggler."

Jacob threw open the door. "You know what, man? In my experience, that's what makes a criminal so successful. No one suspects them. Let's stop jumping to conclusions and check this woman out."

Linc went to straighten his shirt and realized he wasn't wearing his blazer or tie. What had he done with them? Had he left them at the restaurant? Probably. Not that it mattered. He'd get them later. He scratched his head as they approached the front door.

Jacob put out his finger to ring the doorbell and Linc winced. "It's nearly midnight. What if she's sleeping?"

He shrugged. "Then we wake her ass up."

He banged on the door with his fist, for effect.

"Hey," Linc said. "Cool it. If she's an old lady, it's going to take her a while to get down the stairs."

Jacob looked over at his friend, disappointed. "She also could be a criminal. So why should I be nice, again?"

"So you really do believe what Kylie's saying?"

"Yeah. Well, you have to admit. She's got a nose for this business. Her intuition of late has been pretty spot-on. She hasn't really led us wrong before."

He had to admit, Jacob was right. And as much as he didn't like hearing it, it was true. It was like the business had found her. Like she was meant to be in it. And things that were meant to be couldn't be stopped. Why had he even tried?

"She's not answering," Jacob muttered after a minute. He banged on the door again.

"Okay. What does that mean? You going to bust down the door, or what?"

"No. It means I'm going to file for a warrant so that I can search the offices of the Southern Hills Child Welfare Society. So that we won't be breaking any of the laws I'm supposed to be upholding and anything we find will be admissible in court. Sound good?"

Linc nodded. "Where do you think she is, this late at night?"

Jacob started to go back to his truck, and Linc followed. "Hell if I know. Bingo party? Visiting family?"

Linc got in the vehicle and sat there, a sick feeling slowly overcoming him. He'd gone with Jacob hoping to confront this person, ready for action. And now, they were just cooling their jets, with nothing to do. Not to mention, the killer who'd shot Elise was still on the loose, and he'd gone off, willy-nilly, leaving Kylie.

He'd left his wife. And babies.

What the hell had he been thinking? If that killer was still out there, he might come after her.

He lifted his phone and put in a text. *U ok?*

He really would've liked to get an answer right away. She was good at replying quickly to his texts, since she was a slave to her phone. But nothing came in. He punched in a call to her and lifted the phone to his ear.

"Can we get back to the hospital?" he asked when Jacob turned the ignition.

The phone rang, again and again. A moment later, his call went to voicemail.

"As fast as we can?" he added.

Jacob looked over at him. "Where's the fire?"

"I'm just…my whole family's back there. I shouldn't have left her."

"Gotcha, man," he said, and pressed harder on the gas.

29

After a few minutes of quiet conversation, Elise finally nodded back off to sleep with the help of a sedative a nurse had given her only a few minutes ago. Kylie checked her phone, hoping that Linc would let her know how things were going. But he hadn't sent her anything.

She had to wait for Linc to come back, so she spent a few minutes almost nodding off, trying to watch an episode of *Friends* she's seen a thousand times.

Then she got up and paced around, but her feet hurt too much because of the heels she was wearing, and because her legs and feet had just recently begun to retain water, another delightful pregnancy side effect. She slipped off her shoes and inspected her red toes. They looked like little sausages.

She yawned, wondering if the guard outside would be interested in conversation. She needed someone, anyone to talk to. Even if that officer looked young and his only interests were NASCAR, beer, and chicks, it was better than twiddling her thumbs.

As she was preparing to peel herself up off the pleather

chair and strike up a conversation with him, a nurse walked in.

"Well, good evening," the woman said brightly, glancing at Kylie as she went to check Elise's IV. "I didn't think it was visiting hours."

"Oh, it's not. I'm just friends with the detective and the patient, so he told me I could stay here with her. She's had a rough time."

"Yes, yes. It's such a shame."

Happy to have someone to talk to, Kylie said, "She's a really nice person. And it's sad that she was shot in the arm. I hope she can get better soon because she's a waitress. She needs both arms."

"Hmm," the woman said. "We'll treat her like a princess here. She'll be right as rain before you know it."

"I hope," Kylie said, inhaling sharply. As she did, she caught a whiff of strong perfume. At first, Kylie thought nothing of it, but then she remembered where she was. Nurses didn't often wear perfume, as it sometimes interfered with their patients. At least, she thought that was correct.

She craned her neck to look more closely at the nurse, who was still working on the IV drip. The first thing she saw was blonde hair, pulled back in a tight bun.

And then she noticed the woman's hands, complete with pretty, long fingernails. Pink, shiny, and definitely shaped like claws.

Kylie's blood went cold.

She tried to be nonchalant, but her hand instinctively went to her stomach, protecting her babies. She had to protect them. As she glanced around the room, she knew it was up to her.

The guard.

Her eyes slowly flitted to the door.

There, she saw the man slumped in the chair, his chin resting on his chest. Was he asleep? Or had this woman harmed him? Killed him?

Kylie stiffened, her heart a locomotive in her chest. *She's killed the guard. She's going to kill Elise. And then she'll kill me. And my babies.*

When she looked back, the woman dressed as a nurse was facing her. A small black gun was in her hand. It might be small, but at this distance, it was as lethal as a nuclear bomb.

Kylie raised her hands. "What are you doing?"

The gun raised by several degrees, now pointing between Kylie's eyes. Leda Butler laughed. "Well, I hadn't expected to see you here. You threw a little wrench into my plans, but that's okay. Obstacles can be overcome."

There was a call button on the bedside table, but it was between them and a couple feet away. Could Kylie move faster than a bullet and summon help? No. A few months ago, she might have tried, but now she had her babies to think of. She needed to be smart.

Kylie splayed her hands out and said, "I'm pregnant. Please, don't—"

"Oh, I know. I know all about you, Kylie Coulter, and not just the lies you told us when you came to visit the agency. I know that you're pregnant with twins. I know that you haven't had the easiest of pregnancies. I know about that husband of yours. But don't worry. I don't plan on killing you."

"Y-you don't?" Kylie stammered, disbelief in her voice.

The woman reached into her purse and pulled out a clear vial. "No. Once I get done with Elise, you and I are going to take a little walk." She smiled, pleased with herself. "I've never actually kidnapped an adult before, but I don't see it as being a problem."

Kidnapping. At first, Kylie didn't understand, but then her hands went down to her belly, and she gasped. She wasn't being kidnapped out of mercy.

This horrible woman was kidnapping her for her babies. "You can't do that. I'll—"

"Don't worry. I'll take very good care of your babies. I'll give them the best homes that money can buy."

Kylie shook her head slowly, speechless, as a cruel smile spread over the woman's face.

"I can't kill you, dear. You understand that each one of your babies is worth five-hundred thousand dollars? You're worth a million dollars to someone. Or at least, your babies are," she said.

Kylie's stomach roiled. Her morning sickness came back with a vengeance. She doubled over, nearly retching. Where she'd been researching Leda Butler, it was clear Leda Butler had been researching her too. More than just researching.

Had she tapped into her phone calls? Had her followed? What resources did this woman have available that allowed her to get away with these heinous acts for nearly fifty years?

But, how else would she have known that she was pregnant with twins? They hadn't told anyone except their family and friends. "You can't do this," she pleaded.

"Oh, sweetheart. I've been reconnecting precious bundles of joy to proper families for fifty years. It's my calling. My mission. And no one has caught me yet."

Kylie laughed, a bark of sound that echoed through the room. "Your mission? You're delusional to think what you've been doing is in any way altruistic. You're in this for the money, you selfish and psychotic bitch."

Leda's mouth tightened. "Think what you will. Your opinion changes nothing."

"You can't kidnap me," Kylie said, her voice tight with

determination. "We'll never make it out of this hospital. I'll scream these walls down. I will."

Leda lowered the gun until it was pointing right at Kylie's stomach. "The second you do is the second you and your babies die. If I go down, it's because of you. And I promise you, I won't be going down alone," she snarled, her face twisted in a way that was anything but grandmotherly. "If you move or make a sound, I will shoot you. Do you understand? The staff know me here. They know my kind heart. I'll make them believe that you pulled a gun on me and that I was able to defend myself, take the gun away, and..." the woman's eyes filled with tears, her face a sudden mask of pure grief, "I was forced to shoot you. I had no choice, officer. She attacked me."

The act was so believable that, when Leda laughed, Kylie could only stand there in continued horror. That was how this woman had managed to do these horrible things for so long. Not only was she psychotic, she was quite the fine actor to boot.

It had to stop here, but how? She had her babies to think of. Linc. Oh, Linc. This would kill him too. She had to stop this somehow.

Kylie watched in horror as Leda pulled out a syringe and used it to take out the contents of a vial, then insert it into the port of Elise's IV bag. Kylie willed the woman to wake up, but Elise continued to sleep through this entire hellish scene, looking like an angel.

When Leda was finished, she wiped her hand on her uniform and smiled at Kylie. She motioned her to the door. "Shall we?"

Kylie swallowed and took a step toward the door. As she did, she saw the guard's body more clearly. His chest wasn't moving.

"Come along," she said, thrusting the gun into her back. "And if you want your babies to live, you'll not call attention to yourself. If I don't get out of here in one piece, neither do you and your babies."

30

Lights flashing and siren wailing, the police truck pulled up at the front of the hospital, smoke pouring from the squealing tires. Linc jumped out of the car and barreled through the front doors, looking for Kylie. The lobby was largely empty, except for a few solitary people in chairs, noses buried in their phones. The receptionist at the front tried to stop him, but Jacob came through a moment later, telling her to let him go.

He pressed the UP button a number of times in quick succession, as if that would get the elevator to come faster. When it didn't, he bounded for the stairs, taking them two at a time.

On the ICU floor, Linc exploded out of the stairwell, Jacob on his heels. He spotted a nurse sitting at a computer. "Is Elise Kirby okay?"

The nurse gave him a shocked look, leaping to her feet and backing away. When Jacob held up his badge, she stammered, "Y-yes. She's sleeping. Why wouldn't she be?"

Linc let out a momentary sigh of relief and inhaled a

lungful of air as he hurried down the corridor to Elise's room. He needed to see for himself.

"What the hell?" Jacob said from beside him.

Linc knew exactly what he was referring to. The young guard was asleep, his chin resting on his chest.

Jacob shook his shoulder. Nothing. When he shook him again, the officer fell to the floor.

As Jacob called for help and crouched to check for a pulse, Linc rushed into the hospital room. Elise was lying there, resting peacefully, but…no Kylie.

Fuck, Linc thought, tearing out of the room, just as a herd of nurses came running down the hall.

"Get this man looked at right now," Jacob barked. "He's been drugged."

Linc froze. Maybe Elise wasn't resting so peacefully after all. "Check Elise Kirby too. Now!" He glanced frantically around. "Kylie's gone. Where do you—" He saw the door at the end of the corridor with the bright red EXIT sign and lunged for it, shoving it open with all his force and racing down the stairs.

He flew down the staircase, not thinking of anything else but Kylie and their babies. He pushed the door to the emergency exit open, and as he was taking a second to collect his bearings and figure out where he was, a bullet whizzed past his ear, burrowing in the wall behind him.

Instinctively, he dove behind some bushes, out of sight, as he heard Kylie's high-pitched shriek. As he strained to see between the branches, Kylie's captor fired another round.

The exit had let him out at the front of the hospital, about a hundred feet away from the main entrance. Linc could see Jacob's truck parked out front, where he'd left it. The woman was in the parking lot. She was only seconds from getting into her car and leaving with Kylie.

He needed to do something, and quick.

"Leda Butler!" he called. "We know it's you. We know everything. Let Kylie go and we'll talk this through."

There was no response. Linc slowly peered up over the edge of the bushes and gnashed his teeth.

The woman was standing in the parking lot, holding a gun to Kylie's temple. Kylie's face looked as white as the moon, but she wasn't trembling, and she didn't look scared. Maybe she'd been through things like this enough that nothing scared her anymore. Whatever it was, she seemed strangely accepting of this. The woman, however, clearly looked upset.

Leda nudged her toward a silver Mercedes. "I'm leaving with her. Don't try to stop me," she called out.

"Leda Butler," a voice rang out over a loudspeaker. It was Jacob, speaking from the bullhorn in his truck. "It's over. Let the girl go."

"No. I'll kill her first."

Jacob glanced Linc's way and gave him the signal to sweep wide. Linc understood, but he needed a distraction. Like an answered prayer, the answer came in the form of Faith and her cousin, Sky Stryker.

From the other side of the lot, Linc could see Faith rushing from vehicle to vehicle, keeping low. Thinking through the situation, Linc frowned as Sky jumped up from behind a car and began screaming at the top of her lungs. "Gun! Gun! That woman's got a gun!"

When Leda moved the gun away from Kylie and toward the screaming woman, Linc advanced, crouching below the line of bushes. It was chaos, meant to confuse and disorient the suspect. It seemed to be working, and Linc picked up speed.

In his periphery, he noticed Faith only a few yards away as he closed the distance—Faith Dean now, Jacob's wife, who looked completely at home readying herself for a takedown.

It shocked him all over again that the Faith he'd known in college was now his best friend's wife and an FBI agent. Faith held up three fingers, then counted them down.

Three.

Two.

One.

Faith popped up, distracting Leda. The second the gun was pointed away from Kylie, Linc lunged, tackling the woman from behind.

Faith advanced, kicking the gun from the woman's hand as Kylie moved forward and punched the old woman in the throat.

Any struggle left in the psychotic bitch drained away as she gulped for air. As Jacob and Faith detained the woman, Linc went to his wife, pulling her and their children into his arms.

"Just in time, as always," she said with a watery smile.

"Nice move," he said with a laugh. "Where did you learn to throat-punch like that?"

"Old ladies I can handle," she said, breathing hard. Her hands went to her stomach, and her eyes widened.

"Everything okay?" Linc asked, alarmed.

"Yeah, I just…we need to get to Elise. She put something in her IV."

"I know. The staff was checking on her when I went to search for you."

Linc turned at the sound of handcuffs snapping closed, and Jacob pulled Leda Butler to her feet. "Now you know not to mess with the Coulters," he said, winking at Kylie.

Leda kept her mouth firmly closed, almost hissing air in and out of her nose as Jacob began to recite her rights. Linc and Kylie walked away, not looking back at the hateful woman. She wasn't worth a second glance.

They went back inside the hospital to check on Elise. The

girl was alive. Kylie sagged hard against Linc when they were told the news. Leda had given her an overdose of a strong sedative, which they'd been able to reverse. Had it been a poison, the end result could have been so much worse.

An hour or so later, they were told they could visit with Elise. The girl looked around, confused, still clutching her stuffed dog. "What happened?"

Kylie leaned in and patted her hand. "I'll tell you about it later. Just get some sleep."

Linc wrapped his strong arm around her, and together they walked toward the elevators. But as they walked, he noticed she still had her hand on her belly and was stroking it, her brow wrinkled in concentration. "Are you sure you're okay?"

She nodded slowly.

He stopped. "Are you sure? Because we're at the hospital. You can get yourself checked—"

"No. Wait," she said, her eyes lighting up as she ran her hand over her belly. "I feel them. Linc. I feel them!"

His jaw sagged in awe. "Really?"

"Yeah. It was just a flutter at first. I thought it was gas or something. But it's here." She took his hand and laid it on her belly, just where her hand had been.

At first, he felt nothing, and then, just the tiniest ripple caressed his palm. His mouth opened. "Is that it?"

She nodded.

"Holy shit."

"Language, Daddy," she scolded.

He laughed, tears springing to his eyes. "You think they can hear us now?"

"Maybe. But why take chances?"

"Yeah?"

When they got to the parking lot, more police had

arrived, and sirens were screaming in the distance. "Do we have to stay?" she asked.

Linc shook his head. "Let's go. Jacob can get the report tomorrow. You need your beauty sleep."

He walked her toward her Jeep, and when he put her into the passenger's seat, he planted a quick, dry kiss on her lips as he fastened her seat belt securely under her belly. Then he leaned down and kissed her stomach through her shirt. "Listen here, kids," he said very softly. "You have one fierce mommy. She's going to make you feel very safe."

She grinned at him. "Just like you make me feel."

31

The Leda Butler/Southern Hills Child Welfare laundering case ended up being one of the largest in the country. FBI investigators took over the case once Coulter Confidential put a crack in it. It turned out, Leda Butler was only a small cog in the wheel, but further investigations uncovered dozens more involved parties. Twenty-three people from across the southeast were arrested: nurses, child welfare agency employees, doctors, and more. All of them had aided Leda in profiting off stolen babies.

In jail, awaiting trial, Leda had confessed to arranging at least two hundred child kidnappings over a fifty-year period. She told investigators that she'd done so because she believed it was the best thing for the child. Even as she was indicted, she told the judge that she truly believed she'd only done good.

The morning after the indictment, Kylie read the news on her phone and groaned aloud. "This woman is delusional! Purely delusional! Trying to paint herself as a victim. The nerve!"

Linc poured her a cup of decaf coffee and shrugged.

"Well, she can have those delusions in jail, because that's where she's spending the rest of her life."

As she continued to read, her phone buzzed with a call from Greg. She answered it. "Why are you not sleeping in? You're retired."

"Funny, the fish don't sleep," he said, making her grin. "So, I read the papers this morning. Would you look at that. Coulter Confidential is in the news, and my little protégé is a star."

Her smile grew wider. "I owe it all to you. You taught me everything I know."

"Are you going to thank me in your acceptance speech? 'I'd like to thank Greg Starr and all the little people…'?"

She laughed. "Yeah. Something like that."

The tone of his voice changed from teasing to proud. "Well, you did it again, short stuff. I'm thinking I'm out of a job as your adviser. You probably know more than I do, at this point."

"Greg, I hope you know that job is *always* open. Even if I don't need your advice. I still need you."

"Aw, honey. Don't make me get emotional. Fish sense emotion, and I'm going out with the boys this afternoon." There was a pause. "How are the kids doing?"

"Good. Still cooking. But good."

"Excellent. If I know you, I know you won't take this final bit of advice from me, but take some time off. You deserve it. I'll talk to you soon."

She hung up, smiling at his abruptness. She'd expected nothing less.

Linc poured a second cup of coffee. "Greg?"

Kylie nodded, took a sip of her sweet and milky brew, and went back to the article. She stared at the picture of the woman. "Isn't it sad? How for so long, everyone thought she looked too innocent to do wrong, and that's how she got away with everything? It makes me a little sick. Like, you never really know a person, do you?"

Linc nodded. "That's exactly the story of how I ended up marrying you."

She smacked his arm and held up a fist to him. "I'm going to mess your face up."

He raised an eyebrow. "Yeah? Come at me, bro. I'd like to see you try."

She wrinkled her nose. "Did you just call me bro?"

"Indeed I did." He checked the clock on the microwave. "But enough of that. We've got to get ready. We have to be there by noon."

Kylie's eyes lit up. She'd been waiting for this day for a week, and now it was here. She sprang off her stool and charged up the stairs. Her belly was not so large yet as to be preventing her from a lot of things, but now as she walked, she was fond of holding it, as if it might pop off at any second.

When they both finished showering, they took Linc's truck to a park in downtown Asheville, where the first of many reunions was about to take place. Kylie's heart was beating a steady drumbeat from the nerves, and she wondered if she felt that way, how was Elise feeling? She'd texted Elise a few times, and Elise had said she couldn't wait, but it had to have been nerve-racking.

They pulled up to the entrance of the park, where there was a small lot, and a pond with a fountain in the center. When Kylie stepped out of the truck, she was holding tissues, already a little teary-eyed. She saw the social worker she'd met with earlier in the week, as well as Daisy's adoptive parents, and waved. The father held Daisy, dressed in a pink fairy dress, in his arms.

According to the police reports, the parents who had adopted children from the underground adoption ring were told that their children needed special care and that their adoption "fees" of up to $500,000 were for surgeries or other necessary medical treatment, transportation, and care of the child.

Parents, eager to adopt a baby, were willing to hand over whatever amount of money it took in order to have a child. This family, the Smiths, were one of many who had been duped into an illegal adoption, domestically and all across the world.

When the news broke of the case, the Smiths were more than gracious. Worried that they might lose Daisy, they offered Elise as much support and visitation as she'd like, as long as Daisy would be allowed to remain with them. They'd even offered to take Elise in for a time, until she found a better place to live.

But all of this was decided over the phone, since the Smiths resided about two hours away, in Georgia.

Today was the first time they would all meet in person.

As they said their hellos and made introductions, another car pulled up. This was Elise, along with the attorney who had arranged to represent her.

Elise stepped out of the car, wearing her nicest dress, her fingers laced in front of her, holding the stuffed animal Kylie had given her. Biting nervously on her lip, she approached the waiting group, her eyes on the curly haired two-year-old with the big blue eyes.

"Hello," she said to the little girl, a tear running down her cheek. "I'm Elise."

The little girl popped her thumb from her mouth and reached for the stuffed dog, which Elise held up for her to see. Mr. Smith put the little girl on the ground, and Elise crouched to talk to her.

Linc leaned over and whispered into Kylie's ear, "This is

all you, you know. You're responsible for this and all the others that will come after this."

Kylie started to bawl. She lifted the tissue to her eyes to cover the ugly cry she was currently having. "Yes," she said when she was finally about to talk, "but it's my bleeding heart that's going to put us in the poorhouse. Remember?"

He smiled. "I like your bleeding heart, and all your other parts. I wouldn't trade any piece of you for anything in the world."

Linc kissed her lightly and laid a hand protectively on her belly.

They watched as Elise walked off, hand in hand, with her daughter, to the edge of the pond. Elise pretended to attack Daisy's nose with the dog, and the girl giggled.

Linc whispered, "What do you say we go get some lunch?"

"Oh, yes," Kylie said, licking her lips and winking at him. "I thought you'd never ask."

EPILOGUE

Six months after Leda Butler and her cohorts were arrested, Linc stood outside with the dogs, playing catch. Now, the puppies were nearly full grown, and for the past few months, training had been going well. Oh, a few of the dogs still had a Vader-side to them, but they each had a unique personality and had become part of the family.

For now.

Kylie had admitted, that as much as she would miss them, it would only be selfish to keep them from fulfilling their destiny and going to live with their own SAR owners. Linc would train them, then one by one, they'd have to say goodbye.

Except for Roxy, who they'd decided to keep.

Kylie watched from the porch swing, and even though it was a chilly spring day, she was wearing short sleeves. She was always hot now. In the last month of pregnancy, she'd gotten so big that he sometimes looked at her and wondered if she'd pop.

Because she could barely move, she'd decided to put

Coulter Confidential on a couple-months-long hiatus, so Kylie and he could get the hang of parenthood. Ever since the Leda Butler case broke, business had been booming, so much so that she'd had to turn away work and was considering hiring an assistant. But for now, she wanted to enjoy her babies and concentrate on bonding with them.

If they ever decided to burst from their warm and snug world.

From the yard, he could see her sitting on the porch, her feet up, hands clasped over her enormous belly. "That's good!" she called. "I think Riot's aptly named."

Riot might have been one of the more rambunctious ones, but Kylie was right. He was definitely the fastest. He'd gotten about half of the hundred balls he'd tossed out to them, because of his sheer speed. "Yeah. He's fast."

The dogs had started to get tired, and the sun was going down, so he took the ball and said, "No more, guys. My arm's getting tired." He rubbed his shoulder and rolled the joint in a circle as he jogged up to the porch, where Kylie was sitting, looking a little pale. "You okay?"

She nodded.

"I'll make dinner."

"Actually, I'm not hungry."

He stopped with his hand on the doorknob and simply stared at her. She hadn't really eaten very much all day. "What?"

"I think...maybe I should go to the hospital."

His eyebrows shot up to his hairline. "What? Now?"

"Well, I've been timing my contractions, and you know how they've always been five minutes apart? Just now, this one was three minutes apart. And I'm feeling a little queasy."

They'd been planning for months, just what to do when this moment came. There was a list of a number of things.

But right now, he couldn't remember a single one of them. The only thing he could think of was packing her into the truck and getting her to the hospital. He reached for the keys and then bent down to help her up.

"Suitcase?" she reminded him.

"Oh. Right."

He rushed into the house and returned a few moments later with her packed suitcase, which he threw into the back of the truck.

Then he stood there for a moment, a deer caught in headlights. "What else?"

She shrugged. "Me?"

"Right." He rushed up to meet her, took her arm, and guided her down the stairs and into the cab of the truck. When she was safely inside, he went to close the door.

"Don't forget to put the dogs inside and lock up the house. And put the heat up a little because it's supposed to get colder tonight."

"Right." He dashed back inside. Kylie was usually the one spacing, and he was the voice of reason. But not today. Right now, his mind was not capable of any coherent thought. He wondered if he'd even remember how to drive.

As they drove down the curvy mountain, Kylie winced for a period of about thirty seconds. She glanced at her phone, then folded her hands over her belly.

"Was that a contraction?"

She nodded. "Getting closer together, I think."

Linc couldn't understand how the hell she could be so calm. "Okay, hold on." He pushed on the gas.

"Relax. They're closer together, but it's not like the babies are coming now. I'm sure we have time."

"But how do you know?" he asked, tense.

She shrugged and turned on the radio, probably to calm

him down because he was getting insane. Some Jason Aldean song was playing, and he tried to get into it, tapping his hand on the steering wheel to the beat.

It didn't help.

"You know," he said. "I know we've been planning for this for months, but I have a feeling I've forgotten something."

"That's just because we've never done this before," she said calmly. "But we'll be fine."

"Yeah." If she believed it, then he'd believe it too. "We can do anything."

"Just...no matter what happens, stay with me. Okay, Linc? Don't leave me." She looked pleadingly at him, so much so that he almost couldn't drag his eyes away from her and put them back on the road.

He took her hand. "Never."

They made it to the hospital at around their normal dinner time, but Linc couldn't think about food. All he could think of was getting Kylie taken care of. Every time she winced, he had a flash of guilt, knowing he was the one who made her this way.

They were brought up to a room, and when Kylie was checked, she was seven centimeters.

"Epidural," she yelled.

The nurse frowned. "We'll do our best, but there was a multi-car pileup and our anesthesiologist is busy in the operating room."

He watched the terror appear on her face and took her hand. "Look. You can do this. You can do anything."

After another contraction ripped through her, this one making her nearly scream, they asked her if she wanted to walk. She got up to do just that, but when another hit her, she slumped down, and there was a gush of fluid from her water breaking.

They helped her back into the bed, and the nurses got the room ready for delivery. In less than an hour, the doctor checked her and told her it was time to push.

She pushed, she screamed, all while nearly massacring Linc's hand. She didn't let it go for a second. And in the next hour, she pushed out their babies—a boy followed closely by a girl.

He wiped the sweat from her brow and kissed her, relief and excitement making his smile tremble. "See, I told you. We have a boy and a girl."

"They're okay?" she asked breathlessly, her eyes half-closed.

"Yes. They're beautiful. Do you want to see them?"

She nodded.

The nurses brought them over and showed them to the new parents, and Kylie's eyes, fighting to stay open, filled with tears. "Oh, they *are* beautiful."

"Watch them, okay, Linc? Don't let them out of your sight," she said, drifting off.

Even though Leda and her cohorts were behind bars, he supposed she had a right to worry about that. He kissed her forehead. "Don't worry. I will."

The babies were cleaned and given their initial exam and determined to be completely healthy. Linc watched them in the nursery, as promised, and meanwhile, he contacted all of his family to let them know the news. What seemed like a split-second later, the grandparents—Rhonda and Jerry, Jonathan and Linda—all arrived to see the babies in the nursery.

They were all thrilled and wanted to know the babies' names. Linc had to break the news: Though they were prepared for everything, they still hadn't one hundred percent agreed on names. They knew Kylie and Linc Jr. were out, and though they'd been tossing around a number of names, they hadn't decided on anything firm.

A few hours later, Kylie woke up, and the babies were brought to her to be fed. As she held them at her breasts, one in each arm, Linc was amazed at how motherly she looked from the very start.

"I wish my father could be here to see them," Kylie said suddenly, taking the little girl's hand in hers.

Linc was surprised to hear her father's name mentioned. Kylie rarely spoke of her dad. To say their relationship had been strained would be an understatement, since she hadn't known him growing up, and only when she found him did she discover the shady business he was in.

William Hatfield had been sentenced to five years in prison for charges stemming from his ties to the mafia, but from time to time, he'd write her a letter. She always kept those to herself, but she'd said once that he was very apologetic. "He'll be out in another couple of years."

She nodded. "He told me he's happy for me and can't wait to meet them. He feels bad about missing my childhood and wants another chance."

Linc had no doubt she'd give it to him. She'd forgiven her father a long time ago, which was why each time she received a letter from him, she hurried up to the bedroom to write one back, emerging several hours later with the sealed, stamped envelope, ready to go into the mailbox. "Well, it'll happen soon enough. Don't worry."

She smiled. "I'm not."

Good. He didn't worry about William Hatfield leaving anymore, either, which was what he'd done to Kylie when she was a baby. Their babies were born into so much love. Family and friends had been sending gifts and notes of congratulations all evening, and when the Coulters left the hospital and arrived back at the farmhouse, there'd be a herd of furry faces to welcome them. Their children would always know the love and comfort that only dogs could bring.

SHE KISSED their baby girl's head and said, "We should name her Maggie. She looks like a Maggie. Margaret Aravis Coulter."

His heart squeezed in his chest. "You think so?"

"Yes."

"Well, then, this one looks like a Trey."

She smiled. "Trey Gavin Coulter?"

"I think that's it." He laid the little bundle in the crook of her other arm. "And…done. Let's get that birth certificate form written out."

She cooed at them, "Maggie and Trey. Welcome to the world. Welcome to our family. I'm your mommy, and that man over there is your daddy. He's a careful one, so I can promise you, he's never going to let you two out of his sight."

He leaned over and kissed her forehead. "If they're even half as much of a handful as you are, you're damn straight."

"But guess what?" she said with a smile, leaning in as if whispering a great secret to them. "It's actually a very good thing."

The End

AUTHOR NOTE: We hope you loved Kylie and Linc (as well as Storm and Vader) as much as we loved writing these characters. Next, our mysteries shift from North Carolina to New York where you'll follow the journey of Sky Stryker, a true crime writer who gets more than she bargained for when she dives into the seemingly untouchable world of wealth and celebrity in hopes of uncovering enough skeletons to write the bestselling tell-all that will set her career on fire. **The Sky Stryker series is coming soon.**

Find all of the Kylie Hatfield books on Amazon.

ACKNOWLEDGMENTS

How does one properly thank everyone involved in taking a dream and making it a reality? Here goes.

In addition to our families, whose unending support provided the foundation for us to find the time and energy to put these thoughts on paper, we want to thank the editors who polished our words and made them shine.

Many thanks to our publisher for risking taking on two newbies and giving us the confidence to become bona fide authors.

More than anyone, we want to thank you, our readers, for clicking on a couple of nobodies and sharing your most important asset, your time, with this book. We hope with all our hearts we made it worthwhile.

Much love,
Mary & Bella

ABOUT THE AUTHOR

Mary Stone lives among the majestic Blue Ridge Mountains of East Tennessee with her two dogs, four cats, a couple of energetic boys, and a very patient husband.

As a young girl, she would go to bed every night, wondering what type of creature might be lurking underneath. It wasn't until she was older that she learned that the creatures she needed to most fear were human.

Today, she creates vivid stories with courageous, strong heroines and dastardly villains. She invites you to enter her world of serial killers, FBI agents but never damsels in distress. Her female characters can handle themselves, going toe-to-toe with any male character, protagonist or antagonist.

Discover more about Mary Stone on her website.
www.authormarystone.com

Bella Cross spent the past fifteen years teaching bored teenagers all about the Dewey Decimal System while inhaling the dust from the library books she loves so much. With each book she read, a little voice in her head would say, "You can do that too." So, she did.

A thousand heart palpitations later, she is thrilled to release her first novel with the support of her husband, twin girls, and the gigantic Newfoundland she rescued warming her feet.

Made in the USA
Las Vegas, NV
04 February 2022